1

THE GENE HACKERS

First American Edition July 2011
Second American Edition September 2015

Manufactured in the United States of America

Text set in Adobe Garamond Pro

ISBN: 978-0-9968034-0-3

10 years from today…

"A Bump Forward"

Speech given by Raymond Weily for
The New World Extropy Center

"Scientific literacy too often proves to be a costume worn by the scientifically illiterate, specifically by those desperate and impoverished minds that lack a sound scientific argument to oppose *a sound scientific argument.*

"There is a lot of pseudo-science out there, most of it coming from pseudo-experts who make portentous claims, lacking in both reason and evidence, about the effects modernization and technological development have on the human species and its environment. Why do I call these detractors 'pseudo-experts'? Because their conclusions about these exaggerated effects are, in a word, *wrong.* Why are their conclusions wrong? Because their science is, not wrong – that would be understandable – but their science, frankly, is *false.* Their conclusions derive, not from any scientific process, but from their own predilections. They don't bother with aggregating actual evidence for their arguments, choosing instead to conjure them up. Worse still, they call these fabrications *science.*

"By doing so, they hurt us all in three ways: they blemish the reputation of science; they mislead those who could be the beneficiaries of science; and third, which I believe to be the worst offense, they delay the progress of science. They create illustrations of mankind's malicious tools and malignant technology, forgetting that tools and technology are the very threads of our history. Our environment made us to be makers of our environment.

"Unfortunately, it seems to be the nature of pseudo-experts to claim that the sky is falling. When they do so, it is in the nature of humans to panic and run for cover. Sadly, it is in the nature of government to just stand there, scared stiff. Our government is paralyzed when trying to make decisions about how technology will impact the people. It is too often true that, when government is paralyzed, so too is technology. This paralysis has a scientific explanation: *inertia*. It is the inclination of governments and the public to remain in place, receding into the past, until an unexpected, external force comes along and *bumps* them forward into the future.

"Today we have felt a bump. We have been pushed forward. A push is never a pleasant experience; it can feel threatening and confrontational. Sometimes it even incites confrontation. It seems to be a rule of our kind to punish the pioneers and castigate the catalyst. It is only after we realize that neither the sky nor our species has fallen, but instead it has moved forward, that we thank and remember the innovators who were brave enough to bump us into a new world.

"This bump has taken many forms throughout our history, and though its velocity varies before each bump, the consequence is always the same – *progress*."

"The Tree of Enlightenment"

Speech given by John Drayton for
Mount Ararat Anglican Church

"In the beginning…was innocence. Then Adam ate from the *Tree of Knowledge of Good and Evil*. From that day forward, man has been plagued by his own arrogance and his own sense of entitlement. Modern Man, of course, has a different spin on this story. His version of history tells us that in the beginning was, not innocence, but *ignorance*. With knowledge came…*enlightenment*. Yet, when I turn on the news, when I read about wars being fought with scientifically engineered bombs, designed to induce even more suffering and kill even more people, well, excuse me if I'm not convinced by his claims of *'enlightenment.'* It seems to me that the word we should be looking for is *'stupidity.'*

"Modern Man says that we are civilized. Primitive Man lived in the cold, huddled together as a tribe around a bonfire. Today, the Modern Man – *the Enlightened Man* – builds fancy homes and buildings that keep us warm in the winter and cool in the summer. Yet Modern Man doesn't build them for every man. Millions of men, women and children are kept out in the cold, with no fire to huddle around. Some die from the elements, others from hunger. Despite our abundance of food, we fail to even feed every mouth in this 'civilized society.'

"This does not sound very *'enlightened'* to me.

"Modern Man has a very high opinion of himself. It shows in his history books. He makes himself out to be the savior of the sick and the helper of the weak. Yet, if you want the truth, don't read his history books. Read his résumé! There you will find a long list of crimes he's committed against humanity. Despite his so-called enlightenment, he's too *stupid* to realize that a crime against humanity is a crime against himself.

"Modern Man uses his science to show that religion occurs in the same parts of the brain as schizophrenia. We believe in God, so we are, he says, delusional. If he's right, then surely his *'enlightenment'* must be a close neighbor. Which is more delusional: praising God or playing God?

"You see, God has made, *for all of us*, a Heaven to escape the madness of modern civilization. Modern Man has made, *for all of us*, a Hell rife with war, poverty, and homelessness…but he calls it a Heaven. Too many of us out there believe him. Now, if that isn't delusion, then it sure as *HELL* must be *denial!*"

"Us versus *They*"

Speech given by Sohra Vardi for
Fannie Lou Hamer Community Center

"There's a reason I am talking to a lay audience and not to an academic one. The reason is simple: I am not a scholar. Nor am I an academic, an elite intellectual, or any other *class*ification that would secure my place at their round table.

"I am a human being.

"Of course, such sentimentalism holds no currency in their scientific economy. So let me revise my proclamation to something more…demographic:

"I am a minority woman. I work in a non-specialized profession earning $25,000 a year, living in a neighborhood where half the residents make less than that. I constitute some number or pie chart that says I am to be included in some social privileges and precluded from others.

"I am what *They* call '*Them*.'

"Who are '*They*,' you ask? I love that question because every time people ask it, they think they've put me on the spot. However, I'll tell you who *They* are.

"*They* are vanilla in flavor, masculine in temperament, and patriarchal in agenda. They are American in their rapacity, British in their personality, and Nazi in their intentions. *They* are very rich… That's who *They* are! If *They* feel that this is an unfair generalization, well, now *They* know how we feel when *They* decide who we are.

"I am not defined by *Their* patronizing science, *Their* cold technology, *Their* lifeless statistics, *Their* vague theories, *Their* abstract philosophies, or *Their* baseless currency.

"I am human, and, whether *They* like it or not, so are *They*. Until *They* figure this out; until *They* stop dismissing the very idea of God while pretending to *be* God; until *They* stop claiming ownership of everything and reducing it all to product and property; until *They* stop trespassing upon our lives, our bodies, and our future…it will always, always, always be Us versus *They*."

Chapter One

The ground controller looked up at the underbelly of a private plane. *These rich bastards*, he thought. He waived the light signals and cued the pilot to taxi the jet, making sure to give them the finger as the plane moved slowly past him.

On board, two middle-aged white executives looked down at the quickly disappearing LA lights – man-made fluorescent stars that soon vanished behind a condensation of clouds. The plane was bound for Thailand. James Price, CEO of GAIA Pharmaceuticals, looked across the table at Merritt Lee, his lawyer. They had known each other for quite a while and had done a lot of business together. Yet Merritt never quite got used to Price's imperious presence and over-confident body language that, no doubt, was the result of too much wealth and power. Then there was that freaky eye of his, permanently shut by a biological eye-patch. His disfigured appearance was just a reflection of his character. He was a man ugly inside and out. Merritt never understood why Price's wife hadn't yet left him.

The flight attendant's sexy voice brought Merritt's attention back to now.

"Another drink, Mr. Price?" she asked. The same question never found its way to Merritt. It was as if he weren't even there.

"Yes, same as before, one for myself and one for Mr. Lee," Price replied.

Merritt could have punched Price for patronizing him like that. He didn't like the idea of having his drink ordered for him. He took a deep breath and looked away contemptuously. Merritt was ambitious and confident himself, or, at least, that's the image he worked hard to exude. Yet Price's brand of alpha-male arrogance had a way of betraying Merritt's deeper feelings of insignificance. Merritt's only one-up on Price was knowing that *he* knew the business of peddling pharmaceuticals better than this jackass in front of him.

Let's see how he'll deal with the latest bad news, Merritt thought and dropped the bomb: "The FDA hasn't yet responded to our IND's." He paused. "I think they're preparing to do an audit. Ever since the Hybrid-Division those guys are growing a bigger set of balls."

"Any balls they grow are because we engineered them." Price's armor didn't even crack. There was hardly a trace of worry in his response. He knew he had all the key lawmakers under his thumb. This included the FDA. He had them benched just like all the other government watchdogs. He was sure it was his game. However, inside Merritt's briefcase was a proposal that proved otherwise. Their 8,000-mile flight to Bangkok was really an escape from litigation and that word "proposal" just a euphemism for *payoff*. Price watched as Merritt pulled the "proposal" from his briefcase, grinning at his anxiety.

"I wouldn't worry about it, Merritt," he said almost reassuringly. "The Hybrid-Division is just a sign that the HGE Bill is working. Nobody at the White House or the FDA wants to be the guy who said 'NO' to the most important medical breakthrough in history. Everybody wants this."

Yet Merritt wasn't fooled so easily. "Everybody wants a pharmaceutical brand," he countered, "not a pharmaceutical god."

Of course, that was exactly what guys like Price thought of themselves: they *were* gods, walking on earth among the sick, or flying high from the profits made on their illnesses. Price looked out the window at the majestic view of the clouds, rhythmically glowing from the blinking wing lights. His hubris was at home at such heavenly heights.

"We heal the sick," he replied with no shame or sacrilege in his voice. "That's what gods do."

Merritt couldn't help but smile in response. "Okay," he said, while digging through his briefcase. He pulled out a single sheet of paper: creased, cracked, and crumpled. It looked archaeological. "Then you'll appreciate this." He extended the paper to Price.

"What the hell is this?" Price asked, looking at what seemed to be an antiquated Middle-Ages engraved illustration of a mountain view. The beautiful background landscape was interrupted by rotting corpses piled on top of each other. Drawn into the foreground was a robed priest holding a cross while praying over a dying man. The illustration carried a handwritten passage from the Bible:

"Are any among you sick? They should call for the elders of the church and have them pray over them, anointing them with oil in the name of the Lord. Their prayer, offered in faith, will heal the sick, and the Lord will make them well. Anyone who has committed sins will be forgiven."

1: 14-15

"It's a reproduction of an old drawing of the Black Plague, which happened in Europe during the Fourteenth Century," Merritt explained, leaning forward. "Look at the priest. Somebody's always playing God," he pointed out. "Over half of the population in Europe was wiped out," he continued, reclaiming the paper from Price. "And do you know from what? They died from fleas. Fleas got the bacteria from biting rodents. A simple fleabite took millions of lives. The human immune system has always been inadequate against nature. The human body is obsolete."

The flight attendant returned with their drinks. As she walked away Price took in an eye-full of her engaging and well-shaped bottom. He retorted lustfully,

"Not entirely."

***

Price and Merritt emerged from the plane at the Don Mueang Airport in Bangkok. Two vehicles were waiting for them.

"Two limos?" Merritt asked suspiciously.

"I've got another business to look into," Price answered stepping into one of the limousines and shunning Merritt's suspicions.

Merritt held up the operations proposal defiantly. "Mr. Price, what you do outside of business is none of my business. The only business that concerns me right now are GAIA's gene patents and the finalization of our clinical trial contract with this country. What business is more important than this?"

"We're in the pharmaceutical business, Lee," Price fired back, hardly giving the proposal a second glance. "It shouldn't be that hard to get a doctor's note."

Price's car pulled off, leaving Merritt with his futile objections. He checked his phone and saw that he had missed a call from Maria Price, James' wife. He was as earnest in returning the call as she was in answering it. As usual, she truncated their conversation to curt questions only, restricting Merritt to a series of short, no-frills answers.

"Your husband is ditching the meeting again."

"He's not headed for our hotel; I'm pretty sure of that."

"Don't worry. I already set up for him to be watched."

"I'll know tonight what he's up to."

"I'll see you after the trip."

"I love y–"

That last part never reached her ears. With all her questions answered, she had already hung up before having a chance to humor Merritt's mawkishness. The poor sap just stood there, a lone man surrounded by open space, waiting for "*I love you too.*" Realizing that the other end of the line was dead, he put his cell away and silently stepped into the limo.

"Take me to the hotel, please," he said to the driver, who was already pulling off.

***

For a big boy, Price seemed to eject almost effortlessly from the back seat of the limo. He hurried to a golden palace hotel, by-passing a doorman, who offered to take his bags, and brushing past every other accent-free English greeting that waited for him inside the lobby. The elevator door couldn't close fast enough; the elevator car couldn't move fast enough. He was eager. Hungry.

Exotic motifs defined his luxurious suite – a regal temple for the sybarite, with pillars glowing from the natural light. Price entered the room, and the aura became fiercely primal. He dropped his bags, then removed his suit jacket and shirt, revealing a physique of a large man padded with middle-aged fat. He rushed to the bedroom to find a young girl, no older than sixteen, waiting for him in bed. Just the way he liked it. Translucent white sheets clung to the contours of her bare body. Her large, puffy nipples occupied most of her small breasts. Her young face and small body were without any sexuality.

"What is your name?" he asked while approaching her with a sordid look on his face.

"My name is Aroon," she replied with a voice trembling in the face of this animal-man staring at her. She tried not to look at his bad eye, but she could feel that behind this patch of flesh was a ravenous eye voraciously clawing for her tender form. Like animals always do, Price could sense the fear in her voice. He placed himself gently next to her shamefully small body, hoping to set her at ease. She made a point to resist recoiling from the touch of his large hand running down her cheek. She knew that she could repress her repugnance of his scarred face, his flesh covered eye, and his middle-aged smell, but she could not force herself to demonstrate any emotion. That was too much. Even offering up her name was too intimate.

"Aroon," Price repeated her name, trying to taste its rhythm.

"That's a beautiful name. Aroon," he indulged the sound of her name again. "Do you know what it means?"

She didn't want to tell him. She considered lying, making something up. Yet as quickly as she thought about it, she abandoned the idea. She was about to concede her body; concealing her identity now seemed pointless. Her reply was rather stoic, lifeless.

"It means...*Dawn of the Day.*"

***

Inside the towering white Wilshire federal building, Office 220 of the FBI already looked empty. It used to be Stan Medes' office, but now the empty nameplate on the door was patiently waiting for the name of the next occupant. Stan, a burly, broad-shouldered black man, was trying to fit all of his belongings into a rickety box.

Too busy meddling with the box, trying to seal the damn thing shut, Stan didn't notice at first that Amber, a beautiful Asian woman, his friend and partner, stepped into the open doorway. Friends they were, but that didn't stop her from stealing a few glances at his broad back and firm butt. Still standing in the doorway, she kept both hands casually behind her back, hiding something.

"So you're being re-assigned to the FDA. Does that mean you're being demoted?" she asked with a hint of tease in her voice. Stan turned to face her.

"It's the Hybrid-Division, Amber." He couldn't hide his frustration. "The Bureau has collaborated with the FDA before. They're just making it official, that's all. I'm still FBI."

Amber laughed. She loved jabbing at his ego. He always had the same response: "Stop screwing with me."

To Amber, this kind of defenseless protest only invited more jabs. Her next easy target could have been his obvious inability to pack and seal a box properly. The flaps scarcely contained his small mountain of loose belongings. Instead, she decided to be all girly.

"You know you're never going to find a partner like me again," she coquetted.

"Yeah, I know," he admitted. "Good women are hard to find."

Amber shook her head. "That's because they all left when they realized that the same was true about good men," she joked, but Stan barely heard a word of it as he frustrated himself more with the box.

"So who is he?" she asked, changing the subject.

"You already sound jealous."

"Well?" she insisted.

Stan turned around to face her again and almost tipped his box over. A few items slipped free and scattered across the floor. "Goddammit!" he exclaimed and bent down to fetch his junk. A magic eight ball rolled free, stopping at Amber's feet.

"I remember this," she said smiling, "the infamous eight ball that vanished from your office."

"*Vanished* my ass. You stole it." Stan wasn't going to give up an opportunity to tease her back.

"I didn't steal it. I brought it back."

"You didn't bring it back. Marius brought it back."

"No, I brought it b–" She stopped mid-sentence, re-thinking the fuzzy event. "Shit. You're right. It was Marius who brought it back, wasn't it?"

"Yes!" Stan bellowed.

"But wait a minute! I gave it to Marius to give it back to you."

"Instead of bringing it back yourself? You knew I was pissed at your stealing ass."

"My *fine* stealing ass," Amber retorted in that sexy, flirtatious voice of hers.

A fine stealing ass indeed, he thought. *Oh, how I'd love to...* He interrupted his own thoughts, shaking his head and returning back to the impossible task of boxing all of his crap.

"Okay, so now that we've settled that, tell me about this new guy, who thinks he can replace me."

"Addison Calvin. White guy, which means he has no soul. He's also a scientist, which means I probably don't have a soul either. We talked on the phone. Kind of a dry guy."

"I'm sure if you cut him open, you'll find a heart of pure gold," Amber said, inching closer.

"Screw the gold. How about just cutting him open?" Stan

quipped, chuckling. He faced Amber again, now ready to leave with his half-ass sealed box.

"Damn. So that's it. Your office is empty." She looked over his shoulder at the empty space behind him. As he turned his head for one last look, she quickly moved her hands from behind her back and slipped a book on top of the box.

"What the hell is this?" he asked, swiveling his head back.

"Your going-away present. I thought you might need it for your new position."

He frowned at the title:

Genetic Engineering for Dummies

***

Addison pressed his mouth against the lips of a new lover, immediately diagnosing the pressure and texture of his lips, ruling them as acceptable and then pressing harder. His lover, Simon, responded in kind, running his hand up Addison's chest and gripping at the side of his face.

Fully clothed, they managed to get their arms tangled in a confusion of trying to undress each other. Simon laughed, then paused while wondering why Addison was not laughing with him. Addison's exterior was permanently unsociable, even during intimate moments – the only explanation of why he had so few of them. Past lovers were easily put off by it; one had even abandoned him mid-ritual. Yet this one was determined. Addison, after all, was a catch: a lean Greek statue vertically elongated to six feet, but he covered all of it with layers of rigid professional neutrality. Simon kissed at Addison's neck while grabbing firmly at his arms, realizing how limp his body felt. Not sure if this was a sign of a ready lover or a reticent one, Simon decided to detour his hands down Addison's body, stopping between his legs, pleased that this particular limb was anything but reticent. It was ready and stiff.

He zipped down Addison's pants, reaching inside and groping. Finally he heard a response from Addison – a moan. Yet this was deliberate. Addison gave him this moan. He knew what his new lover was thinking and decided that he didn't want another episode of suspended sex. He did want this; he just wasn't sure what *this* was. A fling? A lover? A partner? Or was he simply after another memorial artifact that he could present to himself later as evidence of some kind of sex life. The question became moot as soon as the member between his legs became warm and wet. *Well, whatever this is, it is happening*, he thought to himself. *I can decide what this is later.*

While time dissolved for Simon, Addison felt every minute. As they lay on the floor, post-coital, Addison came to the conclusion that this was neither a fling nor a lover or a partner. It wasn't even an artifact. It was biological. His body craved it, as it had craved this before, only now he was able to do something about it. Sure, maybe it was untimely that they did this inside his office, maybe not. Some people consider office sex to be a good time.

Still lying on the floor, fully clothed, Addison re-situated his penis back into his pants. Finally, he began to laugh. Simon, excited to hear evidence of joviality from his new lover, looked at him and laughed too.

"Are there cameras in here?" he asked Addison.

"You know what?" Addison paused. "I think there are…"

Simon rose up on his elbow, looking at Addison as if begging for a retraction. *Tell me you're joking*, his eyes exclaimed.

"No, really, I think there are cameras in here," Addison reassured him. He looked around and pointed to a corner. "In fact, I think that's a camera."

Simon began to laugh, mostly in disbelief. "You're surprisingly cavalier about this."

"Yeah… I've been on YouTube before. After the first time, you get used to it." Addison now noticed Simon searching him for a poker face. "I'm kidding, I'm kidding. There are no cameras in here."

"And YouTube?"

"Never been on it."

Simon exhaled, relieved, and sprawled himself back out across the floor. They lay in silence and Addison began to reconsider if this had been only biological after all. Simon seemed to have read his thoughts and began probing him circuitously.

"I think I know why you did this," he said.

"Why?"

"Because you're quitting. You wanted to know what it was like to have sex in this office before you never set foot in here again."

"I will be setting foot in here *tomorrow and tomorrow and the day after that.*"

"What? I thought you were quitting to work with the FBI."

"Everyone gets that wrong. I'm not quitting. It's a collaboration of divisions."

"A demotion?" Simon said with a mocking smile.

25

"Fine. It's a demotion."

"I was kidding."

"No, no, I confess. You're right. That part you got right," Addison relented. "You know, I remember once when the FDA had to work with the DEA on a raid of a manufacturer of drug generics. I was there, and I saw how the officers went through their protocol of photographing and cataloging all the evidence. I remember thinking two things: one, how very similar and procedural that process was. I mean, it was almost identical to the very careful and methodic systems that we use, but *two,* what I also noticed, was how unnatural it was for those guys. I mean, I don't know what the experience levels were of the people who were brought in on the raid, but I saw why lawyers are so vigilant in looking for loose-ends in the acquisition of evidence. It's because there are so many of them. I mean these guys were so used to drug raids with the buffoons on the streets that a Pharma raid was almost like asking them to speak a new language."

"C'mon. I'm sure that wasn't their first time kicking open the doors of a pharmaceutical manufacturer."

"That's my point," Addison insisted. "How many times do you have to do this before you decide to establish a unique protocol for this kind of situation?"

"Did you do anything about it?"

"Not right then and there, no, but I did put together a recommended manual of best practices and protocol to obtain and catalogue biological evidence. Well, at least, the best way of acquiring evidence for FDA standards."

"A manual?"

"For future consideration, yes," Addison replied, completely serious.

"Gosh, what would they do without you?"

Addison, offended, picked himself off the ground, objecting in total silence.

"Hey, if your position with the Hybrid-Division is writing manuals then, yes, maybe this is a demotion. You said yourself that it was. I'm just agreeing with you now," Simon replied smiling, situating himself on his side.

"I didn't say it; *you* said it. *I* was agreeing with *you*. Now I'm disagreeing with you because you missed my point."

"What did I miss?"

"You're implying that a manual was a triviality."

"Okay, that was *my* point, and *your* point was…"

"That the manual was *important*, but not exactly the best use of my time. That's my point," Addison said, his tone putting a definitive period at the end of his point. Simon nodded his head, his wheels spinning, gearing up for his counter-point in this game of verbal joust.

"Okay… *But*…if it's not exactly the best use of your time, in your own words, then that would mean that *yes, it is a demotion*."

"I won't be writing manuals for the FBI. At least, I hope not."

"Have you met the guy you'll be working with?"

"Yeah."

"Is he cute?"

"No. I mean, correction: *No, I haven't met him.* I just spoke with him."

"And?"

"Okay, fine. It's a demotion!" Addison said throwing his hands up. "Are you happy? I admit it."

"You already admitted it. We're past that. We're talking about your new boyfriend, remember?"

"No, *you're* talking about 'my new boyfriend', or, at least, that's what you're pretending to talk about. What you're really doing is indulging in an adolescent game that you picked up in high school but forgot to leave there. You poke and piffle around until you find out if the other person feels the same way you do. Here, let me help you out." Addison grabbed a paper and pen from his desk and quickly scribbled a message on it, folded it up, and handed it to Simon, who now picked himself off the floor.

"*I like you. Do you like me? Please check a box,*" he read aloud, then crumpled up the letter and threw it in the trash bin. "You're a dick, you know that? I mean, I kind of expected that when we talked. You were so dry. Now I know for sure."

"I checked 'yes' in the box," Addison replied. Simon looked at him, first in stubborn protest, then he cracked a smile. He bent down, reaching into the trash bin to retrieve the crumpled paper. He took the pen, scribbled an addendum, and handed it to Addison.

"*Maybe,*" Addison read aloud, crumpling the paper and tossing it back into the trash bin. "Okay, so now what?"

"I poke and piffle," Simon said, gathering his personal belongings, "and then I get back to you."

28

Shijea Patra, a Contract Research Physician for ETGR, GAIA's genetic research facility, hurried down the long clinical corridor to David Lee's office. She needed to find out how to get hold of his brother Merritt or even Mr. Price himself. In their absence, David, the Investment Finder for ETGR, liked to pretend that he had decision-making authority, but this emergency was much bigger than him.

"I don't mean to be rude," she said to David, mixing apology with impatience, "but the information I need to discuss is highly confidential and potentially of a legal matter. It would be best if I talked with Mr. Lee directly."

"You are talking with Mr. Lee," David snapped, ignoring the urgency in her voice.

Oh no, she thought, *I don't have time for this.*

"I mean the other Mr. Lee, Mr. Lee." She looked at him with panic and desperation in her face, but he was much too concerned with maintaining his appearance as the man in charge.

"Call me David. My brother is in Thailand…with Mr. Price," he responded coolly. "Needless to say, I don't think right now would be the best time to burden my brother with problems that I'm sure you and I can resolve together," he added confidently.

Shijea actually felt his coffee breath traveling across the small space and hitting her face. Not only was David not the guy to talk to, but he didn't even look like the guy to talk to. He had the appearance of a guy whose very touch makes dirty money even dirtier; a guy who could never discuss legal matters because he was too busy dodging them.

David noticed her hesitation. "Ms. Patra," he tried a plea to win her over, "both men are meeting about setting up research facilities in Bangkok. So as important as your issue is, it's not likely to be as important as that."

"I'm afraid if they heard my report, they would disagree."

David was startled, but he still tried to muster up some executive confidence. He put his hands in his pockets. "I see. Well, I think you should know that I am brokering the investment that GAIA is making into ETGR. I have connections with both companies. So you can trust that whatever issues I can't resolve, I can relay them rather efficiently to either man." He paused. "Fair enough?"

Shijea sighed. She knew he wasn't going to like what she had to tell him, nor would he be able to do anything about it.

"Can we talk in my office?" she asked with resignation in her voice. "I need to show you something."

***

David stared in silent dismay at a letter Shijea handed to him. He allowed his body weight to drop down violently into her office chair. "How could the Hybrid-Division know about this?" His calm and measured façade was now shattered. His voice was shaky; in his eyes – *fatal panic.*

"They could be responding to the public concern about genetic engineering." Shijea was still on her feet. She handled her own distress better while standing. It made her feel that she was not idle; that things were getting done.

"Shijea, they use the word 'cloning' in here!" David continued, almost screaming. "Why would they do that?"

"The term is often confused."

"The FDA wouldn't confuse the terminology! Is there a leak in this building?"

"It's not a leak. At least, I don't think so." She paused before going ahead with the next part. "JOI…is gone… I think someone may have helped him escape."

David's face went from white to pale. "What?" he barely whispered.

He stormed out of her office and jumped in his car. His foot suddenly became heavy as lead, pressing down relentlessly on the gas pedal. Driving like a maniac, he wasn't sure what he was doing or even where he was going. He told himself that he was looking for JOI although it was just as plausible that he was looking for a cliff, hoping to drive the car clean off the ledge. It was a little bit of both. He was hoping for dumb luck: to drive recklessly until fate brought him to the boy, or until some fatal accident freed him from what would happen to him if the boy was never found – or worse still, *if he was found by someone else.* These very thoughts had questions racing through his mind as he accelerated down Gemelo Road:

How did JOI escape?

Who let him escape?

Who tipped off the FDA?

How do I kill whoever tipped off the FDA?

The boy walks as slow as he talks… How far could he have gotten?

Where the fuck is he?

David noticed that he was doing over 100 miles per hour. He slammed on the brakes, nearly veering off the road. Finally, the car came to a stop; for better or worse, nowhere near the cliff he had hoped for. Nor was the boy anywhere in sight. He began battering the dashboard with his fist, summoning every profane word in his arsenal. After one too many punches, he could no longer ignore the pain. He grabbed at his hand, trying to bring his breathing back to normal. He wasn't calm, just exhausted, scared. He looked through his window at the surrounding California hills. The boy could be anywhere out there. He hung his head low in resignation, releasing one last expletive,

"Shit."

Chapter Two

"More coffee, Dr. Shapiro?" The velvety voice of the waitress interrupted Allan's thoughts. He had been buried in his notes for the last hour and still had a long way to go, so both, another cup of coffee and the interruption, were more than welcome, especially from this beautiful mature woman, whose face had become so familiar to him in the last months.

He stole a glance at her cleavage, peeking out through the V formed by her open shirt. She pretended not to notice. *She might be the last natural woman in Los Angeles,* he thought.

"You love your long hours, don't you?" she asked, noticing his lethargic pudgy face and not really needing an answer. Allan had long since made a habit of postponing sleep, and it showed.

"How could you tell?" He wiped the tired away from his face. She threw her hand on her hip, smiling at his sarcasm. *He deserves a freebie*, she thought.

"Well, since you're a steady customer, I'm going to treat you to a free sample of our famous pie. It's a secret recipe and it's on me." There was that velvety voice again. "Actually, it's on the house, but you can think of me while you're eating it," she added flirtatiously. The sight of her walking away woke Allan right up – much more powerful than a sip of fresh coffee. He found it difficult to pull his eyes away from her. Of course, he wasn't the only one looking. The look he got from the old, devilishly grinning, overweight man at the next table was shouting *you lucky bastard*. Lucky indeed.

"There you go, sweetie." The waitress was back already. "Our Famous Key Lime Pie." The free second sneak peek at her delicious cleavage was a much sweeter treat. Allan looked up at her, forcing himself not to return his eyes on her cleavage, but her face seemed to say: *You can look if you want to*. As if to prove it, she bent over, picking up Allan's fork, unwittingly giving the old guy behind her the best show he's ever seen in a small, out-of-the-way diner like this one. She pronged the pie and held a small portion only a few inches away from Allan's face.

"Uh, honestly, I don't trust secret recipes. I have to know what I'm eating."

"I just told you: *Famous…Key…Lime…Pie,*" – she wasn't going to let him off the hook so easily – "but I'll tell you part of the secret recipe – *limes*." She inched the pie closer to his mouth. "Today's lesson is about trust," she said, gently forcing the pie into his mouth. "Trust me."

"I TRUST YOU!" the older man called out from behind. She smiled but mostly continued to ignore him, focusing on her little flirt with Allan.

Finally, Allan conceded, biting down on the pie and swallowing down the guilt that comes with knowing he was not exactly a free agent. She knew, of course. He wore his wedding vows on his finger and the strain of these vows all over his face.

"Always trust a woman who keeps secrets," the waitress added matter-of-factly while walking back to the counter. "It means she's keeping yours," she concluded, looking Allan directly in his eyes.

Their eyes remained locked until the old man interrupted them again, this time pointing at a small TV mounted on the back wall. "Can you turn that up?" he asked, noticing the breaking news title:

PHARMA SCANDAL

"James Price stepped down from his position as CEO of GAIA Global, a multi-billion dollar pharmaceutical. Price's resignation occurred earlier today, after FBI reports surfaced, implicating him in an underage sex scandal during a business trip in Thailand."

The report showed a series of spy camera photos of Price sharing the bed with Aroon.

"Upon learning of these allegations, GAIA Pharmaceuticals requested an immediate resignation from Price but would not issue a statement or give further detail about the incident."

The report continued with a full screen photo of Price holding hands with his wife Maria, a handsome woman with a sexy yet powerful figure, and then cut to a close-up of Maria Price. Her eyes showed little evidence of emotion, but behind her stoicism was a weathered beauty.

"Last year James Price and his wife, Maria Price, were separated following rumors of infidelity. The couple claimed that there were other factors that lead to their decision at the time. Neither James Price nor Maria Price was available for comment."

The waitress lowered the volume again. The old man leaned back in his chair in total disgust. "Sick bastard! Why would a man that rich do something like that? He can have any woman he wants!"

"He's already had every woman he wants," the waitress countered with little surprise in her voice. "Next in line are young girls."

"I wonder how his wife must feel." The old man seemed genuinely sorry for Maria Price.

"I wouldn't be surprised if she was the one who leaked it," she said to the old man but then looked directly at Allan.

"He should have gotten himself a woman who can keep secrets."

***

Driving down Gemelo Road, Allan could barely see anything. It was late, and the many cups of coffee had already worn off. He was tired and felt the wall of night closing in on him. He pulled the car over and wiped his eyes. He thought about taking a nap right then and there. Instead, he opened the door, hoping the fresh air would wake him up long enough to finish the ride home. He looked at the many surrounding hills glowing with a blue-black varnish from the evening darkness. His eyes gazed up at the myriad of stars over head – a majestic view. *Once, these were portraits of gods,* he thought to himself. *Now they are light bulbs carelessly left on and burning out. All gods are dead.*

Allan breathed deeply, contemplating. The chilly air was refreshing and he felt a tad more alert. He stepped back into his car, reached for a CD, inserted it into the player, and pulled off. It was one of his favorites – an audio book he himself recorded. No one but him and a few friends had ever bothered to listen to it.

"Mnemosyne, the goddess of memory, was also the mother of the nine muses. Though herself a Titan, her presence in Greek mythology is comparatively rare, but at one time, Mnemosyne and her sister Lesmosyne both were prominent figures of Western cosmology.

"Memory was held in high reverence with many ancient cultures."

Allan's thoughts drifted away...

"In Greek mythology, Mnemosyne couples with the great Zeus to bring the nine muses to the world. The sudden flashes of inspiration that fuel the arts, sciences, music, and philosophy were all said to come from one of these nine muses. This means that the Greeks understood inspiration to be founded upon the mysterious connection between divinity and memory."

His eyes remained fixed on the road, but his mind wandered...

"Furthermore, the presence of Lesmosyne in mythology means that the Greeks were sure to give attention to the opposite of Memory. Lesmosyne can be thought of as a paradoxical twin sister of Mnemosyne. Just as Mnemosyne was the personification of memory, Lesmosyne represented..."

His car drifted slightly to the wrong side of the road.

"Loss of memory."

Bright lights flashed into Allan's eyes, snapping him out of his slumbering trance. "Shit!" he exclaimed, slamming on the brakes and bringing his SUV into a spin. He felt his middle-aged heart pounding in his chest. He looked down and noticed that his hands were shaking from the adrenaline of a near accident. He forced himself to breathe deeply, silently cursing at his own stupidity of nearly getting himself killed. As the excitement lowered, he dropped his head forward on the steering wheel, nearly fainting from the rush of blood to his head.

"What the hell is wrong with you???" David Lee shouted through the passenger window, causing Allan to snap into attention. Allan looked to his right and saw the face of a man who was, doubtless, as tired and weary as him, but behind David's fatigue was a lingering panic that seemed to keep him awake. The men paused in a silent, awkward stare down. The few seconds felt like minutes to Allan.

"I'm sorry," was all he could think to say to break the awkwardness. David took a second look and immediately recognized the tiring stress in Allan's face.

"It's okay," he said, taking pity. "You look the way I feel."

"Yeah," Allan replied, relieved at an opportunity to laugh, "well, that sure as hell woke me up."

"Both of us," David admitted, pulling a cigarette from his pocket and placing it in his mouth. "I think that pretty much gave me my second wind. I can do an all-nighter now."

"You on your way to a graveyard shift?" Allan asked, trying to be friendly.

"Nah, just the graveyard," David chuckled from behind the cigarette. Allan tried to smile back at this, but the graveness in David's voice made him retract his laugh into a rictus of leeriness. As David lit a small fire, bringing it to the tip of his cigarette, Allan got a chance to see the many beads of sweat that glistened on his face and neck.

"What did you do?" Allan asked rather abruptly, and David looked at him sharply as if he were a trespasser. Immediately, Allan regretted the invasive question. "I'm sorry, I meant to say... 'What *do* you do...for a living...' I mean..." Allan retracted, hoping David would go along.

"I'm an investment finder. I help biotechs find money, yada, yada, yada," David said. Allan nodded his head, relieved.

"What about you?" David asked.

"I'm a dinosaur," Allan replied. David looked at him with a perplexing frown that begged for an explanation. "Translation: I'm a cognitive psychologist. The science community has a diminishing need for dinosaurs like me."

Now David nodded his head. He spent enough time with scientists to know exactly what Allan meant.

"You're a *Soft Scientist!*" David smiled, pulling the cigarette from his mouth and exhaling smoke off to the side.

"That's right."

"Gotta upgrade, my friend," he joked. "You just need to put the word 'neuro' somewhere in-between 'cognitive' and 'psychologist'. Nobody gives a shit about the *mind* anymore. It's all about the brain," he said, tapping his head with a finger.

"Yeah, I know. Problem is, I meant it when I said I was a dinosaur. I'm part of that rare species that still gives a shit about the mind. In fact, I happen to believe the brain and the mind are two, not one."

"Yeah? Well, I'm part of that not so rare species that doesn't give a shit if they are." They both laughed.

"Right," Allan conceded with a smile. It was nothing new. Laughter was the usual response to his archaic schemata. "I'm stuck in the past. Although, in my own defense, I think, at some point in the future, my theory will make for good science, or, if nothing else, good science fiction. Maybe someday someone will even write a novel about my theory."

"What theory is that?" David asked, though he didn't really care.

He wasn't even trying to be polite. He just appreciated the distraction.

"You work in the biotech field, so you might find this somewhat interesting. I happen to believe that every cell in our body is a thinking cell. That intelligence and self-awareness pervade the entire body." Allan paused, noticing that he had already lost David, who was now occupied with something on the road. *Whatever.* He decided to keep going. "I posit that somatic intelligence is dividing from monism into dualism; that the brain and the mind are evolving from one into two. When this happens, the body goes from an instinctive self-awareness triggered by external stimuli to an intrinsic self-awareness triggered by internal stimuli, for instance, knowing that one has a name."

David didn't even offer up so much as an *"uh-huh."* He was too distracted by the sound coming from up the road. Allan turned around in his seat, following in the direction of David's eyes. At first he was confused, but then he could see it too…

A silhouette of a kid.

David started walking towards the silhouette.

Allan opened his door, ejecting from his seat.

David started running. His hopes began to flare up. *Holy shit, I found him.* David couldn't believe his luck. *I found him!* Blanketed by darkness and maintaining the surreal stillness of a statue, the boy's shrouded, silhouetted appearance commanded David into a sudden stop. Seconds later, Allan caught up with him, breathing hard from the short run. Allan froze up too.

"Oh my god…" Allan's words barely came through as a whisper. He saw the same thing that had brought pause to David. This was the obvious form of a young boy, but he stood in place, motionless, as if dead on his feet. Allan turned to look at David and was bewildered at the absence of surprise in his eyes. David's face was almost entirely without expression – just the blank stare that comes when one's mind begins to replay every damned incident that equated to *right now*. David immediately felt Allan's eyes probing him for some kind of reaction, and he looked back at Allan with little change or affect in his gaze. He felt the sinking sting of a tantalizing luck that would bring him to find the boy, but with a witness present. David went glassy-eyed while premeditating how to kill the fat fuck in front of him.

The sound of dirt grinding broke David from his trance. He looked to see if the boy had finally moved, but he hadn't. David suddenly realized that the sound was coming from Allan, who was now slowly advancing forward.

"Wait, don't scare him!" David hissed, throwing his arm out to stop Allan, but it was too late. Allan had already gone into doctor mode, trying to be helpful, asking a number of questions.

"Are you OK?"

"Are you lost?"

"Are you hurt?"

The boy neither responded nor moved an inch. Allan stepped closer, very slowly, taking his time, making sure not to startle the boy. David, meanwhile, found himself teetering on an impulse to pounce upon Allan. He looked down and saw a large enough stone that could easily pound through Allan's skull, killing him, or, at least, separating him from consciousness.

"Can you tell me your name?" Allan asked, again breaking David away from plots of murder. *Fuck!* David thought to himself. *No, don't tell him your name.*

"Joey2" the boy answered flatly.

David looked over at Allan for a reaction, immediately thinking to himself: *I can take him. I have to take him. I don't really have a choice.* David crouched down and picked up the rock, confident that the cover of darkness would keep it concealed long enough to make the attack.

"Joey2?" Allan asked. "You mean Joey *the Second*? Is that your father's name? Is his name Joey also?"

I'm his father! David heard those words blaring in his mind – a plan he quickly aborted, knowing that it was just plain stupid. So stupid that it wouldn't even raise questions of suspicion, just immediate answers of incrimination. His mind illustrated the only remaining option:

He launched the rock from his hand.

In the span of a second, it hurled like a small invisible missile through the air.

It cracked into the side of Allan's head, splitting it open.

He fell to the ground claimed by the darkness of death.

Joey had witnessed it all, but forgot it just as quickly as it happened.

David grabbed Joey, hurled his ass into the car, and took off.

He blinked, waking up from this scenario. Joey was still there. So was Allan.

Okay, so maybe murder didn't seem like much of an option after all. There was plenty of dirt on his hands, but never blood. He dropped the stone from his hand, not surprised that Allan hadn't

43

even noticed its clunk-and-roll sound. He was simply too preoccupied, even fascinated, by the mysterious boy in front of him.

However, the fascination in Allan's eyes quickly vanished when he inched himself just close enough to see behind the dark curtains that had masked the boy's face. The asymmetrical proportions were subtle, yet still noticeable; however, this wasn't what startled Allan. He had seen, observed, and analyzed every oblique feature the human body has ever offered. What concerned him was the obvious disconnect in Joey's eyes. He appeared to be unaware of the danger of being lost. Even worse, he was detached from the potentially greater danger of being found by two strangers.

"My name is Allan Shapiro, Joey. I'm a doctor. Do I have your permission to approach you?"

Joey, of course, didn't answer. The lack of affect in Joey's eyes had brought Allan to expect this. It was a formality that was meant to put a person at ease. *Ask for permission; let the subject know exactly what you intend to do.*

Allan turned back to David. "My phone is in my car. Do you have a cell phone on you?"

"For what?" David asked, somewhat absently.

"To call the police." *You moron!* Allan resisted attaching that last part to his reply.

"Right, call the police." David pulled his phone from his pocket and checked the screen. "I don't have a signal. We're too far into the hills." He paused, his eyes lighting up from the idea that had just fallen into his lap. "I could...drive him to the police."

Allan paused at this idea – leery. "I'd better take him. I'm a doctor."

David's heart sunk. He thought about murder again: *Maybe a little blood on my hands won't be so bad after all.* Allan looked at him, waiting for a response.

"Okay." The tension in David's voice dissipated from concession. "Okay…"

Allan nodded his head, understanding David's doubts, but also knowing that between the two of them, he was the better option.

"We can drive together," he suggested. "I mean, you could follow me to make sure…"

"No, no, you're right. You should take him, but…" – David extended his hand – "Do you have a card on you? You know…so that I can follow up with you."

"Of course," Allan said, reaching inside his jacket and extending his card over to David.

***

Sickness had challenged Claudia Shapiro's ability to wait any longer for Allan to return. After hours of fighting back restless worry, her frail body was having the final say. Gabriella, her caretaker, used the wheelchair to roll Claudia into her bedroom, then relocated her to her bed in a series of measured motions. Then the door opened and they both turned their heads in the direction of the sound, knowing that it was Allan finally coming home. Gabriella hurried from Claudia's bedroom to find Allan dragging himself into the living room.

"Allan! What happened? We've been waiting to hear from you all night!" Gabriella exclaimed.

45

"We found a lost kid. I had to take him to the police…"

"We?"

"Me and another guy, whom I almost drove into… It's a long story, Gabriella. I'll fill you in on the details later," Allan said, his voice saturated with exhaustion. "How's Claudia? Is she asleep?"

"No," Gabriella replied as if the answer was obvious, "she's in bed, waiting."

"Okay," Allan said, walking past her towards the bedroom, "thank you for staying. I'll take it from here."

"Of course." Gabriella started gathering her belongings to leave.

Allan stood in the doorway of his bedroom, looking at the dichotomous arrangement of two beds and two lives. His wife occupied the half that looked entirely clinical: a hospital bed, chairs with steel arms for gripping, a night stand that was filled with pills, a small mirror, and a bedside-organizer stuffed with hygienic items.

"I could hear you from here," Claudia said indifferently. "I can wait for details too."

Allan stepped inside the room. He bent over and kissed his wife on her forehead, but not her lips – a rote gesture. Weary, he walked over to his side of the room – the side that resembled a regular bedroom. He threw himself on the bed. The disturbance of his weight rattled the wall, causing a small brush painting of the seventeenth letter of the Hebrew alphabet – *"PEI"* – to fall to the ground.

Allan exhaled, exasperated. He stared at the image…

He heard Claudia's voice.

"Take a shower, Allan."

***

Allan let the hot water wash away his day, his thoughts, and his worries. He found himself fantasizing about the waitress from the diner. His hands drifted lower; started stroking. He didn't feel shame. He didn't feel much pleasure either. It was mechanical – a release, quick and uneventful. He turned the water off and waited for his body to air dry. He put on a T-shirt and pajama shorts. He went back to bed. Claudia was already sleeping.

***

"Allan," Claudia's words woke him up the next morning, "can you help me into the wheelchair? Gabriella's not here yet."

It had been a while since Allan had to do this, but he remembered all of the techniques he had once mastered. As he lifted her from the bed, he noticed how much weight she had lost. He eased her into the wheelchair and rolled her into the bathroom.

***

They sat together at the kitchen table, eating a simple breakfast that Allan had prepared. As Allan sipped his coffee, he looked up and saw the simplicity of his wife's face as she concentrated on spreading cream cheese on her toasted bagel. Next, he remembered the waitress at the diner the previous evening and his thoughts about her while masturbating in the shower. He realized that these pleasurable images would not make for pleasant memories.

"No office for you today?" Claudia asked, breaking him from his rumination. He looked at Claudia and could tell that this was not so much a question as it was a request. Before he could answer her, his cell phone rang. He looked at the screen.

"It's the police," he said. "I have to take this. Must be about the kid from yesterday." He stood up to answer and walked away. Claudia overheard him giving only yes and no answers. Then she heard the back door open and saw Gabriella enter. Claudia held her breath, knowing what would come next. Gabriella took her job seriously, too seriously at times, assuming the role of a care-taker one minute and a diet lector the next.

"Mrs. Shapiro, you're supposed to avoid refined foods and coffee." Gabriella frowned as she noticed the remains of their breakfast. Claudia ignored her, biting into the bagel in a deliberate act of protest. Gabriella responded by walking over to the pantry. "I'll prepare a proper breakfast for you."

"Sit down, Gabriella. My *improper* breakfast will do just fine for today."

"Mrs. Shapiro, I –"

Allan returned to the kitchen breaking the tension – an interruption that Gabriella welcomed. Claudia, too, shifted her attention to her husband.

"Well?" she asked him.

"The police need help with Joey."

"Your help? Why?"

"Apparently the boy is amnesic," Allan said, grabbing his car keys from nearby.

"How do they know?" Claudia asked, dubiously.

"Well, I think that's why they're calling me back, so that they *can know* for sure. Apparently, the boy has no recollection of what happened yesterday."

"He doesn't remember being lost – *and alone* – in the middle of the night?"

"Nope, and now I'm going to see if he remembers driving alone with me, a complete stranger, for an hour in my car."

Though Allan tried to feign frustration from the call, Claudia could see right away that his agitation was paper-thin. He wanted to go. So much so, that he forgot a few things in a hurry: to finish his breakfast, to greet Gabriella and to thank her for adjusting her schedule, though she was paid to do so. More importantly, he forgot to kiss Claudia, though such passing kisses had grown thinner with time. Just like that, he was out the door, leaving Claudia and Gabriella to finish their clash over what exactly constitutes a proper breakfast.

Allan was ambivalent about Joey's amnesia. That was not what had him rushing out the door. He was going to tend to that, of course, to satisfy the police. Hell, he was going to do every test that was needed if it helped Joey, but that's not what had him rushing out the door.

As Allan hurried to the police precinct, he imagined the questions he would ask Joey, perhaps doing a reverse recollection exercise. It sounded easy enough, just like walking backwards, but when one actually tries it, the mind stumbles.

Do you remember driving to the police station with me?

Joey would reply, *No.*

Do you remember being lost on an open road yesterday?

No.

Do you remember the two men who found you?

No.

Do you remember how you got yourself lost yesterday?

No.

Do you remember me?

No.

Then the next question: *Do you remember your name?*

To this, the boy would reply: *Yes.*

"Nomen est Numen" Allan recited aloud to himself while driving. Those words rushed to his mind as he remembered a historical anecdote from the Nineteenth Century political philosopher Dr. Francis Lieber, who recorded his observations of a doctor and a young "Negro" boy, who was only a mere generation removed from the culture of his ancestors. The doctor could always find the young boy feeding mockingbirds by hand and wondered why the boy had not yet allowed the birds to feed themselves on the proper diet of worms. The doctor eventually approached the boy and asked, "Would they eat worms?" to which the boy replied, "Surely not. They are too young. They would not know what to call them."

They would not know what to call them.

How strange, Allan thought. It was not the primitive ideas of the "Negro" boy he found perplexing, but rather how the importance of a name – and the act of naming – had passed from memory in modern society. How strange that a name has become little more than a mere nomenclature – an appellation and nothing more. "Verum Nomen."

Allan's thoughts returned to Joey and his last question.

What is your name?

No doubt, the boy would know the answer to this.

He would remember.

He would answer.

Joey2.

Chapter Three

Allan leaned forward at the conference room table. He looked at his colleagues, trying to read their thoughts about his theory. Dr. Pearson Fueller, a middle-aged black man with receding hair, knew Allan all too well. He gave him an encouraging look. Dr. Kohei Hiroshi, a thin small statured Asian, was a different story. He anchored his head into the palm of his hand, impatiently listening to what he considered to be more of Allan's pseudo-science. Nevertheless, Allan continued:

"Joey retains semantic memory but not episodic memory. If a dog barks, he'll probably remember that the sound is coming from a dog. Yet if the dog bites him, shortly thereafter his memory of the experience is gone. His length of memory is considerably short. His semantic memory isn't entirely functional either. He doesn't remember names…

"Except his own. I ran scans on his brain to monitor his electrophysiological response to words and images. One of the words I used was his name. I did several tests and averaged them out to account for background noise. There's a widespread increase in cortical activity when he hears his name."

"I'm sure that's applicable to everybody, not just your subject," Kohei added skeptically.

"That's my point, Kohei," Allan replied. "Names embody an intrinsic identification –"

Kohei sighed.

"Kohei, you don't have to be here. I didn't ask you –"

"I asked him, Allan," Pearson cut in.

Allan leaned back, scratching his head, thinking.

"Listen. The boy is amnesic," he said. "The police asked me to do this. I would like to do more examinations on his medial temporal lobes."

"You can keep testing him at this hospital, Allan," Pearson replied. "Nobody at this table is objecting to that. However, we've all known each other for some time and I don't think you're here to discuss his amnesia."

Allan leaned back in his seat again, suddenly feeling ashamed at his own trepidation to say what was really on his mind. The courage of his convictions escaped him, as it always did the moment he found himself speaking among his "peers" – those professional academics who have made their brand of objectivity into an upgrade of religious dogma. Every time Allan opened his mouth or committed a word to paper, a programmed instinct kicked in and overwrote him, editing his tone, rearranging his words to be commensurate with the scientific presupposition that all exposition must be neutral in tone and mundane in description. He could feel this vapid voice swelling in his lungs, forcing its way to his larynx. He swallowed it down…

"Long before Darwin, a Swedish botanist made the connection between man and evolution," he began. "His taxonomy of life grouped humans with primates. However, for humans he made a distinction, classifying them with the words *Nosce te ipsum.* These words are also found at the Temple of Apollo at Delphi. They mean, '*Know Thyself.*'"

"It's been a long time since anyone has sacrificed goats at the Temple of Apollo, Allan," Kohei said smugly.

"Kohei." Pearson's voice, though not elevated, was firm enough to censure Kohei's sarcasm.

"No, he's right." Allan waved it all away with his hand. "Forget that I said that part; or maybe you can't forget it at this point. Both of you already know that I do an absolutely terrible job of disguising myself with scientific language."

"I know where you're going with this, Allan," Pearson said, leveling with Allan. "I'm not trying to insult you when I say that you're a *closet mystic.* You've been one for as long as I've known you. Who knows? Maybe I am one too and don't know it. You want to believe that there is some essential self that is distinguishable from the neurological self –"

"How did we arrive at a *neurological self*, Pearson?" Allan forced in his rebuttal. "We've evolved from primitive responses to environmental irritants to a complex 'neurological self' as you call it. What makes you, or any of us, think that it stops there? Why couldn't this neuro-self take it a step further?"

"As you spout your solipsist unified theory," Kohei interjected, "there's no doubt in my mind that your temporal lobe is having a Fourth of July fireworks festival."

"Actually, Kohei, this isn't a unified theory. Quite the opposite," Allan replied. "Humor me, Kohei. Using your finger, show me 'you.' Point to the entity that is '*you.*'"

"Is this philosophy 101 now?" Kohei quipped at Allan.

"Yes," Allan returned, not missing a beat, "so you should scarcely be intimidated by this little exercise."

Kohei didn't appreciate this trick, but his ego responded faster than his mind. He looked objectionably at Pearson while making a deliberately approximate point in the direction of his body.

"Let me guess. Now you're going to say that this isn't me. It's only my body." Kohei was trying to get the upper hand, but Allan didn't respond. He just stared at Kohei, who stared back as if they were having an intellectual stand-off.

"Kohei," Pearson's voice broke the silence.

Kohei looked over at Pearson, immediately realizing from the soft grin on his face that Pearson had made himself an accomplice to Allan's "exercise."

"I think we just found 'you,'" Allan said, smirking a little. "Lower organisms do not respond to a name, because the only sense of self they have is a somatic one. For them, self and body, brain and mind, are one. For higher organisms, this somatic-self unity is dividing into two. Like Joey, a name is how we retain our sense of self after such a division. A name is the 'finger' we can use to point to the Innate Self."

"Dogs?" Pearson retorted. Now it was his turn to be the skeptic.

"What about them?" Allan asked.

"My dog knows his name. Hell, my cat does too. There's nothing special about it."

"I'm not suggesting that, in order for a quality to be special, it has to be exclusive to humans," Allan replied, looking at Pearson. Next he turned his attention towards Kohei. "This is not a 'solipsist unified theory.' This is more like those Chinese boxes that the British philosopher AJ Ayer used to describe the Intrinsic Self.

You open one box only to discover another box inside. Then you open that one, and therein is another box.

"I compare the largest box to the human body. We open that box to find another box. Maybe this second box is the human brain. And when we open that box, there is yet another one, a third one, inside which is the human mind. Now we open that box, only to find a fourth one, and written on the face of this box is our Name – our singular Name."

"Okay," Kohei leaned forward, "then, when we open *that* box – then what?"

Allan remained silent.

"Another box, or just *nothing*?" Kohei added. "It's not that I don't admire your tenacity, Allan, but I can't help questioning it. I wonder..." Kohei paused to notice the look of undivided attention on Allan's face. "Are you afraid of the possibility that this last box, the one with *your* name on it, has absolutely nothing at all inside of it?

"No soul, no spirit, no ghost.

"Just nothing, Allan...

"A void."

***

Hours later, Allan sat alone at his office, still ruminating on Kohei's words. A nerve had been struck. He was suspicious of his own agenda. *What was this really all about?* he wondered to himself. *Am I really just making a case for the soul?*

Allan's eyes looked down at the old typewriter that sat in front of him on his desk. It was the perfect symbol for a *"closet mystic,"* still clinging to obsolete ideas like *self* and *soul*. Inside the typewriter was a sheet of paper, half filled with ink letters. *Kohei was right,* Allan thought to himself. *I am tenacious. So much so, that I'm writing out my antiquated thoughts on a piece of technology that I could only get at a flea market!*

Kohei had always been harsh with his words. He had never been patient with "existential nonsense" as he called it, and often he was right. There was a great deal of unsubstantiated crap still lingering around. Most of it was rightly ignored. The Twentieth Century was the Age of Physics when it had finally been confirmed that our once mysterious universe was wholly mechanical. The Twenty-First Century was now the Age of Biotech. It seemed that what physics had done to the universe, biotechnology would do to the body.

Then Allan thought about David Lee, the guy he almost hit on the highway. David was the guy who told him that nobody gave a shit anymore about the mind; that it was all about the brain. He was right. Allan had studied Michael Persinger's brain experiments, in which he had recreated religious experiences in the heads of unreligious people. He did this by stimulating parts of the temporal lobe, triggering his subjects to "see" the face of Christ or "feel" the presence of God. *Products of the mind,* Allan thought. *Spirituality is a sham. That David guy was right. I should call him and tell him.*

Call David!

Allan suddenly remembered that he had never followed up with David about Joey.

Joey!

He now suddenly remembered that he wasn't alone in his office. Joey was here with him.

Allan swiveled in his chair and looked over at Joey, who sat still, in a blank meditation that rendered his face and eyes into a void-like gaze. Allan watched his face, wondering if Joey would eventually feel his stare. We've all felt such a thing before – that quiescent message that turns our eyes in a seemingly random direction, confirming that, yes, we were being watched. Sometimes our eyes snap to the face of a comely stranger and we romanticize the experience as *love at first sight*. Other times it is an unwelcome face and we feel as if we're being stalked. We've all experienced this, even Joey. He must have. Allan counted the seconds waiting for Joey's eyes to snap to his. They never did.

"Joey," Allan called softly. Joey's eyes turned in the direction of his name.

Allan smiled. He stood up and grabbed a small mirror. He walked over to Joey, bringing the mirror in front of him.

Joey stared into the mirror, but Allan couldn't be sure if Joey knew the person he was seeing was himself.

"Please close your eyes, Joey," Allan asked softly.

Joey obeyed.

"Make a picture in your head, Joey – a picture of yourself."

Allan looked at the reflection of Joey in the mirror, wondering if Joey was now creating that same image in his head.

"Do you remember who that person is?" Allan asked.

"Joey2," he replied.

"Thank you, Joey," Allan said with a satisfied expression on his face. His experiment was over. Though Allan had not convinced Pearson, Kohei or even himself about the value of a name, he was, at least, convinced not to abandon the argument.

As Allan swiveled back to his desk, he stopped to notice that Joey's eyes had returned to an idle expression, or had they? Allan squinted, as if observing more acutely what was behind Joey's eyes. This was not a void. This was more akin to the look of daydreaming. Allan gazed within himself, whispering a Hebrew word – *"Tzafah"* – not realizing that in his moment of sagacity he resembled Joey.

Holding his thoughts in mind, Allan returned to his desk and began punching at the keys with his fingers. He did this for over an hour before he was satisfied with breaking away from this ritual. He turned once more to look at Joey, whose expression and posture hadn't changed. He turned back to add four verses from a poem he kept in memory:

> *"There slumbers a song in all things,*
> *dreaming on and on…*
> *and the world set out to sing,*
> *if only you strike The Magic Word."*

The manuscript was finished; all except the title, which he could decide on later. He placed in a new sheet of paper and punched out the most tentative name he could think of:

"UNTITLED"

Allan held Joey's hand as he entered his home at a late hour. Once again, Gabriella had to stay late, attending to Claudia, helping her into her bed, then waiting for Allan.

Usually, when Allan arrived, she'd stand to greet him. Today, she was tired, frustrated. She remained seated, greeting him by his first name in a flat tone.

"Hello, Allan."

She glanced down at Joey, the kid who had started all of this, but it wasn't his fault. She forced an exhausted smile from herself.

"Hi, Joey."

Neither Allan nor Joey responded. Allan just looked at her, expecting her to reprimand him or just quit. Gabriella, in turn, was expecting Allan to volunteer an explanation for coming home late – again. Neither met the expectation of the other. The silence was clumsy. Finally, Gabriella looked at her watch, rapped her hands against her thighs, stood up, and excused herself from her work.

"Gabriella," Allan called out to her. She turned to him. "Please take tomorrow off." She said nothing, her eyes asking for an explanation. She wondered if she was being fired.

"I'm finished with my analysis on Joey," Allan continued. "I'm taking him back to the police tomorrow."

"But Claudia…"

"Claudia will come with me, for some fresh air."

Gabriella looked at him.

"Thank you, Gabby." Allan turned around to get Joey situated.

He had never called her that name before, *Gabby*. It was a pet name he must have just invented, perhaps to let her know that she was no longer just an employee, but officially initiated into the family. It was a nice gesture, one that she might appreciate in the morning when she was not so tired anymore.

As Gabriella closed the door behind her, Allan made Joey comfortable in the TV room, then left him to watch a rerun of **Star Wars: *The Clone Wars***.

***

Claudia was asleep. Her sickly body looked fragile in her home hospital bed, but her sleep was peaceful. Allan stood in the doorway, looking at her, debating if he should wake her to let her know that he had come home. Her hollowed appearance that seemed so much to mirror the stillness of death made Allan think about Kohei's question again. *Did he fear the void of death?*

"Claudia."

She opened her eyes at the sound of her name.

"I'm home."

She looked in the direction of Allan, but she didn't smile.

"How did it go today?" he asked.

"Fine, it went fine, Allan. What time is it?"

"I don't know. I wasn't paying attention. It's late."

"Of course it's late. It's always late when I'm in bed and you're just getting home."

Allan said nothing. He had no defense other than to just change the subject.

"How did it go with Gabriella? Is she taking good care of you?"

"It would be easier for me, Allan, if you asked me asinine questions in the morning, and not while I'm trying to sleep."

Again, Allan gave no reply. He sighed mildly, knowing that even his silence would be met with sharp rejoinders.

"Yes, she's taking good care of me. She gave me a pep talk today. *'Don't be defined by your disease.'* Ugh. Did you hire a caretaker or a motivational speaker?"

"She's just trying to help, Claudia. She's young."

"Young I can handle. Stupid is unacceptable."

"She's not stupid," Allan replied listlessly, not sure why he was even playing into this argument. Claudia had made idle threats of replacing Gabriella before, but right now she seemed serious. Why? Maybe she hadn't been asleep at all. Maybe she heard him call her *Gabby*.

"If she's not stupid, she's certainly patronizing," Claudia continued. "'*Don't be defined by my disease.'* What the hell does that mean anyway?"

"It means just that...if that's what you want it to mean."

"*If that's what I want it to mean?*" Her voice heightened. "This isn't a Zen disease that I have, Allan. If this disease doesn't define me then what does it do? The young and healthy are defined by what they can do, the old and sick by what they *can't* do."

"Is that how you choose to see this, Claudia?" Allan asked, now hearing his own voice heightening.

"*Choose?*" That word almost gave Claudia enough strength to raise herself up in her bed. She pulled herself up just enough to get a better view of Allan – and to give Allan a better view of her,

her body, and her sickness. "I didn't know that I had chosen this, Allan."

She dramatically squeezed her eyes shut, almost looking like Dorothy trying to get back to Oz. "Okay, let me 'choose' something else. I am not Claudia anymore…"

She opened her eyes, "I am…SUPERWOMAN!"

Allan's face fell silent as he absorbed the sarcasm. Despite the sharp needles in Claudia's words, there was no irony in her face. Her own words wounded herself as much as Allan.

"Well, that didn't work. Maybe I need to *choose* a different perspective. That's another one of your favorite buzzwords, right? *Perspective.* So give me some other buzzword, Allan, that will help me re-package how I see things. Psychologists are good at that. What's the magic buzzword I'm not thinking of?"

Allan had stopped looking at Claudia; at the deep malaise of her body. Instead he looked up at the *"PEI"* painting that hung silently on their wall.

"A magic word… " he said, almost whispering.

Finally he looked back at her. "How about…*Claudia?*" he said with mocking revelation in his eyes. "Sounds like the perfect name for Superwoman."

That was the best he could do at a rejoinder. He wasn't nearly as good at it as Claudia, but it was enough to bring them both to a dead silence.

Allan realized that he hadn't even stepped past the doorway all this time.

Silently he entered his half of the bedroom, and, without so much as removing a single layer of clothing, he climbed into his bed and lay in sleepless silence.

***

"...Police are still hoping for someone to come forward with any information about a boy named Joey the Second, who was found lost along Gemelo Road. Joey was carrying no identification with him, so police say they don't know his last name, age, or address. Police are having difficulty finding the parents or a guardian of the child. If you have any information about Joey, please call Precinct 19 at..."

A photo of Joey's face appeared for a fraction of a second before vanishing as James Price hit the "OFF" button on the remote, cancelling the report. The image of Joey was quickly replaced by his own reflection from the vacant black monitor of the TV screen. He looked away, having no interest in seeing himself.

He sat on the edge of a bed in a rented luxury suite – an exile from both job and home. Secret thoughts hung over his head. His head lowered, his eyes deeply troubled, he solemnly deliberated his situation.

He was fucked.

***

Joey also sat in total silence as the light from the TV made shifting luminary patterns against his body. His head angled low, his eyes shut, sleeping – dreaming.

***

The sound of a vibrating cell phone rattling atop the hard nightstand surface was enough to jolt Allan awake. As he grabbed at the phone, he missed the unspeakably early hour displayed on the phone's screen.

"Hello."

"Dr. Allan Shapiro?"

"Yes."

"My name is Officer Connel. We got a call about a half-hour ago about Joey."

Allan, suddenly alert, rose up in his bed.

"You did?"

"Yeah, from a woman who saw his face on the news. She says she recognizes Joey from a group home in her neighborhood. Is Joey with you now?"

"Of course. Why?"

"We're going over to talk to the woman now."

"Should I be there? I mean, you need my analysis, don't you?"

"We can send a car over to where you live to pick up Joey and your report. You could follow us if you want to be there when we drop Joey off."

Allan tried his best not to wake Claudia as he finished his call, quietly sneaking away from his bed. He entered the TV room where he saw Joey slumped over in the sofa chair.

"Shit!" Allan cursed himself, blaming his stupid argument with Claudia as the reason for forgetting the boy.

"Joey."

Joey's eyes opened to his name.

"It's time to go home."

Most children love to play in a tub of water, but not Joey. He stood mechanically, as if the act of being washed down by Allan was routine and clinical. Allan imagined the procedure differently. In his mind, he was a father soaking a small stream of water in a sponge and showering it over the head of his son. His was a childless home, and this opportunity for parental role play might never come again.

"Okay, I think that's good enough. Let's get you dried off and dressed."

As Allan lifted Joey from the tub, water drained from his body to the clear, porcelain floor. Joey looked down at the sight of his reflection. He said nothing, but the look in his eyes showed evidence of familiarity. Allan pointed to his shimmering image.

"Who is that?"

Joey's eyes studied his vibrating reflection. Small drops, still striking the small puddle, continued to ripple the image. Finally, the puddle steadied and Joey could see his clone staring back at him.

"Joey2."

Allan marveled at this moment of reflection and remembrance.

"That's right, Joey. That's who you are."

***

Pressed for time, Allan struggled with pulling a fresh shirt over his head while his phone, set for speaker, dialed for Gabriella. As luck would have it, she answered while his head was still buried in the body of his shirt.

"Gabby, it's me: Allan," he said, forcing his voice through the fabric.

"Is something wrong? Your voice sounds muffled?"

"I'm rushing to get out the door. The police picked up a lead on Joey and I need to… Well, I need *you* to –"

"I'm on my way, Allan," she interjected, already knowing his request and hung up.

"Son of a bitch!" Allan cursed through his teeth, still fighting with the shirt. He paused, realizing that he heard the sound of a voice chuckling. *Joey?* Allan stared through the cross hatches of the fabric, scarcely making out the silhouetted form of a person standing directly in front him.

"Dr. Shapiro," the voice spoke softly, holding back laughter.

Finally freeing his hands from their entanglement, Allan pulled the shirt past his head to find the face of an intruder watching him. He had the eyes of a dangerous man, but his form and figure were surprisingly staid.

He was tall, slender, bald, wearing glasses; he covered his cruel chuckle with a smile.

"I apologize for laughing," the stranger told Allan. "It's just that… this wasn't the encounter I had expected. Then again, I suppose you weren't expecting an encounter at all, which means I owe you an explanation."

Allan's face dropped, his mind frozen in some surrealistic dimension. Empiricism was a lie. It had to be. His eyes had pulled back the curtain, revealing a man who seemed to have been there all along, yet that simply wasn't possible. Allan had heard no footsteps, no sounds of the door opening. Like an apparition, there was suddenly an unannounced presence, standing there.

It had a voice, a neutral voice that seemed to speak as if nothing out of the ordinary was happening.

"I'm here for Joey," the man continued. "That's the bad news. The good news is that this is all I am here for. I am not here to hurt you or your wife." The bald man took a step back, opening his arms. "As you can see, I have no gun or any other kind of weapon on me."

He paused, allowing Allan more than ample time to appraise the sincerity of his disclosure. It was of little comfort to Allan, who felt the adrenaline pushing its way through his body, obscuring his judgment, transforming reality into a chiaroscurist haze. Allan was sure of this hallucination. His vision began to refocus while watching this man calmly fit his hands with latex gloves.

"Who are y–" Allan's words were cut short by the stranger's gesturing silence. He held a single finger to his lips.

"Shhh…I think your wife is still sleeping. Let's keep it that way," he said.

The shushing sound gave Allan a sinking feeling of vulnerability. Realizing the danger he was facing, he began to back away along the wall, slowly shaking his head in disbelief. The invader followed his every step calmly, with no rush, knowing that Allan, although stout and corpulent, was in no shape to escape his fate.

"Where's Joey?" Allan demanded.

"He's already gone."

"The police are coming."

"No, they're not."

"You are here to kill me, aren't you?" These words slipped through Allan's mouth with a haunting inevitability. He could feel his heart kicking through his chest.

"Who, me?" This response was unusual, unnatural. "No, I am not here to kill you. If you cooperate, you can survive this." From his jacket, he pulled a syringe, then removed the protective cap, avoiding eye contact with Allan, so as not to alarm him. The sight of the syringe caused Allan to breathe heavily again. "The people who made this informed me that the expurgation of your memory will be complete but not permanent. You will have the ability to form new memories when this is over."

"Please…" Allan pleaded. The invader ignored him, reaching out with the syringe in a calculated and clinical manner, neither comforting nor threatening. Allan was surprised when he found himself acquiescing. He wasn't sure what to do, but he tried his best to steady his nerves, to calm himself. The invader noticed the change and took this as his opportunity. Everything about him was mechanical, like a skeleton in motion. His determination to complete this assignment was eerily dispassionate.

Allan raised his head, exposing his neck. His chest was heaving in and out heavily. His body was tense. His mind was trying to make sense of all this. As the syringe came nearer, he became blinded by the instinct to defend himself. With a sudden motion, he deflected the syringe, knocking it from the invader's hand to the ground. Next, he threw his body weight at his opponent, thinking that by virtue of sheer mass, he could overpower the assailant.

Yet he was no match for the invader who held his ground, anchoring his own body weight against Allan's, their arms struggling against each other. Soon, Allan realized that despite the slender appearance this man was clearly stronger.

In a sudden, brutal move, the attacker pulled his left hand free and locked both hands on Allan's right wrist, swiftly snapping it from a rapid twist.

Allan shrieked. He yanked his body away, retreating from the pain and the attacker. While he stumbled backwards, his foot came down on the syringe, shattering it. He collapsed and crashed into the floor.

With sharp pain shooting up from his wrist, pulsating through his arm, Allan writhed in agony, looking up at the invader, who looked down on him, shaking his head at his foiled plan. Yet he remained calm. There was no panic in his eyes as his mind quickly made a re-appraisal of his assignment. With perfect stillness, he studied Allan's condition, perused his remaining options, and arrived at his decision. He knelt down and unequivocally placed both gloved hands around Allan's neck.

The void.

The feeling of this word – the void – passed through Allan's mind. In fact, his whole body suddenly became aware of this feeling as the pressure of steely hands closed in and cut off his air. Without breath or voice, the entire three-dimensional world felt flat.

His injured hand could do nothing for him. His uninjured hand did little to save him as he punched at the man who was squeezing the very life from him.

There were no faces that passed through Allan's eyes – not the face of the diner waitress, Gabriella, or even Claudia. There was only the frightening face of a man with a shaven head; equable eyes; and thin, white, and bloodless lips. Even this image became hazy.

Life did not flash before Allan's eyes, but he felt life. That was the parting gift of death – he could feel life. It was there. Not devoured by the void, but separating itself from it.

He heard his Name.

Not the name *Allan*, but some other undulation that mixed *sound* and *light* with the mystery of *life*. His Name detached itself from its somatic tethers and slipped free into some place of secrecy.

71

Claudia, meanwhile, had mustered all the strength she could find to pull herself from her bed; an ambition defied by her rotting muscles. She tried to retreat into the darkness of her bedroom, but the door opened, and the light pouring inside exposed her slow escape.

She grabbed only the briefest look at her husband's killer from a small desk mirror. Through the mirror, his eyes met hers, and she instinctively looked away.

Defenseless, she said nothing. She took her few remaining seconds to prepare herself for the inevitable. Yet more than a few seconds passed and she wondered how it was that she was still breathing.

The threat still lingered in the doorway. Once again, the nameless invader repeated his ritual of silently and stoically diagnosing his options. Claudia waited on the brink of life and death that was completely in the hands of this man. She could feel his eyes heavy on her frail body. She could sense that her condition was being studied. The tension finally undid her, and she could not help but to petition for her own life.

"Please...don't kill me."

These words always brought a smile to his face. He simply could not help it. He had heard them so many times, and each time he gave the same reply.

"*Who, me?*"

With those words his decision was made, and it was final. He would leave. She would live. She would *remember*.

She would never forget the haunting sounds of this tragic morning and the darkened images that came with it.

She would suffer the memory of Allan.

Chapter Four

Stan's office was empty. The only "thing" he didn't seem to be able to move out was himself. He was sitting at an empty desk reading ***Genetic Engineering for Dummies***, the book Amber gave him. He looked up when he noticed his boss, Joseph Saracki, Director of the FBI-FDA Hybrid-Division, walking inside.

"What the hell are you still doing here?" Saracki asked.

Stan didn't answer. He had no viable reason for hanging around at his old office.

"Is this the silent treatment, or are you still trying to find a good answer?" Saracki asked, sitting down on the edge of Stan's desk and welcoming himself to Stan's book, removing it from his hands. "What is this?"

"You should know. You signed your name on the inside just like everyone else."

"Oh, that's right, your going away present," Saracki mumbled, checking the inside flap for his signature, then placing the book face down on the table.

"Reading this doesn't qualify as work. I hope you know that."

74

Again Stan didn't reply. Saracki allowed the silence. They had known each other long enough not to pollute such moments with hurried answers. Besides, Saracki understood what Stan was going through. He decided to level with him.

"Listen, back when 'Papa Bush' was President, he pushed Congress to loosen the leash on the biotechs, so they could expand from a $4 billion to a $50 billion dollar industry. Only eight years later, 'Baby Bush' took the baton and the FDA's approval process accelerated." – Saracki threw up his hands suggesting an act of magic. – "Ta-da! Today, it's damn near a trillion-dollar industry, the most profitable in the country after oil."

"Maybe we should be shaking down the FDA, not partnering with them," Stan replied.

"Sure, let's do that," Saracki retorted. "Right after we shake down our own agency for doing the same shit. After that, we'll look at *all* the other agencies. Then, if there's time left over, we'll get to the FDA."

"What the fuck, Joe! What's your point?"

"The point is: Stop moping around like you've just been demoted. It's the same fucking game whether you play in this stadium or some other one."

"So you came here to tell me that?"

"No, actually, I came here to throw you a bone. I've got a kidnapping case."

"I thought you wanted me to work with the FD–"

"You will. The FDA's been probing a biotech that may have violated the federal moratorium on human cloning."

"What?" Stan exclaimed.

"The police had a cognitive psychologist walk through their doors with a lost boy. He tells them that he, and some other guy, found the boy late at night on Gemelo Road, just a few miles away from the same biotech that the FDA's been keeping their eye on. The boy is apparently amnesic, so the police asked the psychologist to help diagnose his condition. The psychologist agrees, and within a few days he's dead and the boy's gone." Saracki paused, letting it all sink in, before continuing: "The police are at the psychologist's house now. Head over there and get the details from them.

"Don't forget your new partner."

***

Two cops watched Gabriella help Claudia into her wheelchair and give her an insulin injection.

"What happened to her?" asked one of the cops under his breath.

"Myotonic Dystrophy; it's a form of Muscular Dystrophy except it appears in adults, usually around middle age. Her muscles are rotting."

"Is there a cure?"

"Does it look like there's a cure? The money is never in the cure. It's always in the treatment, and there's no money in treating something as rare as Myotonic Dystrophy. The market is too small. She's gonna die that way."

Both cops looked towards the door as it opened.

Stan walked in with Addison, who immediately seemed out of place at a crime scene, a point evident to everyone but Addison. He interrupted a group of officers from their forensics, holding a three-inch thick manual in front of their faces. One officer accepted, looking past Addison at Stan as if to say *Who the fuck is this guy?*

"Hybrid-Division." Stan answered.

The cop stood up, brushing Addison off, and walked over to Stan. He handed Stan a clear plastic bag, containing shards of glass.

"We're not sure what it is, but smell it," the cop instructed. Stan took a whiff and his face recoiled. "Exactly, it's definitely some kind of chemical," the cop added. "Found it right next to where we found the body – altercation."

"Altercation?" Stan asked astounded. He noticed Claudia and Gabriella in the other room. "Were they here when it happened?"

"The woman in the wheelchair was here. The killer came to her bedroom."

"But he didn't kill her?"

"You have eyes, don't you? You can see that she's over there, still breathing, so no," the cop replied sarcastically. "She said the room was dark, and that he was standing in the doorway. You figure, whatever light was in the house, was to his back. Maybe he figured she didn't get a good look at him, so he didn't see any reason to make a messy situation even messier."

Stan received this conjecture rather dubiously. He walked away, making his way for Claudia.

"Mrs. Shapiro?" he asked, showing his badge.

"Yes?" Claudia looked up at Stan.

"I need to ask you a few questions about Dr. Shapiro."

Stan felt a hand touch his shoulder; he turned around and saw Addison stand behind him.

"I thought we weren't here for a murder case," Addison said, with a hint of impatience in his voice.

"We're not, but –"

"Then why are you here?" Claudia interrupted, irritated by what she had just heard. "Who are you two anyway?"

"We belong to a collaboration unit between the FBI and the Food and Drug Administration," Addison tried explaining.

"Why is the Food and Drug Administration inside my house, asking me questions about my murdered husband?!?!" Claudia's voice rose with each word, her pointed eyes and words aimed directly at Stan.

"Actually, he's FDA. I'm FBI," Stan clarified, showing his badge again.

"If you're FBI, shouldn't you be asking questions about my husband's murder?"

"The police will investigate that. We're here to find out about the boy," Addison replied.

"Mrs. Shapiro," Stan interjected, his agent instincts kicking in and kicking out Addison's anal adherence to protocol. "Did you see the man who did this? Did you see or hear anything?"

"Not really, no. It was too dark and I was afraid to look at him anyway. I only heard his voice. I asked him not to kill me, and all he said was 'Who, me?' and then he was gone."

"Did Dr. Shapiro say anything?" Stan persisted. "Anything at all that might hint at why this man came after him?"

"No."

"Do you remember the last conversation you had with him?"

"The last conversation we had was… I don't know how this is going to help anything."

Stan knelt down, compassionately, to be on her level.

"You'd be surprised how small details will help a case."

"Well…in our last conversation he called me…*Superwoman.*"

Dumbfounded, Stan looked up at Addison, whose only response was a silent, reprimanding frown.

***

"So do you think after tonight she'll fly out of that wheelchair and capture her husband's killer?" Addison asked Stan sarcastically while a security guard escorted them through the busy hallways of Crotona hospital.

"Relax, point taken," Stan replied.

"Please make sure that it is. We're not here for a murder case."

"Oh, yeah? Well the way you walked into Dr. Shapiro's house, wearing your detective face, I would have thought they plucked you out of the LAPD, not the FDA." Stan was quite proud of his little jab but surprised that Addison hadn't entertained it with a response.

The guard dropped them off in a stripped down room with mostly white walls and intimidating technical equipment. There was a strange ambiance to the place, for the sterile room strongly reflected the light from above.

"Please wait here while I get Dr. Fueller," the guard said, leaving the room. Addison, feeling familiar with the setting, exhaled and found a place to sit. Stan wandered around the room until his eyes were drawn in by a life-size reprint of *"Anatomie des parties de la génértion de l'homme et de la femme,"* an illustration of a dissected pregnant woman and her exposed fetus. It was both haunting and beautiful.

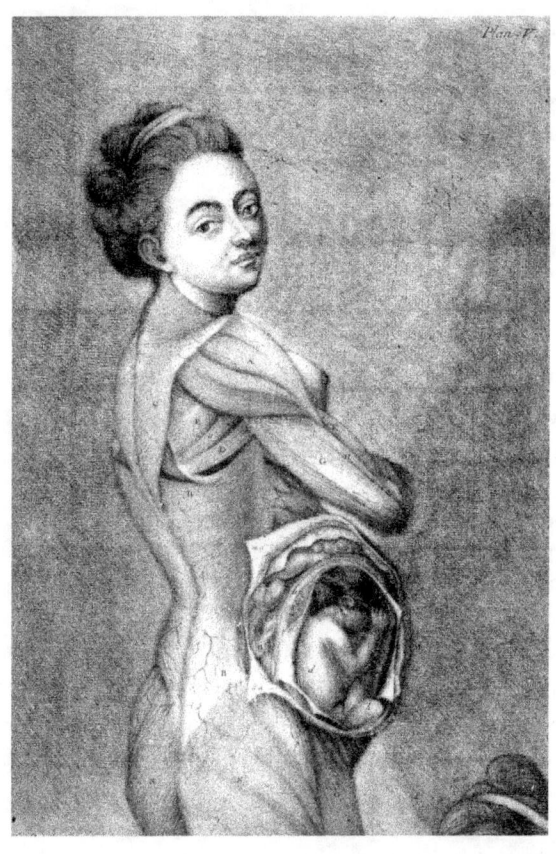

"Hello, gentlemen." Pearson's voice pulled Stan's eyes away from the illustration. Addison stood up. "So you two are part of this new government Hybrid-Division?" Pearson shook hands with Addison. "We just met, so I'll save the bureaucratic jokes for later."

"You gave Dr. Shapiro access to these facilities, so he could run tests on the young boy he found, right?" Addison asked, jumping right in.

"Yes, that's correct. I did. Allan was doing some analytic tests for the police although he was motivated by some of his own curiosities as well."

"Curiosities? Such as?" Addison asked, his face skewed.

"Joey had a very severe, yet remarkably selective, memory disorder."

"Memory loss is common," Addison commented.

"Yes, it is, but I don't think Allan was fixated on what Joey couldn't remember, rather on what he *could* remember – his name, and only his *first* name at that. His last name completely escaped him. Why would Joey remember his first name and nothing else?"

"How could he not?" Stan chimed in. "People hear their first name a dozen times a day."

"Well, that would mean that the cure for his memory loss would simply be repetition of usage. Yet every time Allan left the room and returned, he had to re-introduce himself to Joey. There's something about a name. Allan felt it was something of a milestone in our evolution from stimuli-awareness to self-awareness."

Hearing this, Stan turned around and looked again at the haunting illustration behind him. This time he took special notice of the divorce between the body of the woman, de-skinned and dissected, and the sense of self that seemed to linger in her eyes. More unnerving was the eye contact that this dichotomous image made with its viewer. While Stan fell into a trance, staring at the image, Pearson's voice continued to run through his head like an ambient commentary.

"Allan once told me a Jewish mystic story:

A Rabbi dies and stands before an Angel, waiting for entry into heaven. The Angel looks into the Book of Life and begins reading the names of all the souls entitled to afterlife. As he reads the names, the faces of the souls appear before the Rabbi in an instant, but the Rabbi never hears his name and begins to weep.

The Angel tells him: 'Do not weep. I spoke your name, but you did not recognize it. Return to earth and live out your life, knowing that your purpose is to know your true name and thereby know your true self.'

"Joey was Allan's excuse for re-opening his closet mysticism."

"Joey?" Addison asked.

"Yes, Joey the Second," Pearson replied. "That's the boy's name."

"In Western culture names are just practical labeling systems," he continued. "The nurses here often joke about the colorful names of our foreign patients. Americans don't appreciate the significance of a name. We give them to our children very carelessly, being either oblivious to their meaning, or treating them as a mere novelty to the life of the child.

"We have a lot of demented elderly patients here. Some of the newer nurses try to wake them by addressing them with their surname…and they don't respond. You can use your loudest voice and you will get no response. I tell them to use the first name. When you do that, they wake right up."

Stan walked away from the illustration, approaching Addison.

"You can't win today," he said jokingly. "You jumped right out of a murder case and into a philosophy class." He obnoxiously slapped Addison on the shoulder, chuckling.

"Sorry?" Pearson asked, recognizing that he was standing on the outside edges of an inside joke.

"Like you said, Dr. Fueller," Addison began clarifying. "We're part of the new Hybrid-Division, so we're not really here about Dr. Shapiro's murder. We're here about Joey."

"So his anomalies are of no importance to you?"

"They will be if we confirm some details about the boy."

"Which details?" Pearson asked.

"We can't discuss that; not until we know more ourselves. Even then, I'm not sure we'll be able to discuss it."

To this, Pearson remained silent.

"Out of curiosity," – Stan leaned against the wall, looking at Pearson – "do you know what your name means?"

"I do. Are you familiar with the Bible?"

"More familiar than I would prefer; had it pounded into my head by my parents," Stan replied, smiling.

"Then you're familiar with the fisherman Simon, whose name was changed to Peter by Jesus. Pearson is my first name; it is a variant of the Biblical name Peter. It comes from the Greek word *Petra*, which means *Rock*. 'I say also unto thee, that thou art Peter, and upon this rock I will build my church.'"

"You've had scriptures pounded into your head too, huh?" Stan joked.

"*Pounded?* No. Whipped? Yes," Pearson retorted with a cynical curve in his voice.

"What do you mean?" Stan asked.

"Do I look like a 'Pearson Fueller' to you?" Pearson pressed his fingers into his face as if to exhibit his dark skin. "Blacks had their last names imposed on them by their slave owners, and their first names by a slave religion."

Stan remained silent, suddenly reconsidering this "philosophy class" he had mocked only a few minutes earlier.

"Now I'm curious… What is your name?" Pearson asked Stan.

"Stan Medes."

"Right," – Pearson smiled – "you don't look like your name either."

Addison, the only white man in the room, felt discomfited by where the conversation was going, but he also couldn't resist wondering about the etymology of his own name.

"I'm not a religious man, Stan Medes," Pearson continued. "I had no scriptures 'pounded into my head' as you did, nor am I a closet mystic as Allan was. Yet I don't believe you have to be either to have some sense of conviction about your own identity."

Pearson turned to walk towards the door.

"Wait, what about Joey?" Addison called after him.

"Everything I know about him I've already told you."

Before he could leave, Stan quickly added: "I have one more question."

"Yes."

"If identities are a point of conviction, tell me… Do you know the patients in this hospital by name?"

Pearson smiled, shaking his head slightly.

"Of course not. Since when has any institution known any of us by our names?" Pearson walked away, stopping in the doorway to look back at Stan and offer his last words. "We know them only by their numbers."

With those words, Addison and Stan stood alone in the room, silently looking in the direction of where Pearson left.

"Well…" Stan said, breaking the silence, but as he searched his own thoughts, the room was once again quiet. A minute passed. "So…" Stan continued, "What do you suppose your name means?"

"*That which we call a rose by any other name would smell as sweet,*" Addison replied, quoting Shakespeare. "Besides," he continued, "we're American. Our job titles are more important."

Whatever, Stan thought and moved back into their investigation: "Do you want to head over to ETGR?"

"Yes," Addison replied, "but let's head over to Dr. Shapiro's office first."

"Dr. Shapiro? Don't you mean…*Allan*?" Stan winked.

"Same difference."

***

"The FDA is on a kidnapping case?" Mae, Allan's assistant, asked as she stood in front of Stan and Addison, looking the two men up and down.

"He's FDA. I'm FBI," Stan thumbed over to Addison. "Please direct all of your sarcasm over to him."

Stan walked away, over to Allan's bookshelf, pretending to have any interest in the hodgepodge of titles:

GREEK MYTHS, MEMORY,
ANCIENT EGYPTIAN CONCEPTS OF THE SOUL,
THE HIDDEN MYSTERIES OF NUMBERS

Stan's eyes stopped at the last title, written by Sheikh Habeeb Ahmad. He reached up and removed it from the shelf.

"Excuse me; if you're not the police, then maybe you shouldn't snoop through Allan's stuff."

Stan, irritated, replied by holding up his badge.

"I'd like to have a look at Dr. Shapiro's reports and the results from his tests on Joey." Addison got straight to the point. Mae instinctively thought to protest but suppressed the idea when she saw that Stan was still holding up his badge. She conceded and left the room.

Stan, finally, put the badge away and began scanning the pages, stopping at one particular paragraph that brought to mind Pearson's last words before he bailed on the investigation.

"To an ordinary mind a name is no more than a mere label, but a student of the mysteries of science and nature thinks differently. He knows that every letter in a name has a value, both phonetically and numerically, and that it has an aggregate value which can be made to yield a single digit...

"Everyone knows that a name is a compound of so many letters or sounds, but very few are aware that every letter has its numerical value according to a certain scale of progression..."

1 2 3 4 5 6 7 8 9
A B C D E F G H I
J K L M N O P Q R
S T U V W X Y Z

While Stan surveyed the book, Mae returned, handing over a small folder to Addison.

"Mostly PET scans," she said, "I'm not sure if this is what you were expecting."

"Thank you," Addison answered. He held the folder to his side, indicating to Mae that he planned to keep the contents and decide for himself if any of it would be useful.

Stan saw his cue and walked over to Addison.

"I know you're probably not at liberty to discuss, but I am going to ask anyway..." Mae wasn't giving up. "Why would the FDA be interested in a boy with amnesia?"

At first, Mae's question was met with silence. Then Stan made a deliberate clearing of his throat, holding a fist to his mouth as if blocking a cough.

"*Ahem...* He's FDA. I'm FBI."

Inside the car, Stan continued reading the book he swiped from Allan's office. "Dr. Shapiro was a strange man," he said, casually flipping from page to page.

"You probably shouldn't have done that," Addison commented.

"Done what?"

"Take his book. It is of no consequence to –"

"Alright, alright," Stan conceded, tossing the book into the back seat of the car. Addison looked over at Stan, hardly satisfied.

"Tossing the book into the back seat is not the solution, Stan."

"I'll return it tomorrow, or I'll donate it to science or something," Stan replied, dismissing Addison's protest.

"Try the library. Science would hardly come near it. In fact, we can't get far enough away from that kind of nonsense."

"Speaking of science, is ETGR next?"

"Tomorrow. I want to drop you off and then head back to the office, so I can go through Dr. Shapiro's reports on Joey."

"A boy with no memory… That's kind of crazy, huh?" Stan said.

"Not really, ever hear of Albert Szent-Gyorgyi?"

"Of course, who hasn't heard of Albert Gy-or-gy-i…" Stan replied, fumbling the syllables.

"Szent-Gyorgyi," Addison corrected. "He's the man who discovered Vitamin C. *'We know life only by its symptoms'* were his words. He also called biology *'the science of the improbable.'* Only when we are healthy, does the body seem like an improbable entelechy: The Intelligent Design of God, but then the body breaks down, like Allan's wife, whose muscles are genetically condemned to deteriorate over time. Now the so-called Intelligent Design of God seems quite flawed. The symptoms of illness remind us that we are neither immune to nor exempt from the cruel probability of gene mutation. We realize that the technology we create, and yet deplore, becomes the only explanation for our improbable victory in evolution."

All of this was a little heavier than what Stan had expected and he had no rebuttal prepared.

"Life for Joey may have begun in a Petri dish," Addison continued. "The idea that life can be engineered commits us to at least one scientific truth."

"Which is what?" Stan asked.

"God doesn't have a patent on life after all."

***

Pearson sat in silence in his office, looking at Allan's finished but forgotten manuscript. Actually, it was *near*-finished. The cover page revealed that Allan had left this world without ever having had a chance to give his book a proper title.

"UNTITLED"

BY DR. ALLAN SHAPIRO

Pearson stared at this word – "untitled" – wondering what Allan would have called his book. His rumination was interrupted by Kohei, who opened the door softly, sticking his head inside.

"Are they coming back?" he asked.

Pearson turned to look at him, then returned to his previous position. With his back turned, he answered Kohei cryptically:

"Does wisdom keep a man home, or does it send him on a journey?"

Kohei rolled his eyes. Pearson was sounding too much like Allan. He closed the door, leaving Pearson alone with the untitled manuscript in his hands.

***

Addison's car pulled up in front of the FBI Building and Stan hopped out of the passenger side, eager to get the hell out and back to familiar territory.

"Don't forget this," Addison called out.

Stan turned around and saw Addison hold the book from Allan's office. He rolled his eyes, dawdled back to the car and reclaimed it. He turned to walk away, but Addison's voice grabbed at him again.

"Take this too, Stan."

He turned around again. This time, Addison was holding up the plastic zipper bag with the shard of glass in it. Stan grabbed the bag somewhat forcefully.

"We'll head to ETGR tomorrow." Addison sounded as if he was giving an order. He pulled off without waiting for a response.

As Stan watched the car travel away, he grabbed at his nuts as if to say: *Fuck you,* knowing that even if Addison did see him in the rearview, a tightie-whitie like him would hardly know what the gesture meant. Of course, this hardly satisfied Stan as he grumbled to himself while marching towards the entrance and past the security check-in. He continued muttering futile insults while walking up the hallway.

"Arrogant prick."

"*Who, me?*" a voice answered.

These familiar words grabbed Stan from behind. He instinctively swiveled around in a self-defensive stance that relaxed at the sight of Heinrich, a balding agent from the BioEvaluations Department, who stepped out of the restroom, wrestling with his zipper.

"What did you just say?" Stan asked.

"You just insulted my prick," Heinrich replied, smiling and bringing way too much attention to his crotch as he finally managed to zip up.

"I wasn't talking to your pr–"

"I know, I know. I was just joking. So what got you all wound up like that?"

"Tell me something," Stan said, while he and Heinrich walked together. "What makes scientists think they know every fucking thing there is?"

"The name," Heinrich quipped.

"What?"

"It's the name – *Scientist*. It comes from some Latin word that means something to the effect of *Knowledge*."

"That means you know everything?"

"We wouldn't be called 'scientists' if we didn't."

"Okay, so since you know everything, tell me something about this." Stan forced the plastic zipper bag into his hand, "Take a smell."

"No, thanks… I trust hard data over anything my nose can tell me.

Let's head over to my office, so that we can take a peek."

They stepped inside the BioEvaluations Lab. Heinrich immediately got down to business with gloving his hands, masking his face, and draping himself in a lab coat. He tried talking, but Stan motioned to his mask, letting him know that he couldn't understand a single word.

"Sorry," Heinrich said, pulling the mask to his chin, "what I said was: 'I have a joke for you. You'll like this.'"

"Okay," Stan said, waving his hands inward.

"So three doctors die and go to heaven. Now these are three different types of doctors, and all three of them are standing in front of God, who is looking down on them from His throne. One's a witch doctor, okay? The other is just a straight-up quack, and the last one is a surgeon. Follow me?"

"Yeah."

"Okay, so God looks at the witch doctor and says:

'Why the hell should I let you into heaven? Look at the crazy voodoo shit you've done to people. Doctors are supposed to cure people, not put hexes on them.' God said this with a booming voice and the witch doctor got scared and begged and pleaded. 'Okay, okay,' God said, taking pity on the bastard. So He let him in.

Next was the quack. God said in a booming voice, 'Why should I let *you* into heaven? You've deceived people all your life, selling them snake oil when you should have given them cures.' So the quack begs for forgiveness, and God takes pity on him and lets him in too.

Finally, God comes to the surgeon. He leans back in His throne and looks at the surgeon and smiles. He says, 'Ah, my child. You've helped people. You've saved lives. Ask anything of me and it shall be granted.'

The surgeon looks at God and says, 'You can start by getting your ass out of my chair.'"

"Good one," Stan said chuckling.

"Glad you liked it; now get your ass out of my chair."

Stan looked down, abashed, then stood up as if he had been given an order.

"Thank you. There's a chair over there by the computer. This might take a while, so you can surf the web or do whatever you want while I run a check on this."

"Right."

Stan took a seat at the computer. His fingers poised in front of the keyboard, but then he paused, realizing he had no idea where to go online.

"Got any suggestions? You know, good websites?" Stan called out over his shoulder.

"*Google.com*, then type in 'porn,'" Heinrich replied.

"Fuck you," Stan mumbled, but, of course, he did indeed go to Google and typed:

P...O...R...

His fingers paused, tapped the backspace key twice, then typed in a new search query:

P...E...A...R...S...O...N F...U...E...L...L...E...R

Stan leaned forward, scanning the results. He clicked a link that snagged his attention. His eyes narrowed in on a few details.

A grin broke across his face.

Addison drove in silence.

Though it was late as hell, he had no intentions of going home. He was anxious to study Allan's reports on Joey, and the best place for him to do that was his office. His mind moved through a path of ruminations, thinking first about Joey and the investigation. Then he wondered if this collaboration between the FDA and FBI would bear any impact at all, or would it simply be a joke.

His thoughts were abruptly broken at the sight of a white van approaching him up ahead from the wrong side of the road. Addison pressed the horn lightly, but as the light drew closer, he pressed down harder, then started beating it with his fist, hoping to alert the other driver. The van persisted at a rapid speed.

Addison veered to the other side of the road, only to see that the van changed its course to match his. This encounter was no accident; that much was clear. This whole time he had been followed. Addison slammed the brakes, thinking there was time enough to turn the car around and make an escape. The plan abated within seconds when he realized that the van purposely accelerated as if to make a direct impact. Abandoning the car seemed hopeless, so Addison shielded himself for a collision. Seconds passed.

Nothing happened.

He lowered his arms to find that the van had stopped only a few feet away from him. There was not much Addison could do to save himself, but, whatever his fate from here, he could make it easier for someone to find him. Thinking fast, he pulled a cell phone from his pocket and punched quickly at the keys. He turned on the phone's GPS and forwarded his position to Stan.

The van door opened and a man emerged from the passenger side. The headlights, sharp and directional in the thick of night, were blinding. Addison could scarcely make out the man's form.

The shadowed, slender body was enveloped by beaming lights. The man stopped at the driver's door and suddenly bent down, bringing himself to eye level, allowing Addison to see his face: slender and bald, with steely eyes behind glasses and a dispassionate voice.

"I need you to stay calm, okay?" the man asked. Addison didn't reply. "Okay?" he asked again.

"Okay, okay," Addison reasoned. "I'll cooperate."

Addison watched the man pull a syringe from the inside of his jacket and remove a protection cap. Immediately, his mind began to race through escape options; the most obvious one being to slam the gas and take off, but take off where? The van blocked the way forward.

"Put the car in park," the man demanded, practically reading Addison's mind.

Addison obeyed. His next escape option flashed through his head. Without a second thought, he acted on it by quickly grabbing the car handle and pushing the door open into his abductor. The plan failed. The attacker intercepted the blow, catching the door and forcing it shut. A steel-like skeletal hand reached inside and grabbed Addison by the neck, squeezing.

"No," Addison said choking, "don't kill me."

"Who, me?" he replied, smiling.

Hard fingers dug deeply into Addison's throat; he instinctively froze up knowing that any movement would result in a crushed larynx. He struggled to breathe past the pressure points; all sound and motion came to a halt. His vision blurred, and just before collapsing out of consciousness, he felt a syringe needle puncture deeply into the side of his neck.

The blackness that soon followed felt like death.

Chapter Five

"Addison."

Addison heard a quiet voice in the darkness of his mind. The darkness dissipated slightly as he heard his name a second time. The voice heightened:

"Addison."

A vague demi-consciousness was returning to Addison. His eyes remained closed, but somehow light found its way inside his mind. As he focused on the light, it penetrated the darkness and uncovered a near perfect simulacrum of the outside world. He wasn't sure if it was real, or if his mind created it, or if there was even a difference. Either way, he did not question this mind-world that had managed to generate a face: a face he remembered, slender and bald. It was bold and steely-eyed, but somewhat hazy, as if summoned from a distant memory.

He heard his name repeatedly, which caused the sound to blur into a hazy, ambient, pervasive voice. He tried focusing on the sound, but he couldn't quite make out the words anymore, hearing only scrambled syllables: *Son-i-Adda.*

Next, the images in his head began to shuffle; the bald face disappeared, and suddenly he stood in front of Allan's home. He saw Claudia, Allan, and photographs of Joey. As the images panned through his head, making him dizzy, a voice that was not his own seemed to be at the helm of his consciousness, demanding answers:

"Are you here about Allan's murder?"

"*No.*"

"Are you here about the boy?"

"*Yes.*"

"What agency are you with?"

"*FDA.*"

"Your partner… Is he with the FDA as well?"

"*No, he's FBI.*"

"Do you remember his name?"

"*Stan.*"

"And you… Do you remember your name?"

"*Son of Adam.*"

Addison heard whispers: "*He remembers too much. Give him another injection.*" He felt a second puncture, followed by a saturated darkness.

He wasn't sure how much time had passed. He only knew that the darkness surrounding him had not fully claimed him. His mind was fighting, *remembering* his name: *Addison*. He was lingering inside the deep, clinging to his name as if it were the edge of an abyss. He knew if he lost his name, he would be gone too.

He'd stop existing. He knew he had to save it. His mind kept repeating it.

He felt his muscles move. He felt a chill. The darkness was still there, but of a different type. It was no longer the blackness of the abyss but of interminable consciousness…

He was waking up.

***

Addison's eyes opened to a placid sky mixed with cumulus clouds and a flock of birds passing in the distance.

He looked around and saw a terrain of dilapidated architecture. Buildings decayed from age and abandonment. This was an economically staggering environment, where the space had been engineered to no space at all. The design here was "massification" – an attempt to cram the enormous population called "the poor" into a segregated enclosure. Addison had never envisioned himself waking up in such a place. Nevertheless, there he was, pulling himself off the ground – a foreign organism in an environmental *geo*nome rife with malignant mutations. He didn't know where he was or how to get back home. He just knew he didn't belong. He felt a jolt of panic as his analytical mind kicked in, taking an inventory of his surroundings:

A black man was inside an abandoned car, sleeping.

Another man passed by on a bike, riding with one hand while using the other to balance a cinder block on his shoulder.

A third man was pushing a cart loaded with trash.

A young black woman carried a child.

These were ghosts in a fringe society, long forgotten by technology.

Could I ask any of these people for help, he wondered. His thoughts were interrupted by a voice:

"You can find 'King' just around the corner."

Addison's head swiveled in the direction of the voice. It belonged to a man whose face was heavy with lines and age. He looked like an artifact of decades past.

"Find whom?" Addison asked, dazed and bewildered.

"Whom?" the old man laughed, noticing Addison's proper English. He then continued with a pompous curve in his voice, "Pardon me, *my Queen*, but the *King* will see you around the corner."

"King?" Addison asked again, his mind not quite able to follow.

"Quit playing stupid, white girl. I'm not the police. If you're looking to buy, then King is right around the corner."

"I'm not looking to buy anything!" Addison protested in utter confusion. The old man laughed at him.

"That's the only reason white folks come around here. Follow me." The old man began walking away, then stopped, realizing that Addison hadn't moved an inch.

"Come on, white girl. I'm not gon' keep askin' you."

"Why do you keep calling me a white girl?"

"Because I can see that your skin is white, and I can hear the sugar in your voice. Now come on, so I can get paid."

Addison was surprised to find that he was actually amused by the old man. He watched him hobble away and decided that going with him was a much more comforting option than staying where he was.

This feeling left him the moment he caught sight of where the old fool had taken him – an abandoned building completely hollowed with large rooms that felt like caves. Tucked away in the shadows were three men, standing – waiting.

"KING!" the old man shouted.

A man emerged. He was broad-nosed, thick-lipped, and dark-skinned. King had the features of a mean boxer. His muscle shirt revealed a lean form, though not entirely intimidating. His minions, behind him, were of a heavier stock, with faces as mean as his.

"I got somebody over here who lookin' for you." The old man thumbed over to Addison, who immediately felt the heat from suspicious eyes upon him. These were black men that Addison had never encountered before. Until now, he had seen them only as media images and mythical parodies of actual inner-city poverty. Usually he shook his head at these images, not taking them too seriously. Now these "images" were standing right in front of him. Their faces reeked of animal poverty; their yellowish eyes were fixed and fierce, yet strangely vacant from drugs. Their expensive sneakers and baggy-branded jeans embodied an ephemeral wealth that did more to reflect their poverty than to ameliorate it. The fear that swelled in Addison's stomach told him that these men were not images. These three men were real.

"Who the fuck is this?" King barked.

"Come on, King. I just found him outside. He's lookin' to… You know…" The old man stood off to the side as a spectator. It made Addison feel as if he were standing alone to face his fate.

"Old man, who the fuck did you just bring into my shop? I saw a van drop this nigga here last night! Get him the fuck outta here. I don't know him!"

"I didn't say you *know* each other. I said he was looking for you. Come on, King, you know what I'm talkin' about." The old bastard sounded like a cheap lawyer. Addison would have been happy to obey King's orders, but the sudden motion of King stepping into the face of the old man compelled him to stay put.

"I don't pay you to bring no fucking heat to my shop. How you gon' bring him in here and you don't even know him?" While King screamed, spitting in the old man's face, Addison glanced at the two bodyguards, discovering that they had been staring at him the whole time. He quickly looked away.

"I do know him!" the old man pleaded. "You cool, right? Tell him your name."

My name, Addison searched himself, looking for his name. "My name is Addison."

"Addison who, nigga!" King demanded.

"Addison… Addison…" Addison's last name escaped him. King motioned to his two men.

"Get him the fuck outta here."

One of the henchmen grabbed at Addison's arm. Entirely by reflex, Addison pulled back, triggering one of King's men to bury a fist in his stomach. The sinking feeling caused him to buckle and collapse to the ground.

"Check him," King ordered.

Hands tore open Addison's jacket and pillaged every pocket until snatching up an ID badge. The henchman tossed the badge to King, the only one among them who could read. The old man became nervous, knowing that this didn't bode well for him or Addison. King sounded out every syllable from Addison's ID.

"Add…i…son…Cal…vin. Food and…DRUGS!!!"

102

King dropped the ID, pulling a gun from the small of his back. His two goons followed his example.

"You undercover, mutha-fucka?!?!"

From the ground Addison looked into the metal eye of a gun barrel, knowing that no answer he gave would save him, but an unexpected voice from behind did.

"No, he's not." Cool as ice, Stan stood in the doorway with two P-226 guns of his own, one aimed at King, the other at his gunmen. "He's FDA. I'm FBI," Stan added. "I'm getting tired of telling people that."

As Stan confidently walked forward, King's men began losing their courage. Stan's eyes showed no signs of fear. This was his element. He knew how to handle these boys.

"He's coming with me," Stan stated in a stern voice.

Footsteps pattered away. King turned his head to the sound, finding that his boys had turned tail and ran. He turned his head back to Stan, who now had both guns fixed on him.

"All you have to do is leave. It's the best offer you'll ever get from a federal agent, believe me."

King thought the offer through, stepped backwards, and retreated in the direction of his men.

Addison looked at the stranger who had just saved his life. *What just happened?* he thought, trying to hold on to the blurry event. He felt that the ordeal was just barely clinging to his memory. It was escaping him.

"Just relax, Addison. We'll get some help."

He heard his name one last time before succumbing to a hypotension that pulled him back into unconsciousness.

***

"Addison."

Addison's eyes awakened to his name.

"You know your name," Pearson said, surveying Addison's condition. "That's good. Do you also know your last name?"

Addison remained silent.

"No? How about me? Do you remember who I am?"

Addison's voice was weak. "No."

"Your partner is here. Maybe you'll remember him."

Stan stepped into view, but Addison's eyes showed no signs of familiarity.

"I ran a blood test. There was a large concentration of an enzyme inhibitor," Pearson said to Stan.

Stan handed Pearson a printed report. "Did it look anything like this?"

"What is this?" Pearson asked as his eyes made a cursory scan of the pages.

"It's a sample that was found with Allan's body. I ran it through BioEvaluation at the Bureau, and they came back with that. Know what it means?"

Pearson paused a moment, his eyes now sucking in every detail of the report. He looked up at Stan and inhaled deeply.

"Well, my friend... If you've seen such oldies but goodies as *The Matrix,* then you know that the brain is host to a whole lot of electrical activity. That electrical activity travels down a nerve fiber, triggering the release of a chemical neurotransmitter called a glutamate, which has a bridge to cross." – Pearson held up his two fists, keeping a slight gap between them. – "*This* fist is what's called an axon, and *this* fist is a dendrite. The gap between the two, called a synapse, is where we need to produce more glutamates, because the drug you just showed me has destroyed them." Pearson spread out the fingers of one hand so that they touched the knuckles of the other. "So we're going to give Addison some new drugs that tell the axons to hurry the hell up and rebuild those bridges and strengthen them up, so that they keep."

"The question is," Pearson continued, "Will his memories keep, or will he have to form new ones? That's an ancient question, my friend. What are memories? Where are they? Where do they go after we die? The answer to those questions... I have no idea whatsoever. As is the case with most science, we'll have to try it out, wait it out...and see."

Pearson continued studying the report, "You certainly don't get something like this from a drug dealer," he muttered to himself.

"Oh, it came from drug dealers all right," Stan replied, "just not the kind you think."

Realizing what Stan was referring to, Pearson found himself out of words.

"I ran a check on you too, *Dr. Pearson Fueller,*" Stan continued. "Ever heard of the Biotech Lab ETGR? You must have. Your name is on their list of principle advisors."

"Mr. Medes," Pearson began, "I think, at this point, we can be straight with each other."

"You don't think I'm being straight with you?"

"I know why the FDA is probing a kidnapping case –"

"No, see, you have that wrong." Stan stepped closer to Pearson, cutting him off. "The FBI is probing a kidnapping case. The FDA is probing a cloning case. It just so happens that, by some strange coincidence, the two are connected." Pearson fell silent again. "Now," Stan continued, "something tells me that Dr. Shapiro had no idea that Joey was a clone, but something is also telling me that you did...

"Am I right, 'Mister Ethics Adviser'? I'm sorry; I meant to say *Doctor* Ethics Adviser."

"Yes, I'm a member of their Ethical Advisory Board," Pearson snapped, "and *NO*, I had no idea about Joey. Since you seem to be implying that I'm somehow an accomplice to what ETGR *may* have done, let me point out to you that it was my recommendations, which were summarily excluded from their IND's, that tipped the FDA off in the first place."

"*Your* recommendation?"

"Yes, *not* to go through with it."

"If ETGR excluded your recommendations from their report, how did the FDA find out about it?"

"Allan always talked about the power of the spoken word," Pearson began, grinning at Stan's question. "In the world of corrupt government, there's even more power in the *written word*. It's amazing the response you get when you commit what you know to paper."

"Think you're ready to take what you know to the public?"

Pearson's grin vanished. He didn't answer right away. He just looked at Stan as if Stan were nuts. Stan's expression offered no concession – he was serious. He wanted Pearson to blow the whistle.

"After what has happened to Allan?" Pearson exclaimed.

"Yup."

"And your partner?" Pearson pointed at Addison, pleading.

"Yup."

"Sorry, but I think I've done my part." Pearson waved his hand, ending the conversation and walking away.

"So you sent your 'paperwork' to the FDA, right?" Stan called after him, before he could exit the door. Pearson stopped in his tracks, knowing where this question was going. He turned to face Stan, his eyes darkening with contempt. "Did I fail to mention that I'm working for the FDA now?" Stan continued. "How hard do you think it will be for me to dig up your smoking gun paperwork?"

"You said you were FBI."

"I know what I said, but nobody listens anyway."

Pearson looked up at Stan angrily. "You're willing to gamble with my life – a witness who's tried to help?"

"We do it all the time," Stan replied smugly.

"What will the FDA do to ETGR afterwards? Fine them?"

"Something like that," Stan replied, smiling at the sarcasm. "That's what passes for justice when you're dealing with the big boys. If you want, I can tell you about the 'justice' I've seen way up at the top of the ladder."

"No, thanks," Pearson said, exhaling somberly while walking away, "I'll be too busy with the public statement I have to prepare."

Stan watched Pearson leave the room. The door shut and Stan looked over at Addison.

"Get some rest, buddy," he said softly. "You're going to need it. The shit is about to hit the fan."

***

Maria Price marched quickly through a hotel lobby.

She rapped at a door. Merritt Lee opened with an expectant look and a happy smile on his face.

She walked in with no greeting. Merritt closed the door. His smile vanished.

She undressed herself, as if for an audition.

She unfastened her bra.

She removed her panties, exposing a heavy but shapely rear.

She climbed in the bed and looked up at Merritt, waiting.

He had wanted more romance, but beggars can't be choosers. He promptly obliged her look by disrobing, revealing an oblique physique, and climbed in bed next to her.

As he mounted her, he thought to himself: *I beat you Price, you son-of-a-bitch. I beat you. I have less money than you. My dick might even be smaller than yours, but it's inside your wife and that means I've won.*

His victory lasted only a few minutes. His discharge came and went and he rolled over to Maria's side. This was his real victory. He grew to dislike Price over time, but he fell in love with his wife instantly. For too long, only his eyes were allowed to grab at her, but now – right now – his hands were on her, all over her. It did not matter that she seldom touched him back. He ignored her unresponsiveness. It didn't matter.

While he rubbed her shoulder and then her breast, she held up the remote in her hand, turning on the TV.

"New information has surfaced about the missing boy named Joey. The FDA/FBI Hybrid-Division has reported that the Biotech Lab, ETGR, may have violated the federal moratorium on human cloning. ETGR is majority-owned by GAIA Pharmaceuticals. GAIA recently dismissed their CEO, James Price, behind an overseas sex scandal.

"Dr. Pearson Fueller, a former consultant and advisor for ETGR, has come forward as a whistle-blower in the cloning allegations against them. He will be making an official statement, which our reporter, Michelle Linneck, will cover live. We are told that we will also hear statements from the commissioner of the FDA, the Director of the FBI and the Attorney General."

Maria turned off the TV.

"I'll have to disappear for a while," Merritt told her. For the first time, she rolled over and looked at him. Her reply was dispassionate.

"Yeah? That's what James said too."

Chapter Six

The maelstrom of black vehicles encircling ETGR Labs meant that Stan was right. The shit *had* hit the fan.

Shijea watched the cars in perfect silence from her office window. Her outer shell was strangely calm and resolved as she observed a small army of federal agents eject from their cars and stampede through the front door. She stepped away from the window silently, preparing for her fate.

In her hand was the letter from the FDA – the letter that had started it all. She rescanned the words, not exactly reading them. Instead, she focused on what the group of letters clumped together in their government style of packs and patterns alluded to: *You're fucked.*

She crumbled the letter and allowed it drop to the edge of her desk. It rolled to the floor. The sound of feet running in all directions reverberated through the entire building. She could hear them approaching.

She considered leaving her office and going out into the storm. She opted against it. *Better they fish me out of my office,* she thought.

My office. The words sounded strange in her head. Was this ever really her office? She looked around at "her office" and took a quick inventory of all the things she had amassed over all these years. There were no personal items, no funny cartoon clippings, no pictures of faraway places, no family, no friends; only reports and letters and memos and book length applications – work stuff.

"*No,*" she said to herself, "*not here.*"

She walked calmly from her office, not even bothering to lock the door. The hallway was lined with white coats and white faces – confused, concerned.

"No one is to leave this building!" an agent shouted thunderously. His voice traveled through the hallways. It felt like a command not to move at all – a command that everyone, even Shijea, obeyed. All bodies were frozen stiff.

A small cluster of agents turned the hallway corner, with Stan walking in their lead. He seemed strangely reserved as he kept his hands in his pockets. He looked up at the ceilings, as if investigating the place for cameras. Shijea quickly figured out that this was the guy she'd be talking to.

"You've been inside here before?" one of the agents asked Stan.

"No."

"There's nobody in charge here, only personnel," the agent reported. "Who exactly are we looking for?"

"We're looking for the scapegoat," Stan answered with a cynical tone. His eyes wandered from the ceiling to Shijea, "And there she is."

Shijea barely moved, not even shifting her weight, as she watched Stan approach her. Her colleagues stood off to the side like spectators; their eyes locked on her. Shijea took a deep breath, sucking in the last air of confidence she had. She exhaled it all just as quickly.

Stan held up his badge. She glanced at it.

"I'd respond in kind, but unfortunately I don't have a badge to flash." Her cracking voice belied her cockiness.

"Just tell me who you are," Stan replied.

"Dr. Shijea Patra, I'm a Contract Research Physician."

"That means what?"

"It means a lot of things. To ETGR, it means I oversee specific research and clinical trial testing done locally and abroad. To GAIA, it means that my company absorbs most of the research liabilities. To you, it means exactly what you said... *I'm the scapegoat.*"

Stan responded with silence, studying the resignation in her voice.

"Follow me," she said.

She led them up a hallway, stopped in front of a secured doorway, and placed her hand on a print-scanner. A light flashed green and the door slid open.

"This is it," she said walking inside.

The agents paused as their eyes widened.

"Fuck..." one of the agents whispered at the sight of the enormous room, filled with wall-size glass storage freezers. Behind the glass were isolated bodies of various animals and humans; all were born dead or died shortly after birth. Their preserved bodies were haunted with cold inertia.

Stan walked quietly into the freezing cold room, looking at the contents of each freezer. Shijea joined him on his rounds. His eyes were filled with the unfathomable as he paused, staring at the aborted body of a fetus. Its mouth and eyes were slightly agape; its arms and hands bent in front of its chest.

Shijea's own reaction to these bodies was *no reaction*, but she knew that Stan was without the luxury of scientific temperament. *Better I explain to him what he is seeing, lest his imagination do it for him,* she thought to herself.

"This is a six-month fetus, naturally aborted by the body. We preserved it to get a better understanding of what caused the termination." Her voice was neutral in tone, uneventful. She explained and moved on.

"This one is a 19-week fetus with hydrocephalus, which caused the skull to be unusually obtuse.

"This one is only four weeks. At this stage, an embryo resembles a large tadpole. Its only human characteristics are its head and eyes.

"This fetus was born with chest and abdominal defects. What you're seeing are the heart and abdominal organs protruding from his body.

"This girl fetus didn't develop a brain or cranium, which is why her eyes seem to occupy most of her face. It is a result of the top half of her head missing."

Stan's eyes hardened, not at the surrealist bodies, but at the vapid voice and measured tone that had narrated them. He looked over at Shijea, searching behind the window of her eyes for a soul, surprising himself when he realized that he found it. He could see it, right there, in the wakefulness of her eyes that said: *Life is here.* He turned again and looked at the tiny corpses – evidence that life *was* there, but not anymore. It had vanished, but where?

Stan returned his eyes to Shijea as if she might have the answer, but, alongside the soul in her pupils, there was none. What he saw was modulation and measurement, dissection, an analytic search for answers – something not entirely misunderstood. Was his own job any different? How many times had he mined dead bodies for data, sifting through it, sorting it all out for clues that teased at questions that would never be answered?

"I want a list of all of your past and present senior officers and those who served on the Board of Directors." Stan's demands were surprisingly muted. "I also want records of all your cloning developments."

Shijea looked at him, recognizing the withdrawal in his voice.

"Follow me to my office, please."

***

Shijea pushed her door open, with Stan close behind her. Her eyes widened at the unexpected sight of someone else in her office.

"Rosalind? What are you doing here?"

A quick glance at an array of shuffled papers, scattered erratically across Shijea's desk, as if hastily examined, was answer enough. This woman was snooping.

Furious, Shijea attempted to charge forward, but Stan intercepted her rush by grabbing her arm.

"Just hold on a second. Calm down," he ordered. Stan studied Rosalind's face, noticing that she did not seem frazzled at being discovered. In fact, the determined look in her eyes suggested the opposite – she was waiting for them.

Rosalind pushed away her copper hair from her eyes. She bent down and picked up a crumpled paper from the floor. She decompressed it and laid it on top of a stack of papers she had assembled.

"I was looking for this," she said, forcing the papers over to Stan.

"Excuse me!" Shijea protested, but Stan censured her with a stern glance of counter-protest. Satisfied with Shijea's silence, he looked at the papers in his hand. The un-crumpled paper was from the FDA, threatening an audit. Underneath it was a letter of condemnation from a name Stan immediately recognized – Dr. Pearson Fueller.

Stan looked up at Rosalind. Her hair was stringy and sweaty from her rushed excavation of Shijea's private files. Her eyes were strong.

"Who are you?" Stan asked.

"Rosalind Hagen. I'm the one who released JOI."

***

Addison pulled his shirt off his lean, slender body. He caught a whiff of his own smell. After a few days spent in a hospital bed, he smelled worse than he felt. He got up, making his way to the bathroom. He examined his appearance in the mirror and used his hands to re-tame his hair. He was preparing himself to be released.

He heard the door to his room open. Thinking it was the doctor, he rushed out of the bathroom. Instead he saw a man and a woman walk in, which immediately made him remember that his top half was naked. They pretended not to notice.

"I'm sorry. Who are you two?" Addison asked, hurrying to cover himself. The woman pulled a fresh shirt from a plastic bag.

"Courtesy of Stan," she said.

Addison stared, dumbfounded by the gesture, but it also answered his question. The smile on her face told him right away that she was a friend of Stan's.

"My name is Amber, Stan's ex-partner," she said, smiling and then pointing over at the dirty blonde-haired man next to her. "This is my new partner, Carl."

Addison nodded, then covered himself with his new shirt.

"I'm checking out," he said.

"Yeah, I know. We won't hold you up for very long. We just have a few questions," Amber replied.

"Okay."

"What do you remember about the attack?" she asked while taking out a note pad.

"There was a white van, then a guy got out. I couldn't really see him that well."

"It was definitely a man?" Carl asked.

Addison closed his eyes trying to remember the face. As he spoke, he saw a hazy image in his memory.

"It was dark. I didn't see any details, but he was bald."

"Did you see any weapons?" Carl asked.

"Just a syringe. Then the lights went out." Addison opened his eyes. "Dr. Fueller said I was drugged. Where is Dr. Fueller?"

"He's in protection," Amber answered.

"Right. I wish I could give you a better descrip– Wait. I think I remember someone else being there."

Addison closed his eyes again, then reopened them. "Yes, yes, I do remember someone else."

***

The old man hung out at his regular spot, waiting to spot customers for King. He kept a shopping cart full of trash-turned-treasures as his alibi for the police, but they hardly ever bothered with him. Even when they did, they didn't stick around for very long. No one could stand the smell of him. He had long since developed an eye for spotting the police. He knew the black car pulling up to him right now was filled with law dogs.

He prepared himself to go through the routine: *One*, always keep your hands on your shopping cart. Idle hands are restless hands to the eyes of a cop. They want to see the hands doing something non-threatening. *Two*, look slightly disoriented. Nobody has patience for Q&A with a nut. *Three*, never run, but this was moot. The old man didn't have the legs for a fast getaway anyway.

Last but not least, always smile, especially when there's no reason to smile. It underscores the nut factor.

The old man smiled as he watched Amber and Carl step out of the car, looking cool and official.

"Hello there," Amber greeted the old man with the faux-friendliness that was signature of all law dogs, "we need to talk to you."

"Everybody always needs something, officer. People in hell need ice water, but I can't help them, and I doubt that I can help you."

It was a smart-mouth response, but he knew that after following it up with a stretchy smile, she would just laugh it off.

"That's a good one," Amber said, laughing. "I like that. I'll have to use it, but I'm not looking for ice water. You met a friend of mine very recently. I'm sure you'll remember him."

"Do you see how old I am, officer? Now, I don't like giving away my age, but I don't mind giving you a hint. Honey, I'm so old that the last time I was in prison, Abraham Lincoln himself personally gave me keys to my cell and told me 'get out of here nigga, you a free man.'" The old man began rifling through his shopping cart. "I think I still have those keys too. They're in here somewhere... Shit, I forgot where I put my keys."

"Watch the hands," Amber commanded firmly. The old man paused and threw his hands up in the air.

"Oh, that's right. I forgot about that. See? I can't remember shit, honey. Now, what makes you think I would remember your friend?" The old man added an extra helping of his fragmented, near toothless smile.

The rear door of Amber's car opened and Addison stepped out.

"Remember me?" he said quietly.

One look at Addison made the old man's smile disappear.

"You were right," Addison added. "I am looking for King."

The old man's face dropped. He looked down and cursed into his chest:

"SHIIIIIT"

"You see that?!?!? I SMOKED that bitch!!! Yeah bitch!!! That's how we do it over here!!! Lighting those blue caps up like the Fourth of July!!!" King screamed in excitement over his gaming victory. "I'm the *real* KING KOP KILLA, beyotch!"

Practically sweating from excitement, King looked over at the half naked woman on the couch beside him. She clearly didn't share his excitement.

"Stop yellin' King!" she barked; her voice and eyes in a stoned daze. "Shit, you messin' up my high."

"*Yo'* high? You mean *my* high. That's my shit you smokin'. Keep runnin' yo' mouth, bitch, and you ain't gon' have no high!"

"King, stop playin'!"

"I ain't playin' bitch! Get yo' ass off this couch and pay for yo' high." King held out his hand, demanding money. Again, she ignored him and pushed his hand away.

King took an inventory of his small, crusted apartment, littered with everything from beer bottles and potato chip bags to small storage bags for crack.

"Fuck it. If you can't pay for yo' shit, then you better get your crack-head ass off my couch and clean up this shit. Half this shit is yo' shit anyway!"

The woman didn't budge. As her high seeped deeper into her brain, a vacancy in her eyes took over.

"Yo' bitch —"

His protest was cut off by the sound of the front door crashing in and the sight of Amber and Carl barging in with their guns drawn.

"Warrant!" Carl yelled.

With the instincts of an animal in the wild, King dashed off from the couch. Amber, with even faster reflexes, was already after him, but the woman sprouted up in a stoned stupor and stammered in Amber's way, unwittingly buying King a few seconds to make his escape. Amber pushed her aside. Carl grabbed the woman, pinned her to the ground, and cuffed her.

King, moving fast, squeezed through an open bathroom window. He ignored the stray nails that ripped his skin open. Fear of capture reprogrammed the pain. He free-fell, head first, to the ground. Again, ignoring the daze from the impact, he pulled himself up and darted away.

Amber, much leaner than he, effortlessly made her way through the window, but her flesh suffered the same fate as she felt the nails prying inside her. She fell to the ground, gripping her side, but still catching sight of King hurling himself over a fence in his desperate retreat. She dismissed the pain and was after him.

Where the fence had slowed King down, it was but a mere hurdle for Amber, who scaled the barrier with one handless leap, demonstrating her incredible prowess.

King fled up an alleyway with Amber closing in on him. He felt her presence behind him and made a spontaneous detour up a graffiti and gang-ridden alley. A group of thugs saw the pursuit and immediately recognized a federal officer. They scattered, obstructing Amber's view of her escapee.

In King's way was a large pronged-fence. In a fraction of a second, he readied himself for the pain, spring boarded off the ground, anchored one foot on the fence, grabbed at the top just below the prongs, and pulled his body over. Fortune favored his escape, as he was able make the leap unmolested by the small teeth at the top of the gate. Amber, who was only seconds behind him, did not share in his fortune. The prongs bit into her already-bleeding side, causing her to fall to the ground, gripping at her wound.

She let go of her gun.

King seized the opportunity, bending over to reach for the gun. Amber, likewise, pounced upon his distraction, bringing a sweeping kick to the side of his jaw. His head jolted backwards. Another swift blow to his abdomen had him bowing over in pain. Next came a leg sweep that uprooted King's feet, sending him crashing down.

Dethroned, King lay there, still in a daze.

"They call that 'excessive force', bitch!" he yelled out, now struggling to lift himself from the ground. As his vision cleared, he caught sight of a gun barrel aimed directly at him.

"They call this a gun, *bitch,*" Amber retorted, looming over him. As King anchored himself off the ground with his bloodied elbows, he felt Amber press the cold steel against his forehead, prompting him to lie back down voluntarily on the ground.

"It would behoove you to lie back down. It's for your own safety, *your Highness.*"

King fell backwards, finally giving up. The pain he ignored before was now demanding his full attention. He wanted to grab at his jaw and nurse it, but he knew better. He simply turned his head to the side, hoping the chill of the concrete would assuage the throbbing ache. Amber's words only added insult to injury.

"I'm not sure which name sounds dumber: 'King' or your real name...*Eugene.* I'm sorry, but you just don't look like a Eugene. Then again, right now you don't look much like a King either."

"Why you fuckin' with me, miss? I didn't do anything."

"*Miss?* What happened to 'Bitch?' I don't mind being a bitch, especially to dick-heads like you." Amber chuckled.

"What did I do? I'm clean," King pleaded.

"You assaulted a federal employee. Did you already forget about that?" Amber said, still pointing her gun.

"Come on, the old man brought him to me. I didn't know who he was."

"Is that really what you want to tell me, or is there something else you want to talk about with me?" Amber said, kneeling down. King's eyes widened. This sounded like a deal.

"What do you mean?"

"I thought so," Amber said, smiling. "Let's start with the white van you saw. Then you can give me a description of the bald guy who got out of it."

***

Addison unlocked the front door and walked inside. *Finally,* he thought, looking around his very spacious, perfectly manicured home. He walked to the minibar and poured himself a glass of Scotch. He took a sip. *That's better.* He looked into his glass, trying to remember the last time he rewarded himself with a drink. He took his small glass with him over to the answering machine, where he saw that only one message waited for him. He hoped it to be Simon.

He pressed playback:

"Dr. Calvin, this is a courtesy call from Nancy Bailey at the Laylor Street Group Home. You had a Tuesday appointment to pick-up your brother..."

Addison's head dropped backwards as he exhaled. *Not Simon.*

"We understand that appointments can't always be met and just wanted to do a follow-up call to make sure everything was okay and see if you wanted to re-schedule for another day. Please call us back at..."

Addison stopped the message, lifting his phone to make a callback, but immediately aborted the call after hearing his front door open. His head swiveled with fear filling his eyes. The door was ajar, but no one entered.

"Who's there?" Addison called out. An old hand stuck its way through the open cavity and waved.

"It's just me, Addison." Joe Saracki stuck his head inside. "You forgot to lock your door."

"It's not the only thing I forgot," Addison replied, waving him in.

"Yeah, I know. I heard all about it." Saracki stepped inside looking around and immediately noticed how much more alive and well-groomed Addison's home was, compared to his own.

"Have a seat," Addison invited.

"I better not. Your furniture looks more comfortable than mine. If I sit down, you might have a hard time getting me the hell out of here. Besides, you've been through a lot of shit, so I don't want to stay too long."

"I have been through a lot," Addison replied, "so you can stand if you want, but I'm sitting down. I deserve it."

Saracki laughed. It was an uncomfortable laugh and Addison picked up on it right away. The two were silent for a few seconds, trying to find the angle to begin their conversation. Saracki scratched his head and took a shot:

"Well, I'll just come out and say it, Addison. You're fired."

They paused. Addison looked up at Saracki, waiting for the catch.

Saracki held his ground at first. Then he began chuckling. Addison didn't laugh with him.

"I'm joking," Saracki said.

"I know."

"Well, I'm only half-joking."

"I know."

They shared another silence.

"Sure you don't want to sit down?" Addison asked.

"Here's the deal." Saracki forced past his own trepidation. "We've got a conflict of interest with your position. It's something that we should have considered before. It was overlooked somehow… whatever. We're going to deal with it now."

"*Conflict of interest?*"

"Your father, Senator Calvin… Did you know about his connections with GAIA pharmaceuticals?"

"Is that really the question you're asking me," Addison replied, his voice and blood heightening, "or are you asking about pharma planting its own people into the FDA? Either way, not to bust your bubble, but I've seen that documentary too. Frankly, it's getting tired. *I'm getting tired.*" Addison paused, waiting for a response from Saracki, but he didn't get one. He continued: "Okay…so since you're standing there, pretending that the Bureau doesn't have any of their own dirty laundry to hide, can I invite you to sit down, finally, so we can compare résumés?"

"Addison, we're going to run some genetic tests on you and Senator Calvin," Saracki interrupted him.

"What?"

"The Bureau conducted a raid on ETGR, gathered all their cloning records. There's a quite a few of them. We found some stuff on your father. If it turns out that you're a clone of Senator Calvin, well, yes, it will make for a good documentary, but it's not going to look good for the Hybrid-Division."

"So I *am* fired?"

"Not yet, let's get the testing done first. Stan doesn't know yet. Nobody has to know. We'll make it as discreet as possible. Let's get answers and then… Well, whatever bridge we come to, we'll cross it when we get there."

"My father is dead, Joe."

"I know that. No offense, but we don't need him alive for the testing."

Addison fell silent, brooding. His feelings, if they could even be called that, were flat and listless.

"So is that it?" he asked.

"I do have one more question," Saracki replied.

"What?"

"Did Senator Calvin arrange for your position with the FDA?"

"Of course."

"Well, you seemed pretty convicted about finding out if ETGR had cloned Joey," Saracki said suspiciously. "GAIA owns ETGR. Can't knock down one without knocking down the other. Doesn't sound like your father put you in there to do that."

"Do you have any children, Joe?"

"A daughter."

"Is she '*Daddy's Little Girl?* '"

Saracki heard the salt in Addison's voice. He paused as he felt himself swallowing the impulse to throw salt back.

"No, she's not," he conceded, "not anymore."

"Right, '*Daddy's Little Girl*' sounds good, but in the end it's a myth," Addison replied, looking Saracki in the eye. "So is '*Like father, like son.*'"

Saracki was almost smiling as he absorbed Addison's wit.

"I'll see you tomorrow… So we can begin the testing."

Addison remained seated while Saracki turned and made his way to the door. He made a point of turning the lock switch, ensuring that, as he closed the door, it would lock and secure the secret of Addison Calvin behind him.

Chapter Seven

"We have to stand up. We have to stand together. Against the FDA and, dammit, against the FBI if it comes to that too. We have to stop asking, petitioning, and lobbying for what the FDA tells us are scientific privileges. Research is not a privilege. Knowledge is not a privilege. It's a right! It's time we demand our rights as scientists."

Everybody looked in the direction of Linda, the only female research geneticists at the table. Though her face remained neutral and stately, her daring words betrayed the passion boiling inside her. She began rapping her pen against the table, waiting for a response to her plea. The others did not share the conviction in Linda's eyes. The males at the table hardly fit the profile of activists. Their very appearance was more akin to government fashion – rigid, inoffensive hair shaped to the contours of their fatherly and agreeable faces. Yet their usual studied expressions were now absent and replaced with tired features that spoke of hours of futile discussion and debate. Now there was a quiet, heavy brooding. She continued rapping the table, waiting. Finally, someone decided to break the oppressive silence:

"We're not rebels."

"No, but we are revolutionaries," Linda retorted. "We come from a history of revolutionaries – people who have cracked the codes of the universe, the codes of nature, and the codes of the human body. Go back to your history books, and you'll remember that the results weren't always pretty. When we're at our seminars, surrounded by colleagues who celebrate our work, it's easy to fake humility with that old cliché that we 'stand on the shoulders of giants.' Right now is a turning point in history. Whether we like it or not, every one of us is about to find out exactly what it means, not to just stand on the shoulders of giants, but also to defend and preserve their legacy."

Once again silence and stuffy air filled the officious room. Linda didn't back down from the silence. She leaned forward, demanding, even daring, that one of her trepidatious colleagues give her a response. One of them finally did:

"You should hear yourself. You sound like you're leading a battalion into war. We're not soldiers, okay? We're scientists, and while your illustration of a band of revolutionaries is a very romantic one, we're not here for romance. We're here for research. I don't think anyone at this table, including you, is willing to jeopardize their research."

Research, of course, she thought, *it would be like robbing a believer of their faith.* She watched the spark in each of her colleagues' eyes revive as they could no longer remain silent. All at once, rebuffs and rebuttals overlapped:

"For all we know our research is already jeopardized. You don't think that after the FDA is through with ETGR, they won't come after us?"

"You and I know that they don't even have the manpower."

"They'll find the manpower. They won't have a choice. The public will demand it."

"Right, especially after we turn ourselves into desperados and volunteer that we've all got a couple of clones hidden away in our labs. In fact, let's tell them how many are already out there walking around on the streets. That should go over well."

"If we go public with this, we have to expect a reaction – small rallies, protests, maybe even a riot. We can't just think about ourselves here. We have to consider the safety of the personnel and their families, who don't even know what we're doing."

"Then we brief our personnel. We develop a protocol. We don't make a statement for another two to four weeks. That gives everybody time to beef up security at their homes."

"They may not like the idea of turning their homes into fortresses."

"They'll learn to adjust. They'll have to."

"For how long? This isn't going to blow over in a week. This could go on for years."

"Unless we *don't* go public. Suddenly, we've gone from an oath of silence to making public statements about cloning. We cannot let fear force us into making rash decisions. We are men of reason."

"*Men of reason*? Some of us are *women* too," Linda spoke out, agitated.

Silence returned again, interrupted only by the sound of Linda rapping her pen against the table.

"Could you please stop that? It sounds like a time-bomb is in the room." One of her male colleagues couldn't take it anymore.

"Exactly," Linda said, not passing on the opportunity to turn his words towards her point, "you all act as if there's a choice here. The bomb goes off whether we want it to or not."

"That's enough with the hyperbole. Do you have any idea what you're saying?"

"I know what I'm saying. I don't think *you* know what I'm saying. I'll give it another shot: THIS–IS–GOING–TO–COME–OUT! It's either going to come from us, or from some stubborn group of reporters, who are smart enough to know better. At least, if it comes from us, we have some control over the statement and can prepare for the reaction."

There was silence once more.

"She's right."

Linda looked in the direction of the agreeing voice.

"Yes, I am right. So, now that's two of us." She looked around the table. "What about the rest of you?"

One last time, the room was overtaken by silence. This time, Linda purposely rapped her pen on the table, smiling, knowing it had managed to break her colleagues from their spell of consternation.

"Do we each do this separately? Do we do it as group or what?"

Linda stopped smiling. Her next words were serious:

"As a group. We stand together as the Biotech Consortium."

Pearson sat alone in an inconspicuous room inside the FBI Building. He was officially under witness protection. Ignoring the scarce entertainment, he paged through Allan's untitled manuscript in silence, unable to part with it.

The sound of a door opening diverted his attention. He looked up to find Joe Saracki escorting Addison into the room. Pearson greeted them both with silence. He studied Addison's face, noticing that something in his resolve had changed. Saracki left the room. The sound of the door shutting behind him gave Addison his cue to speak.

"What are you reading?"

"It's a manuscript that Allan left in one of my labs. It appears to be finished, except for the title."

"What's the book about?"

"The importance of a name, identity, and knowing who we are. You know, all that stuff that is now obsolete in our modern age. It's an interesting read though. It deserves a title," Pearson said, rubbing his hand across the cover page.

"Maybe you should give it one."

"No. I'll give it to Claudia. She should be the one to name it."

Until now, Addison had kept his distance. Now he was stepping forward and seating himself directly in front of Pearson. The minimal space between them made Pearson feel uncomfortable.

"I came here to finish our conversation," Addison said directly.

"About Joey?"

"About the clones."

"We never talked about —"

"We're going to talk about them now," Addison said, cutting Pearson off.

"What else is there to say?" Pearson said, perplexed.

"ETGR's ethics advisor doesn't have anything to say about the ethics of cloning?"

Pearson paused, looking down, wondering what he could say. He then looked back up at Addison.

"I guess I would say: 'So you're a clone; so what?'" – Pearson threw his hands casually into the air. – "Big deal! Worse things could happen. You were engineered to be smarter, stronger, better looking. That doesn't sound so bad to me."

Addison was surprised by this response.

"Then why did you advise ETGR against it?"

"Because the world isn't ready for that. Science is grisly. We give the public images of a stainless steel future that shines with perfection, but the details behind that are dirty. We don't always get it right. In fact, we almost never get it right, but if we're ever going to get it right, we must accept the trial and error process. The public doesn't want that. They want gods in white robes, disguised as human beings in white lab coats. They want no margins of error, no mistakes, no side-effects. That's not medicine. That's a miracle."

With those words, Addison's expression changed. He too was a man of science. Years at the FDA, where he juggled the demand for expedient drugs with the demand for fail-safe drugs, told him right away that Pearson was right.

"What they want is mediocrity," Pearson continued. "Mediocrity has its moments of passionate conviction, but only when resisting change."

Addison surprised himself with a grin and his acquiescence to Pearson's brand of wisdom, but he wasn't sure how universal this brand of wisdom really was. *Maybe society is right to resist change,* he thought to himself. *Maybe a wholesale acceptance of progress is as naive as blind opposition to it.*

"What about Joey?" Addison asked, softly.

"Science requires sacrifice. You know that," Pearson snapped. "Hell, even a crazy mystic like Allan knew this. He didn't care about Joey. He cared about this." Pearson held up Allan's manuscript. Addison's eyes fixated on one word:

"UNTITLED"

"If Allan had known Joey was a clone –" Addison began, but Pearson cut him off:

"After the shock or novelty of that kind of news…I doubt it would have changed anything for him. Does replicating a body really qualify as replicating a person? If memories, experiences, and personality are inimitable in the cloning process, then what exactly have we cloned? A body? Is that it? Can that really qualify as a clone of a *person*? After this cloned body accumulates new experiences and memories, the result will inevitably constitute a new person. At that point, they might as well have a new name."

"You know," Addison began, standing up looking down at Pearson. "I just wasn't expecting to hear all of this from a guy who, by his own admission, doesn't 'look like his name' – Pearson Fueller."

Pearson stared up at Addison, silent.

"'*Science requires sacrifice*?'" Addison continued, throwing Pearson's own line back at him. "Is that how you would defend the Tuskegee Syphilis experiments, or have you forgotten your own history along with your real name?"

Pearson ejected from his seat.

"Who the fuck are you to lecture me about my history?"

"I was going to ask you the same question," Addison snapped.

Pearson squinted his eyes, not sure he understood what was being implied. He searched Addison's face, identifying the same resolve he saw in his eyes when he first entered the room. Addison, in turn, watched the light-bulb flicker in Pearson's eyes. He decided to leave him with those words, letting him figure it out for himself.

As Addison walked away, he listened to the sobering silence behind him. He could practically hear Pearson thinking, the wheels turning. He could feel it when the bulb finally switched on, radiating with revelation. He felt Pearson's eyes reaching to pull him back, but he had already left the room.

Pearson sat down, exhaling and staring at the nameless book in his hands.

***

Amber and a group of agents sat at a row of Formica-top tables while a digital analyst interpolated Addison's sketch of his kidnapper into a 3-D lifelike rendering. The image projected onto a white wall behind the Special Agent in Charge, a red-haired woman with plain, indurative features, who briefed the other agents.

"We haven't matched a name to the profile, so for now we are going to refer to our suspect with the codename 'The Jackal.'"

Next to the image of "The Jackal" appeared the image of a white van.

"This is the vehicle that 'The Jackal' was driving at the time of the abduction. It's possible that he may be using multiple vehicles.

However, this is the vehicle we identified as being parked, multiple times, outside this warehouse." The SAC pointed at a *Google Maps* image of an abandoned warehouse. "Can we get a scaled back view?" With this request, the satellite image zoomed out to display street coordinates. Using a laser pointer, the SAC specified four entry points for the seize.

"We're going to seal the place off here, here, here, and here. At each of these spots, we're going to have a point agent taking the lead, with two back-ups. Now, in case our guy gets the drop on us, we're going to set up fallbacks at each of these junctures, three blocks away."

While the SAC continued the briefing, Amber guilefully slipped her cell phone underneath the table, away from all eyes, and punched in a message to Stan:

"Want some action?"

"About time you offered. My place or yours?"

"Neither. How about an old warehouse?"

"???"

"I'll forward GPS data to you. See you there."

***

From every direction, dozens of cars surrounded the vacated warehouse. Their doors opened, and a flood of Field Agents rushed inside. Amber took point with her two back-ups behind her. As she moved in, she looked over her shoulder, waiting for her third man.

She saw Stan's car arrive and skid to a stop. The door swung open and Stan barreled out, his gun already in hand. His eyes scanned the terrain and immediately made contact with Amber, who motioned at him with her hands as if to say: *Hurry your ass up and join the party.*

Stan took his place behind Amber. Coupled with the other agents, the four of them passed from daylight to darkness as they entered the entrails of the warehouse. Stan could scarcely make out the sight of his own hand and gun in front of him. Strong beams of light made precision cuts through broken, dirtied windows and interrupted the thick blackness surrounding them. Each time they passed through a beam of light, Stan felt as if he had exposed himself as a target. Seconds felt like minutes before he stepped back into the fleeting comfort of protective darkness.

Eventually his eyes began to adjust. The hidden bodies alongside him became moving shadows. He could now see just how close to him Amber was – close enough to feel her heavy breathing travel the short distance to his skin. For only a few short seconds, he allowed himself to forget the moment and to find her eyes behind the thick ebony veil.

She was afraid. Her eyes were trembling.

She blinked. A wet bead trickled down her cheek – sweat, or maybe a tear.

She blinked again. Her pupils, dilated with tension, were fixed forward.

She blinked once more. Her eyes no longer looked forward but *down*.

Stan noticed her trance and removed one hand from his weapon to reach out to steady her. She stepped away from his touch, advancing forward carefully. Her eyes remained pointed downward. Stan was tempted to break the silence and ask her what she was fixating on, but his nose soon answered the question for him.

Death!

The odorous scent of death passed under Stan's nose. Amber made a motion with her hands, bringing the agents next to her to a complete stop. She moved her head in several directions trying to follow the morbid stench. She moved slowly, carefully tracking it until she found its source.

Behind the darkness, beneath the floor, she saw a body. Her eyes moved slowly until they found the face of the victim.

Joey. Dead.

Hastily buried – a portion of his lifeless face still exposed through a gaping hole. His one eye was closed, his other eye half-shut. Both were void of light or life.

"Oh my God..." Amber whispered to herself.

The scent and sight of the young boy, concealed in the dirt and already rotting from the trapped humidity, was almost overwhelming for her, but a distant sound snapped her from the trance of visible death. The sound of feet cracking against dirt was accidental and subtle, as if someone were hiding.

Someone is here, she thought to herself. Her instinct kicked in and transformed the overwhelming emotions of fear into a combat-ready expression.

Somewhere in the black void of the vast gutted room was movement. It was difficult for her to be sure who exactly escaped the eyes of all these agents, but, whoever it was, he had not escaped detection. Even as the camouflaged suspect remained perfectly still, Amber was able to follow the memory of the sound. She followed her instincts, confident they were leading her in the right direction. She pointed her gun at a steel vertical beam that anchored the dried, decaying ceiling.

Another movement.

Amber fired her gun, hitting the beam and forcing a play. The mysterious figure rocketed away, like a shadow sprinting through the darkness.

"Over there!" Amber called out. In a fraction of a second, Stan and every other agent darted after the fleeing figure. Amber, however, didn't follow after them. She saw an alternate path to head him off. She charged in that direction. A second agent followed behind her.

The phantom runner propelled himself up a flight of stairs and immediately sensed their fragility. Knowing that they may break underneath him, but not seeing an alternative, he continued his escape. He heard shots being fired in his direction and instantly recognized the sharp pain in the side of his leg. He screamed and fell onto the dry, rotten, bullet-ridden stairs. As agents piled up the stairs, they heard the cracking and felt the stairs weaken beneath their feet. A sudden collapse sent one of the agents downward. Stan managed to cling to the remains as a single stair plank refused to succumb to his weight.

The blunder of the agents had just bought this mysterious fleeing man some time. Adrenaline and determination blocked out the pain in his leg as he continued his limping escape.

He changed his course, detouring from the stairs into an empty room, rushed to a window, and looked down. *Shit, it's a long way down,* his eyes told him, but his options were few, and the time to make up his mind was diminishing. He could feel the blood running down his leg. He could feel his heart pounding within his chest, sending more blood to the wound. The pain told him that the jump would mean suicide. His mind told him that *not to jump* would mean to surrender.

With his decision made, he stepped to the ledge of the window. His body almost completely engulfed by sunlight. "*So this is the light everyone sees before death,*" he said to himself. Holding his breath, he prepared for the leap. A voice stopped him.

"You won't survive that jump!"

His face, once masked by shadows, now veiled by blinding light, turned to find Amber's gun aimed directly at him. Behind her was another agent.

"Even if you do, it'll hurt like hell, especially with a wounded leg."

His figure, captured by light, began to pull away slowly from the window and slouch back into the shadows. His body language could speak of only defeat and despair.

Amber watched him as he allowed his body to drop back against the wall and slide slowly down to the floor. He stretched out his wounded leg, resting it. She heard him exhale, almost as if he were relieved to have been talked out of the jump.

Amber approached him. Dead suspects have a way of leaving cases wide open, but this one was alive – a living symbol of the many questions that could now be answered. As she continued towards him, she finally began making out the face of a tired, haggard man. It was not the face she expected. She searched the files of this case in her mind; the names and faces of all "persons of interest" flashing through her head: *James Price, Merritt Lee, Shijea Patra…*

"David Lee!" she said with surprise in her voice.

David looked up at her.

"Someone else is here," he said, half-smiling.

POP!

The deafening sound of a shot, coupled with a flash, cut through the darkness in less than a second. Amber turned her head to find the agent next to her going limp and falling to the ground, dead.

POP!

Another bullet was shot. It ripped through her and she collapsed.

David laughed – a madman's laugh – realizing that he now had the blood of two federal agents on his hands.

"We are fucked." His laugh was cracking into desperate sobs. "We are so fucked."

POP!

A single shot fired out, tearing through David's seated body. He flinched from the nerve shock before his body silently slumped forward.

The sniper emerged from the shadow, with bald head, lanky body, steely eyes behind glasses. He walked slowly over to David and nudged his lifeless body with his foot. Next, he walked over to Amber. He kicked at her side, she moved – *still alive.*

Hovering over her, he aimed his gun for her head but stopped at pulling the trigger when he noticed her fearless eye contact.

"I know you. You're 'The Jackal,'" she said.

"You don't know me. That is not my name," he replied flatly.

"No…I do know you. You're the *'Who, me?'* guy."

He gave no reply. He looked past her indomitable stare, steadying his aim at the center of her forehead where he could be sure to finish her.

POP!

Amber's body was inert. Light seemed to pass effortlessly through the window, falling on her angel body that was completely inanimate.

The sniper stumbled. It had been a long time since he had felt the burning sensation of his own flesh seared by bullets. He looked down and saw where the bullet had passed through his chest cavity. His breathing began to strain, and he immediately knew that a lung had been punctured. Instinctively, he dropped his gun and clasped at the exit wound. He stammered around. His vision was blurry but still succeeded in capturing the image of Stan standing behind with a gun fixed on his crumbling body.

POP!

This bullet passed through his head, toppling his body into a dimensionless *void*.

Stan rushed over to Amber. She smiled at the sight of him. Even now, as she lay on her back with a bullet hole torn through her, she felt the instinct to tease him, but she didn't. Her words were soft and sincere:

"Thank you, Stan."

Chapter Eight

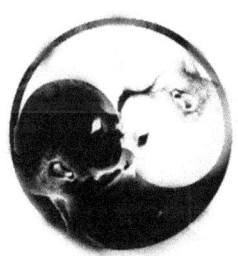

"Amber," a voice whispered.

She squinted and blinked her eyes, as if blinded by light. Gradually, they opened, taking sight of a hazy shadow-like form, standing over her. At first she believed it to be Stan, but as the image took on more definition, she made out the probing face of a male nurse studying her patient records, noting her temperature and placing the records back at the foot of the bed. The look of routine was all over his face, but when he saw that she responded to his voice, he conjured up the best of his hospital etiquette.

"Welcome back," he said, smiling.

"Welcome back? How long have I been in here?"

"This is the second day – not that long," he replied. "Seems to me, you needed the sleep. You're exhausted."

Amber looked around the room and noticed a modest set of flowers on the desk.

"Flowers? From whom?"

"Oh, the black guy; he just left, actually."

Amber smiled at these words and at her fond memory of *the black guy*.

"Stan," she said softly.

***

"Son of a bitch!" Saracki exclaimed at the sight of Stan, who came rushing into his office.

"I know, I know, I'm a little late, but I was checking up on Amb—"

"Not you — them!" Saracki held up a *Statement of Position* letter from the Biotech Consortium. "Michigan, Virginia, Jersey…" he continued. "Biotechs from all over the damn country are coming out of the closet."

"About what?"

"What the hell do you think?" Saracki looked at Stan, annoyed by his obtuseness. He began reading from their Statement of Position: "Listen to this:

The FDA took form in 1906. It took only 30 years after its inception for the laws and regulations they created to become obsolete. That's because in 1906 they could not have imagined the abundance of products that were possible with man's ingenuity. In short, those were regulations that were made with the present in mind – not the future.

The shortsightedness of the FDA and its history of regulatory intrusions still remain. The new FBI/FDA Hybrid Division functions less as health inspectors and more as health policemen and suffers from short-term enforcement goals. While they are concerned with protecting the health of American citizens of today, the Biotech Consortium is thinking about the health of the American citizens of tomorrow.

Science has been restrained before by the short-sightedness of sovereignty. During the Middle Ages, it was a so-called divine sovereignty that placed misguided parameters around the ingenuity of man. With sacrifice came a Scientific Revolution that usurped this era of intellectual limitation. Today, we turn the corner into a revival of that revolution, which will usurp legislative sovereignty with the unified proclamation that the pursuit and acquisition of knowledge is not a privilege to be granted by the State, but a fundamental right that is both instinctive to our species and therefore inalienable to our race."

Saracki tossed the Statement onto his desk.

"That's not so bad," Stan commented.

"The statement includes a list of biotechs that are admitting to, or standing in defense of, human genetic engineering. The biotechs listed are from all over the damn country."

"So, what are we going to do?"

"What the hell can we do? We don't have the manpower for this."

"Isn't that why we have FBI and FDA working together in the first place? Fuck it. There's about a dozen other agencies with overlapping jurisdiction. We rally them together. We organize a series of investigative initiatives."

"I'm with you on that last part," Saracki said, rubbing his hands through his receding hair. "The Attorney General and the President are both preparing their announcements for this. The first question will be 'What the hell is being done about this?' which means we'll need to have a reasonable protocol that can be put into motion as soon as needed. That can only come after they've established and clarified a counter-position."

"Counter-position? We already know what that is?"

"Do we?" Saracki grabbed and waved the Statement of Position. "Do you think this was for our eyes only? This is going to every media outlet in the country, if it hasn't already. Hell, they've already got a website and they published this online."

"How do you know? You've looked at it already?"

147

Saracki pointed to the bottom of the Statement. Sure enough, in small caps at the foot of the page it read: **BiotechConsortium.org**. Their logo was a baby raising its fist.

"They're going to rally public support; as much of it as they can," Saracki opined.

"Let them try. People are freaked out by this kind of shit."

"Yeah, but they were freaked out by 'Frankenfoods' too, and look at how companies like Monstranto turned that around. They established a 'position' just like this one." Saracki drilled a hardened finger on the Biotech Consortium's statement. "Combine buzz words like 'world health' and 'feeding the hungry world' with faces of hungry children from Africa, add a tiny trademark icon to top it off, and suddenly we look like the Big Bad Wolf trying to stop Red Riding Hood from 'feeding' her poor old African grandmother."

"Well, I can sum up a counter-position in one word – Joey! They can write and sign any Declaration of Independence they want. All they're doing is hanging themselves. When we announce that we found Joey dead, we'll see how the public feels about them then."

This perked Saracki's ears. His nerves were still heightened, but it sounded as if Stan had just handed him his trump card. He lit up a cigarette. Carl barged into Saracki's office.

"CJIS ran a profile search on 'The Jackal,'" Carl began. "The guy has no background."

"That sure as hell has the ring of 'government employee,'" Saracki said, exhaling grayish smoke. "Which agency?"

"We ran semantic checks, based on Stan's report from Mrs. Shapiro and the report from Addison. In both reports, he used the phrase '*Who, me?*' Before the OSS reincarnated as the CIA, *'who, me'* was the codename for a liquid issued to Japanese kids to spray on enemy officers during World War II. The liquid smelled like diarrhea on steroids. They called it 'the harassment weapon' because the goal was to kill morale, not people."

"So anyone on their shit-list was sprayed with shit?" Saracki replied while taking another puff of his cigarette.

"Exactly, and, uh…it's the same stuff they use in cigarettes – as a flavoring ingredient." Saracki's eyes widened. He put out his cigarette.

"So this guy murdered Joey?" Saracki asked, looking over at Stan, who nodded. "Who hired him, ETGR?"

"Well, we might have been able to confirm that if he wasn't being cut open in autopsy." Carl couldn't resist his own sarcasm. "Next time, Stan, try to bring the suspect in alive."

"Too late for that now," Saracki said waving it away, having no desire to belabor dead issues or dead suspects. "What about the other guy who was with him, David Lee?"

"He was a 'Finder' for ETGR. Finders are like placement agents that help Biotechs find funding, except they aren't government regulated," Carl explained.

"Okay, and how did ETGR find him? Who and what were his leads?"

"That's an easy one – his brother, Merritt Lee, a Senior Executive at ETGR. You don't get a better lead than that."

Saracki retreated into a pensive stare, sucking his teeth, laying out his strategy. Finally, he looked over at Stan. "Looks like you were right," he began, pointing down at the Biotech Consortium statement. "Carl, get everything you can on David Lee; find out how he got in contact with The Jackal. Stan, I want you to follow up on the ETGR raid. Accumulate any and all data that connects them to Joey. We're going to lay out two roads here, two intersecting roads, and we're going to T-bone whoever the hell we catch at the intersection."

* * *

"So you want me to dumb this down for the stupid public?" Linda asked, tinkering with the mic on her lapel. She was now the official spokesperson for the Biotech Consortium, a position to which she had practically appointed herself the day she declared herself and her reluctant colleagues to be revolutionaries defending the legacy of their predecessors. The fact was, despite the preponderance of males in her newly-formed band of research rebels, she was the only one among them with balls enough to put her face in front of the public via a talk show.

The talk show host seemed rushed as stylists and make-up artists made last-second corrections to the generic sociable appearance all too common among talk personalities. He seemed not to have heard Linda's question, or he was just ignoring it.

"Hello? I'm asking a question," Linda repeated. "Grade B or C?"

"A minus," the talk show host responded, not smiling.

"A minus?"

"Yes, that's what the producers are asking for. They think that is what the public is asking for. They want hard science, not soft science. Don't be afraid of lingo and jargon. You know, words like 'metabolism,' but not too much jargon, not any words that they can't repeat later to their friends. We want them to feel smarter about themselves. We don't want them to feel stupid."

A stylist hurried over to Linda and fixed the placement of the mic that Linda had re-adjusted. As the seconds ticked down, everyone took their positions, including Linda and the host. They suddenly arranged the space between them as if they had known each other for years – a geneticist and a host, long time friends, engaging in a friendly discussion of genetic engineering.

The final second hit and the cameras were rolling...

***

Amber entered her apartment, setting aside all of her bottles of medication. Some of them were emblazoned with the GAIA logo. Instinctively, she wandered over to the TV and turned it on. Linda's face appeared, front and center, on the monitor.

"A gene is a unit of hereditary material that determines phenotypic traits of a living organism," Linda explained with a composed expression. *"The genetic material itself is a chain of nucleic acids which we call DNA. If the organism is a virus, we call this chain RNA. This chain of amino acids is linked by peptide bonds and we call a particular segment of this chain a polypeptide chain. These polypeptides are the expressions of the genes that comprise them. These expressions are what most people know to be proteins. A simple protein can contain anywhere from 100 to 300 amino acid units."*

"So, to be clear here for the public," the host interjected, *"a polypeptide is just another name for a protein?"*

"Proteins are polypeptide chains," Linda responded. *"When you hear the statement: 'genes code for proteins,' it's to this that we are referring. Proteins are the principal building blocks of cells, and a gene can code for more than one type of protein. For instance, some proteins, called enzymes, are useful*

in accelerating chemical activity in an organism. Proteins are expressions of genes. The particular protein expressed is contingent on more than one variable. The temperature of the cell, the presence of bacteria, and environmental factors can determine the protein's location in the cell and with which molecules it will bind. All of this, of course, can be consequential to the organism. Proteins are quite responsive to the environment, especially a changing environment. So, while we might call proteins the proverbial 'building blocks of life,' the environment, we could say, plays a part in how these building blocks are stacked."

"How these blocks are stacked determines us?" the host asked.

"Yes, you could say that," Linda replied. *"Simply moving an active gene to a new location of the genome could render that gene inactive. The environment is a form of genetic engineering. Actually, the environment is the principle engineer. We are the environment. If we take this back to the beginning, from the moment atoms bonded through electron sharing, molecules were born. Molecules constitute more complex substances called compounds. The carbon atom is the most versatile. It can form many types of bonds, in many different ways, to produce a great many types of compounds. As carbon molecules become more complex and larger, we call them macromolecules. For example, a protein is a macromolecule. So you see, we are made by our environment."*

"Some people say 'We are products of our environment,'" the host chimed in again, offering a manufactured smile. *"You're saying that, literally, we are products of the environment."*

"Exactly, we are the environment; we are not separate from it. We are expressions of it, like a tree or animal or anything else. The difference is that the environment is a form of stochastic engineering, which means it works randomly. Human beings, on the other hand, bring an element of order to the chaos.

Genetic engineers are protein engineers. We are products of our environment, and now we are producers of our environment. We have completed the cycle of creation. We are 'Intelligent Designers.'"'

Amber walked away, into the bathroom, and in front of the mirror. She gazed at herself – her phenotypic self. She moved her hand to the damaged part of herself. Pain from the afflicted wound gave Amber a heightened awareness of her body. She couldn't help but stare at the discoloration that resulted from the body's attempt to heal itself.

Miracle, she asked herself, *or simply a machine at work? Perhaps the machine is the miracle.*

Perhaps this was a near-fatal reminder of how vulnerable the body really is. The wound, the blood that seeped, the sharp sting from even the slightest touch gave the addendum that this was a frail miracle, teetering on the pinpoint of life. Yet this wound, these cracks in the flesh machine, might be the opening for a soul that waits a lifetime to escape from matter. Matter is, perhaps, too small a container for the soul. It seeks release through art, poetry, music – or death. An unbreakable soul in a broken body.

These were all decaying ideas.

She looked in the mirror at the exotic curvatures of her eyes and remembered her heritage. At least, she *tried* to remember. She was a bricolage of her native identity, her naturalized identity, and, more accurately, *no identity.*

What she would have guessed to be her cultural selfhood had been vanquished by empirical language. Gods, souls, and ancestors had all, quite literally, been excommunicated to a New Age in this land. The language of her tradition, at least as she scarcely remembered it, was measured and disciplined, but still evoked divinity and life-force.

The words of The West were also quite measured and disciplined, but, to her ears, theirs was an objective language that mirrored their world of objects. Linda's vapid voice, hanging in the background, lacked inflection. There was no reverence, only observation.

The observed becomes the intellectual property of research and the researcher. Research, in turn, *must* be observable if it is to be real, and so the cycle of empiricism goes on.

This was not so in her heritage.

A mountain, a river, a fantastic creature of the wild, a gifted human – all are observable. From observation, they inspire awe and exude a great majesty. Therefore they are *kami* and quite real, but that was pretty much the extent of her recollections.

She resealed the crack in her body and returned to the living room, where the lecture on the bits and bytes of the human body continued:

"The idea of a random environmental creator is difficult for most people. We have fathered the idea of a benevolent creator who, presumably, has created a finely-tuned machine we call the human body. Yet this 'finely-tuned machine' is rife with problems. Consider cancer, muscular dystrophy and its rare sibling, myotonic dystrophy. All of these are a consequence of the fact that the human body is not perfect. It doesn't always work. These afflictions result from aberrant genetic material, which, until very recently, could only be treated – if at all – by destroying the malignant cell, cutting off the blood supply, or cutting it out completely by removing the tumor. These are sledge hammer approaches to treatment. At my lab we have an old saying: 'the genome giveth and it taketh away.' It's that last part of this adage that we seek to change. We want to minimize just how much our genes can take away from us."

"So now you're talking about genetic engineering," the host added. *"This topic, of course, has inspired a great deal of controversy as of late. The recently established Biotech Consortium is taking the*

position that genetic engineering is something the world should not condemn, but embrace."

"We've already embraced it," Linda retorted quickly. *"Farmers are genetic engineers every time they crossbreed plants or animals. However, to make this a bit clearer, you might say that farmers are 'macro-engineering' since they work at the phenotypic level. 'Micro-engineering' works at the genotypic level, where we alter the genetic material, or make enzymatic attachments of one gene to another to produce endogenous proteins with different properties than the original, or we generate new proteins altogether.*

"We can change the way genes 'talk' to each other to make new determinations about, say, the length of your nose, your height, etcetera. These, of course, are cosmetic considerations, but these processes can, and will, be applied to considerations of life, its quality and longevity..."

Amber turned off the TV.

Silence turned her room into a temple. She opened a window, allowing the natural fragrance from the breath of wind gods to sweep through and circulate. A gush forced its way inside; *the wind god sneezing perhaps.* This thought made her laugh. The soft touch of the passing breeze was pleasing to her skin. She sat down on her couch and absorbed the feeling, but somehow this didn't quite seem the way to savor the enjoyment. She groaned slightly as she shifted her body weight to the floor, positioning herself on one knee, completely prostrated as if praying or meditating.

She felt silly. She hadn't meditated before, let alone prayed.

Who am I praying to? she asked herself.

To the gods.

Gods? Which gods? How many gods?

155

Yao Yorozu No Kami.

Okay... If I pray, what do I say?

Say nothing. Let the gods speak, and if they say nothing, then to hell with them.

If I meditate?

Think nothing. Good luck with that, though. The mind will want to speak. If it turns out that it has nothing to say, well, congratulations. That would mean that you are a god. Of course, that also means that someone is praying to you, and you have not answered...so to hell with you too!

She laughed again. *Is meditation supposed to be this funny?* she wondered. *Okay, seriously, let's do this.* She sat silently, feeling her hair respond to the swaying winds. It tickled, and she caught herself smiling again. *I'm a terrible pupil,* she thought. This, of course, triggered a stream of other thoughts. Her mind jumped around, from Stan and his ass, to kicking King's ass, back to Stan's ass, and then to her hair, which had wrapped around her face from another gush of wind. No doubt the wind god growing annoyed with her restless mind that had wandered in every direction, *except* at the slight ache from the wound in her side!

This was a success, she thought to herself, smiling. *I'll quit while I'm ahead.* She broke the meditation, returning back to her world of body and matter, picked herself off the ground, and audibly groaned when she felt the sting of the so-called miracle wound.

"Shit!" she exclaimed, cupping her side with an open palm.

She stood in silence, unsure what to do with herself. She wanted company. Then an idea entered her mind—*Addison.*

Linda's interview continued on Addison's TV. He sat alone, his eyes and ears barely tuned to any of the propaganda or politics. His mind was fixed on his new-found identity, or lack of it, as far as he was concerned. Yet he found himself suspicious of whether or not this was a valid sentiment or just sentimentality.

Do I really want or need to belabor this? he asked himself, but every time he forced the issue from his mind, it seemed to force its way right back in, each time rooting itself even deeper than before.

Don't fight this, own it. Make it yours and then you can control it. He heard a voice in his head. Sentimentality took the opportunity to tell him that this was his father's voice, but his father would never have said such a thing. No, this was the generic and faceless voice of the mind – his own voice. His father was a Senator. Like every politician before and after him, he never made a habit of something as noble, and naïve, as "owning a problem." Problems are buried in sand and marked with an X, so some other fool, believing to have stumbled onto a treasure, will dig it up and "own it."

That's just what he did too, isn't it? the voice told Addison. *He made me in his image and after his likeness, buried the secret, and left me with the shovel.*

His thoughts were interrupted by the sound of the door buzzer. He leaped to his feet, his nerves still recovering from his abduction. The buzzer continued to ring as he steadied himself, walked to the door, and took a peak at his unexpected visitor – Amber.

"Can I come in?" she asked but didn't wait for the invitation and squeezed past Addison. "I see you're watching the clone talk show, too."

"Yeah…and I'm wondering what else they've been hiding from us. For all I know, we could be cyborgs," he said half-jokingly.

She laughed, not noticing the bitterness behind his joke. She wandered through his living space, as if unaware that she was a visitor. Addison watched her rather humorlessly.

"Do cyborgs get lonely?" she asked him.

Taken aback by the question, Addison could hardly muster up a response. He just looked at her, wondering at the implicit layers underneath it.

"Humans do," she added, always a flirt, although Addison could hear a certain degree of sincerity in her voice.

"Maybe it's just restlessness," she continued. "Whenever I finally sit down, I can never figure out if what's bothering me is that I'm sitting alone, or that I just have a problem with sitting still."

Her restless eyes noticed a syringe and small containers of drugs resting on his mantle. She picked it up and then looked over at Addison, demanding an explanation.

"It's all work stuff," he complied.

"Drugs?"

"*Water*," he rebuffed her. "Listen, this is my home, not a prison cell. There's no contraband in here, okay?"

"I'm sorry," she said. "Told you I was restless. It's not personal. I did it to Stan too. I used to pick through his office all the time. Sometimes I'd walk out with something of his, forgetting I even had it in my hand. He'd spend all day looking for it, and then later find it in my office. Pissed him off."

Finally he laughed.

"Cyborgs can laugh?" she asked.

"Humans can." He pointed to the couch, obliging her to sit.

"So, you two have worked together for a while, huh?" he continued.

"Actually, not as long as it seems. Uh, I mean 'long' in a good way. You know, that whole relativity thing."

"Right, '*Time cannot be absolutely defined,*' is what Einstein said about relativity. Talk to a young man who moves in the fast lane and time can't possibly catch up with him. Give him enough time to have life snatch away all of his ambitions, and suddenly life slows to a halt. It's an act of mercy, really. We need as much time as we can get to figure ourselves out, don't you think?"

Amber gave him a curious look. "Einstein said all that?"

"No, that last chunk was me," he said grinning.

As they shared a quiet moment, voices from the interview with Linda filled in the silence.

"You mentioned 'engineering advantages' with this technology, but how do we properly define these advantages? Would blonde hair be considered advantageous? How about blue eyes?" a voice from the audience asked.

"I think blonde hair and blue eyes would fall under the category of aesthetics, not advantages," Linda replied. *"African Americans, or other minority groups, would have the option of their own aesthetics."*

"Would they?" the host picked up the baton from the pointed question. *"Affluence is not equitable in this country. Is it realistic to think that everybody can afford this kind of technology?"*

Addison walked over and turned off the TV.

"If someone just told you that you were cloned…what would you say to that?" Addison turned around, shocked at Amber's question. He stared at her.

"Well…" he began, trying his best to mask the surprise in his face and voice, "I'd say the joke's on them."

"What do you mean?"

"Look at me. I'm the Perfect Man!" Addison remarked, this time surprising Amber with unexpected cockiness. She listened on with a raised eyebrow. "Tall, blonde, blue eyes. I'm a scientist, which has to mean that I'm smart. They got everything right…*except* my sexual preference." – Amber raised her second eyebrow. – "They engineered a fag," he finished, sitting back down, smiling, enjoying his sucker punch.

"You're gay?!?!" Amber said, the shock in her voice coming more from missed opportunity at romance. "Okay." Her open mouth quickly turned into a grin.

They sat together. They smiled together. They shared a second silence together – their friendship firmly secured. But they weren't best friends yet, so Addison made sure to throw in a quick retraction, just to make sure she didn't walk away with the *right* impression:

"Well, anyway, that's what I would say…*if* I were a clone."

***

Stan pulled out a massive folder full of paperwork and spread it out on a desk, sifting through it all until he found what he was looking for – *more paperwork*. Yet this one was special. He even gave it a name. Actually, it pretty much named itself. Rosalind Hagen had been caught red-handed snooping in Shijea's office, digging up an armful of papers that she volunteered to Stan. Her name and her smoking gun equated to the perfect conspiracy title – *The Rosalind Files*. Sounded like *The Roswell Files,* which was exactly why Stan picked it.

The paperwork didn't seem to say anything about Joey. All of its language, though explicit, was incomprehensible to Stan's eyes. Thank God for pictures. He was able to recognize several images of bacteria: a combination of color X-Ray photos, 3-D recreated renderings of the images in the photos, and line art representations of the same images. They were all labeled as bacterium 1, 4, and 5 and accompanied with bulleted information that may as well have been a foreign language to Stan's eyes. He'd have to run it through BioEvaluation for a translation.

His eyes moved to the recommendation letter from Pearson Fueller. That was pretty definitive but hardly sufficient, and said squat about Joey.

He leaned backwards in his chair, stroking the top of his head, cursing himself for not being more perspicacious. His eyes were acute to most things, but with stuff of this level he felt like he was back in middle school.

As he re-scanned The Rosalind Files a second time, his mind wandered back to the departing gift Amber had given him – *"Genetic Engineering for Dummies." Shit,* he thought to himself, *maybe I should have carried that book around with me. Who knows? It might have been useful.*

Stan allowed a self-depreciative laugh, rubbed his face in exhaustion, but decided to plumb himself even deeper until something jumped out at him. He stared intently, studying every abstruse detail relentlessly until finally the words, and more specifically *the numbers*, were staring back at him. Yet this was no triumph of revelation, it was ridicule. The obvious had emerged from the white pages, whacked him over the head, and fell back laughing into their hiding place on the page.

The bacteria images were labeled 1, 4, and 5.

What happened to 2 and 3?

***

Yellow tape surrounded the monolithic ETGR Building. Its vacancy belied the very root of what it was – a Biotech. *Life* Technology, but there was no life here. Everyone was gone, or perhaps, true to the word *Bio*, this Biotech had run the very cycle inherent to all life. It was born, it had lived, it had done its best to survive, and, in the end, it had fallen prey to another living entity, far stronger than itself – *the law,* even if be it a corrupted law. Perhaps there is no corruption in this space of life. There is only the strong and the stronger. Governments, stronger with the law, exist at the top of this food chain. ETGR was just another fallen prey, so there it lay – a vacant space, a decomposing shell.

Moments later, the scavenger of the dead appeared – a white van.

With its headlights dimmed, shrouded in darkness, it slowly prowled around the perimeter as if to scavenge the remains or to protect them from other scavengers...

The headlights from Stan's car approached from a distance. The white van slowly pulled away, crawling around a corner and vanishing into a crevice of the building's exterior. Only a minute later, Stan pulled up at the front entrance, unsuspecting.

The hallways of ETGR were dark. The absence of living and moving human bodies allowed a distinct, seamy smell to seep inside and saturate the hollowed spaces. No doubt, the odor being the consequence of neglected materials claimed by time and the elements. Even the smell from the bathrooms managed to precipitate into the hallways. Stan held his sleeve under his nose to intercept the odor.

He went back to where he remembered Shijea's office to be, deciding to pick up where Rosalind had left off. He came prepared, pulling a small flashlight from his pocket and turning on a precision beam that highlighted the scattered mess left from the raid.

He snooped around, opening drawers and shuffling through stray files – *nothing.*

He left the office, turned the flashlight off, returned it to his jacket pocket, and placed his sleeve back under his nose as he walked through the dark hallways again. Cloaked in night, the place no longer felt like a lab but a labyrinth. He relied almost exclusively on memory to navigate his way to the stairwell, where he climbed to the executive floor.

The most overt feature of the executive lobby was a glass wall that spanned the entire length of the room, framing a hilly background illuminated by soft moonlight. It exuded a sensation of air missing from the lower levels. No longer did Stan have to breathe through his jacket sleeve.

Stan's eyes fell on an office door, specifically on the nameplate:

MERRITT LEE

Immediately recognizing the name, he pulled his phone from his inside pocket, punched in a message to Carl, and sent it off.

The moment Stan entered Merritt's office he couldn't help but notice how the abandoned amenities prevented the space from having the feeling of desertion. The oak shelves, loaded with legal books, documents, biotech journals, and biotechnology books, seemed to transform the office into a private library. The wall of glass in the executive lobby continued, uninterrupted, inside this executive space.

Stan couldn't help but compare this emptiness to the one he left behind at the Bureau – all it took was a few boxes, and the office space that used to be his second home was nothing more than an empty box. Merritt's office appeared, at worst, temporarily unoc-cupied. In fact, all evidence revealed it to be mostly unused, as if habitation were fleeting. The occupant, if he could be called that, was almost always gone, traveling, away. Whether his absence was necessitated by business or litigation, the tenant of this space would be back...someday.

Stan's flash light seemed futile against such enormity. *Fuck it,* he thought and hit the light switch.

The space, including the absence of computer equipment, carried signs of the Feds having confiscated its most vital items. Merritt's remaining possessions, however, seemed not to have suffered the same disarray as Shijea's. With hands in his pockets, Stan cased the place with his eyes, walking around, seeing if anything jumped out at him.

He sorted through paper work on the desk – all of it generic. None of it seemed to have any relevance. The desk drawers were filled with random office stuff: pens, staplers, legal yellow note pads scribbled with notes. Stan leafed through the notes, at first finding nothing, then his eyes stopped at a sheet of paper, folded and wedged inside the pad. As he pulled out the page and opened it, his eyes frowned at the sight of an old engraving of dead bodies and a priest praying over the fallen figure of a dying man – *The Black Plague* illustration.

As Stan's eyes scanned the page, diagnosing how ill-fitted it was to be hidden inside this legal notepad, in this oak desk drawer, in this oak office, and even this whole damn building, he asked himself, *why would this be in here?*

Then his eyes widened slightly as an answer passed through his mind. He shook his head, doubting the possibility, staring at the *improbability*. He looked up, smiling at first, then laughing. Before, the evidence had leapt off the pages of the Rosalind Files and whacked him on the head for missing the obvious; this time it was doing so for *not* missing it.

You're a fool Stan, was his final ruling on himself, before putting away the illustration. Yet he couldn't walk away from it.

He stood staring at it for another second before saying "fuck it" out loud, grabbing up the illustration, folding it, and stashing it away in his pocket.

Then the lights went out.

The entire office went dark. Stan looked up, wondering what the hell had just happened. *Was it a power outage or did Carl get here already?* If it was Carl, he would meet him at the ground level. Stan hurried out of Merritt's office, down the stairwell and back into the odoriferous hallways, where he came to a sudden stop. There was no one there.

No agents.

No Carl.

As he approached the entrance doorway, his face darkened as his eyes confirmed a familiar vehicle, waiting on the other side of the glass door, blocking his exit.

It was the white van.

Chapter Nine

XY XX

Why the hell am I the one running? I'm the federal agent here!
This thought ran through Stan's head just as quickly as he ran
from the sight of the white van.

"This is pathetic!" he cursed aloud after taking a random detour.
Much to his chagrin, his detour landed him in the men's restroom.
Pride almost compelled him to turn back and find a hideout more
befitting his ego, but the sound of footsteps approaching chased
away that idea. What he needed now was a hideout *within* his
hideout, and restrooms, by their very nature, are scant in options.
In fact, there was only one option – the bathroom stall.

The very thought was an insult to his already injured ego, but it
would have to do. He ducked inside, raised his foot, preparing to
step on the toilet seat, but a last minute thought brought him to
a pause, or rather a *preparation.* He grabbed a handful of toilet
paper, wiped the seat of any stray urine (just to be sure), hopped
on the seat, and, of course, he still slipped.

A foolish attempt to break the fall (or perhaps just Murphy's Law)
had his hand slam down on the flusher. The dissonant sound of
toilet water roared around as a miniature whirlpool bounced off

the bare white walls. Stan crashed to the floor, his head striking against the porcelain. If the sound of the flusher wasn't enough of a giveaway, surely the ringing in his head was. As the ache and clamor inside his head finally settled, he heard the unfavorable sound of footsteps approaching.

He quickly rolled underneath the partition, escaping to the next stall, sprung to his feet and onto the toilet seat. This time, he was sure to keep his balance. He sucked in air, holding in any sounds that might betray his position. Not that it was much of a hideout; it would only take the invader a half second to trace the sound of the hissing toilet, discover that the stall was empty, then kick open the stall right next to it. *Then what?* Stan asked himself. *He'll find me standing on a toilet seat like a damn idiot! Screw that.*

Stan searched his pockets for something to fight with and came up with only his small flashlight. At this point, all he could do was exhale and place it in his jacket pocket. He pushed it forward, so that it might protrude in such a way as to be mistaken for a gun. *Yeah, yeah… An* old and outdated trick, but it was all he had. He steadied himself, preparing for who or whatever came through the stall door.

The bathroom door was pushed open with force – a surprise tactic. The same was done with the stall door next to him. Sure enough, as he predicted, his stall door was next. However, what he hadn't anticipated was that he'd be staring into the face of the same man he had plugged in the head a few short days ago.

The Jackal.

You're fucking kidding me! Stan eyes exclaimed as he stood frozen in place.

It was the same bald head, same stoic eyes behind thin glasses. The Jackal immediately noticed Stan's hand buried inside his jacket. He calmly backed away from the stall.

"I don't use guns, so you won't need yours. Step down from off the toilet, please."

Stan stared at him, stupefied. The Jackal showed no signs, not even a hint of the intent to attack. *What the hell is the catch here?* Stan wondered, but, after standing in place for what felt like an hour, he began to realize there wasn't one. This was a legitimate offer.

He slowly stepped down and immediately felt boxed in by the stall walls. He tried to conceal his vulnerability, though he knew there was no deceiving the strong, steely eyes of the killer in front of him. The Jackal, like all animals, could smell Stan's trepidation. In a show of good faith, he stepped back a few more paces, giving Stan room to exit the stall.

Stan obliged but braced himself as he emerged from the narrow walls. He half-expected a second Jackal, or maybe even a third, to club him over the head as he emerged. He exhaled, almost relieved, as no such attack followed.

Finally free from the enclosure, Stan strategically positioned himself opposite the main door, just in case an ambush was waiting for him on the other side.

"So, now what?" Stan asked.

"Introductions," The Jackal replied.

"I don't think so," Stan said, almost laughing.

"I just want to know what name the Bureau gave me."

"Bureau?" Stan asked, raising an eyebrow.

"There's no need to be coy. I know who you work for." The Jackal's expression never changed as he spoke. He was surprisingly civil, though his neutral etiquette seemed to be more akin to professional courtesy.

"I'm not being coy with you. It's just that… Well, most people know us as 'the FBI' or 'the Feds.' We might go by that name in movies but not in our own circle. There's only one type of person who ever refers to the FBI as 'the Bureau' – another agent."

The Jackal grinned, impressed by the guile of his prey. "You're right; kind of like the difference between the 'CIA' and –"

"'*The Company*,'" Stan said, completing the sentence for him.

"Exactly," – The Jackal casually leaned against a sink faucet – "except I never called the CIA 'The Company,' especially now that I'm not a *Company Man* anymore."

Stan wasn't one for giving into his fate without putting up a fight. He began re-diagnosing his chances of besting this guy in hand-to-hand combat. The prognosis wasn't good. He cursed himself for not positioning himself at the door, where he could, at least, turn tail and run. His so-called strategic positioning only succeeded in making him a sitting duck.

"So how exactly did you go from working for one Drug Company to another?" Stan asked, half-wanting to know the answer but really just using a dilatory tactic while planning his escape. The outward chuckle from The Jackal meant that the diversion might have been working – *might*.

"Yeah, I've heard those conspiracy theories before. The CIA supposedly pushes cheap drugs into the black community." The Jackal paused at these words, suddenly realizing who he was talking to – a federal agent, a *black* federal agent. "Although," he continued, "I suppose there are no conspiracies for guys like us, are there?"

"No, there aren't," Stan replied.

"Then you already know the answer to your question. I left The Company to go Corporate; simple as that."

Stan didn't reply. He was too busy trying to figure out how to get through this alive. Having exhausted every idea for an escape, he was back to playing out combat scenarios. With each battle sequence that passed through his mind, his hope for making it out in one piece grew dimmer. He had all the skill he could ever need in a fight, but Company Men were trained to kill and kill quickly.

"So, now that I told you who I am, maybe you can tell me who you *thought* I was," The Jackal continued.

"We gave you the code name 'The Jackal,'" Stan answered.

"The Jackal?" he smiled in response. "That's close, very close. How about 'The Gemini?'"

"How about you just tell me what you want?" Stan countered with impatience.

"Let's start with what *you* want."

"Okay, what is it that I want?"

"Well, initially you wanted some kind of evidence from this building, but during our brief conversation your only preoccupation was to stay alive." – *The Gemini* reached into the inside of his jacket, pulling out latex gloves. – "That shouldn't be a problem." Next he pulled out a syringe.

"Be nice to keep my memory too," Stan retorted, looking at the syringe.

"Then you understand that a direct confrontation with me will not end in your favor?" The Gemini examined the contents of his syringe, waiting for confirmation of his question. Stan hesitated. It took him a few seconds to swallow his pride before he could give his answer.

"Yes."

"Good, so then my proposal should be settled very quickly. In exchange for your life and memory, what I want is simple – information."

"What information?"

"I want to know the first and last name of the agent who killed my brother."

From that single word the air dissipated and vanished entirely.

"Brother?" Stan asked, his words trailing off.

"Twin brother."

The Gemini noticed the change in Stan's biology. He saw Stan's chest noticeably expand and compress. He saw the blood drain from his face. His nose even detected the sharp odor of his instant anxiety. It was his ears that were still wanting – waiting for an answer.

Silence surrounded their stand-off; if this could even be called a *stand-off.* There was nothing about Stan's position and posture that seemed defensive. Quite the opposite, he was defenseless.

The Gemini was relaxed as he patiently waited for Stan to betray the identity of his brother's killer. It was this unflappable composure that Stan figured could be turned against him. *Just come right out and tell him,* Stan thought to himself. *The shock will buy me a second, maybe two...*

"Name?" Stan asked.

"First and last," The Gemini replied flatly.

"Stan Medes."

The Gemini paused, furrowing his brow, suspicious.

"Stan Medes?" he asked, as if the name were sour in his mouth.

"Yeah, I know. It's a pussy name, isn't it? Trust me, it's haunted me my whole life."

It took only a second for that to sink in. It took three times that for Stan to reach inside his jacket, as if grabbing for a weapon.

Two seconds – The Gemini pounced, discarding his syringe and the merciful attack for memory. This blitz was for blood.

One second – He saw Stan's hand emerge from his jacket.

Half-second – The Gemini rocketed an iron fist, cracking Stan in the jaw.

The final second – He snatched Stan's hand, clutched the wrist and snapped it. Stan's hand released the object. He crashed hard to the porcelain floor and quickly retreated by sliding his body into the feeble protection of the restroom stalls. The Gemini mocked him with a sordid smile that soon vanished as he caught sight of what Stan had dropped to the floor; not a gun – a cell phone.

Perplexed, he picked up the phone, and his eyes dropped at the message on the screen:

GPS Data Received

"I just wanted to make a call, asshole," Stan said laughing, holding his injured hand, using his elbow to pull himself up and take a seat on the toilet.

"When did you send this?" The Gemini asked.

"Long enough for the cavalry to kill your ass after you kill me."

Kill me. Those words usually warranted a "*Who, me?*" from The Gemini, but not this time. His calm and cool expression was now shaken. He watched Stan take his injured hand, rest it on the flush handle and painfully press down. The sound of hard water spun around the entire bathroom, bouncing from wall to wall, until finally traveling outside.

The Gemini retreated to the main bathroom door and thanked his lucky stars that there was a latch to lock it on the inside. He slowly backed away, listening for footsteps, but the silence he needed to identify the coming cavalry was sabotaged by Stan's continued laughter.

"Shhhhh…" The Gemini hissed, but Stan ignored the order, still laughing.

"Shut up!" he commanded, but immediately realized his mistake. He turned and looked at the door. It shook as someone tried to force his way inside. Next, several kicks jolted the door, which remained stubbornly shut. Only a second of silence punctuated the time between Stan's coughing laugh and the sound of gunshots ripping through the main door, aimed for the lock. The bullets barely missed The Gemini, who instinctively ducked downward and hurled his body to the floor and inside a stall for protection.

His refuge was interrupted by an injured hand reaching underneath the partition, grabbing him by his collar, and yanking him into the next booth. With his perfectly healthy hand, Stan pummeled multiple times, hurling missile-like punches in the face of The Gemini.

A final gunshot shattered the lock and four agents burst through the door, lead by Carl. With guns drawn, they stood frozen upon the realization that they would not be saving Stan from The Gemini, but instead the other way around. They paired off, with two agents jumping on The Gemini to detain him, and two others leaping upon Stan to restrain him.

"Stan! Stan! Chill out!" Carl shouted into Stan's ear. "Chill the fuck out!"

With daze in his eyes, Stan ceased his retribution and looked over at Carl. His eyes seemed to re-focus from the familiarity of Carl's visage.

"You're Amber's new boyfriend?"

"Partner, Stan, I'm her new partner. Now come on, stand up."

Stan tried to obey, but his injured hand, still filled with adrenaline and defying all pain, refused to relent its hold on The Gemini.

"Let go. Come on, buddy. Let go," Carl prompted. "Jesus, you're like a pit bull with that hand."

Stan eventually freed The Gemini. Carl threw his arms under Stan's, helping him raise himself off the ground. Stan re-oriented himself, reached into his pocket and pulled out a copy of *The Black Plague* illustration, showing it to Carl.

"What the fuck is that?" Carl asked with confusion in his eyes.

"Don't laugh," Stan answered, "but I think it's a password."

***

Saracki sucked at his teeth, staring at *The Black Plague* image.

He looked up at Stan – a pathetic sight with one side of his face swollen. His injured hand was doctored and wrapped up. His free hand was clenching a stack of papers.

Saracki tried his best to look serious, but in reality he wanted to laugh, hysterically, at Stan's hazardous heroism that resulted in his haphazard appearance. The way he sat in Saracki's chair, bruised and broken, seemed reminiscent of a middle school kid, sentenced to the principal's office after a schoolyard skirmish.

Carl, the way he stood there, resolute and report-ready, had the aura of the poor teacher charged with breaking up the brawl and briefing the principal on what the hell happened. Then there was this *Black Plague* illustration in front of him...

Saracki looked down at it, as if it were a cheat sheet ripped right out of a textbook.

"'Are any among you sick?'" he began reading the Biblical passage just beneath the illustration. *"'They should call for the elders of the church and have them pray over them, anointing them with oil in the name of the Lord. Their prayer, offered in faith, will heal the sick, and the Lord will make them well. Anyone who has committed sins will be forgiven.'"*

"So what exactly is so special about this?" Saracki asked, looking back up at Stan.

"I think it's a password to something," Stan replied. "I mean, it could be a typo...but I don't think so."

"Typo? What do you mean?" Saracki asked, scanning the text. "Spelling looks right to me."

"It's not the spelling, Joe." Stan sighed. "It says '1:14-15.' That quote is chapter and verse from the *Epistle of James*. It should read *5:14-15.*"

"Okay, let's say it is a password," Saracki said, leaning back in his chair. "It's moot anyway. ETGR's computers are in acquisition. Computer Forensics have gone through every Senior Executive's secret and deleted data from their computers. So you have a password...so what?"

"Okay," – Stan stood up and placed his stack of papers on Saracki's desk – "the woman who freed Joey gave me these at the ETGR raid." Stan sifted through the pages and segregated the bacteria images, placing them adjacent to *The Black Plague* illustration.

"See here, how they're numbered 1, 4 and 5? Well, initially I thought it meant that images 2 and 3 were missing, but —" Stan paused mid-sentence. He looked up at Saracki, who listened with such impenetrable incredulity that Stan was certain, if his crackpot theory turned out wrong, Saracki would have him committed.

"Okay," Stan said again, waving his hand as if to start his point all over, "look, this is going to sound crazy —"

"*Going* to sound crazy???" Saracki blurted. "*Going* to sound crazy?"

"I don't think the information we're looking for was saved on a computer," Stan continued, sidestepping Saracki's skepticism. "I think it was saved into these little fuckers right here." Stan pointed to the bacteria images. Saracki followed the direction of Stan's finger, then looked up at him, his expression shifting from skepticism to sympathy. His friend was losing his damn mind.

"Maybe I need Addison to help me make sense of the details, but I think these records are telling us that computer information can be interpolated into genetic information."

"How?" Saracki asked.

"By converting the letters of our alphabet into numbers, then assigning those numbers a DNA value — ATGC."

"But you said this was a password," Carl cut in, "a password for hacking into...*bacteria*?"

"I think that's exactly what it is. Assume that each bacterium is like a miniature hard drive. I think the data has been encrypted and spread out across three '*bio-drives*' that are labeled 1, 4, 5; but, after decryption, the data has to be re-sequenced in five parts..."

Stan grabbed and held up *The Black Plague* illustration.

"*11415.*"

A demurring silence followed.

"What's crazier?" Stan added. "My theory, or a guy like Merritt Lee being a closet Bible Thumper?"

Saracki and Carl looked at each other.

"Okay, let's say we have BioEvaluations sequence the DNA. How the fuck are we going to decrypt, decode, and re-sequence the information?" Saracki asked.

"You're asking me?" Carl recoiled from the question.

"No, you're FBI." Saracki directed his voice at Stan. "He's FDA. I'm asking him."

"Well, let me first run this by Addison and make sure I haven't completely lost my mind."

"Good idea!" Saracki concurred.

Stan gathered together *The Rosalind Files*.

"Then we'll talk to the woman who gave me this."

***

"No, you're not crazy," Addison began, wiping away sleep from his eyes, "not completely crazy, at least."

While Addison shuffled through *The Rosalind Files*, Stan allowed himself a few seconds to make a cursory diagnosis of Addison's home. For a single man, he found it to be surprisingly well kept and tidy. Then again, Addison was more or less the anal-retentive type, so maybe it shouldn't surprise him. As he began to wonder about Addison's sex life, his nose caught the smell of perfume – *a familiar perfume,* a smell he had come to associate with…*Amber.*

Instinctively, he raised his head, angling it to allow for a better whiff. Addison noticed his awkward behavior.

"What's wrong?" he asked.

"Nothing," Stan said, lowering his head back to eye level. "What were you saying?"

"Biodrives date back to 2001, but a practical application of this technology came nine years later from a team of Hong Kong researchers," Addison continued. "The data is actually fragmented and spread out across different cells of different extremophilic bacterial strains."

"Extremophilic?" Stan repeated, his eyebrows contorting.

"The term is not as scientific as it sounds, just a combination of the words 'extremus' – or 'extreme' – and 'philia,' meaning 'love.'"

"Extreme love?"

"*Love of the extreme*. Extremophilic bacteria are known for surviving under extraordinarily harsh conditions. They're ideal for storing and preserving information, without worry of losing the data to, say, a nuclear holoc–"

"So it can be done?" Stan interjected.

"Can it be done? *Yes*. Is it being done?" Addison asked with a skeptic tone in his voice, looking again at the paperwork. "I guess we have to find out. Who did you say gave it to you?"

"A woman named Rosalind Hagen from ETGR."

"She *volunteered* this to you?"

"Yeah. Why?"

"Do you know where she is now…so we can talk to her?"

It was 6:30 a.m. and Rosalind Hagen was wide awake. Lately, she had been unable to sleep past 4 a.m. Dreams kept waking her up like clockwork, and after-dream thoughts relentlessly tormented her, forcing her out of bed.

She stared at herself in the mirror – her real, unpainted self. Her lips were thin and stiff, her freckles pronounced, and her copper hair long. Her entire body was peppered with freckles. They stood out against her pale white skin. Even her veins were clearly visible, appearing as bluish embossed tributaries.

She looked down at her hand, holding a pair of scissors. She looked back up at her reflection. Her eyes held no guilt or sorrow, only determination; but determination to do what? As she leaned forward to inspect herself even closer, she tried to decide what exactly it was that she was determined to do: *to die,* or simply *to change*? She felt determined and yet undecided.

Change is the best of both worlds, she decided. *It is death and rebirth.*

She ran her hand through her hair, grasping at a small lock of strands and, in one decided motion, chopped it all off with the scissors. She repeated this again and again, feeling both pain and liberation.

It was 7:30 a.m. as Stan and Addison knocked on Rosalind's door. She greeted them with her newly shaven head and a conspicuous smile. She looked androgynous, and Stan had to re-focus his eyes intently to even remember who she was. She offered them a place to sit, but that was all she offered. She grabbed a cup of coffee for herself. Addison and Stan sat with their hands empty, except for the paperwork that brought them here. Papers she immediately recognized.

"Did you find everything you needed on the biodrives?"

"Not quite," Stan answered, "embarrassing as it may be, we… Well, I…just figured out what they were."

Rosalind nodded her head, understanding.

"Do they do the storage and encryption themselves?" Addison asked.

"No, they outsource, probably to Dr. Martin Parks. His team worked on programming viral-therapeutic vectors for GAIA, but they used bio-cryptology as a profit source."

"Were you responsible for outsourcing the data?"

"No, definitely not, I was pretty low on ETGR's totem pole. Apparently, whenever something was that sensitive, it wasn't stored with conventional methods, let alone shared with someone like me."

"How did you figure out that Joey's information was on here?" Stan asked.

"I was chiefly responsible for Joey's lab administration, his day-to-day schedule and surveillance. The operative word being *'surveillance'* if you know what I mean. Truth is, I don't think I've ever stopped watching Joey, not even after I helped him escape from that God-awful facility. When he wasn't directly within my sight, he was on my mind, until the very end."

"The very end…" Stan frowned, puzzled and troubled by these words.

"Joey is dead," she said in a very matter-of-fact tone.

Addison's eyes widened, he stared at her in disbelief, then turned his head to Stan, who didn't look back at him. Instead, Stan kept his focus on Rosalind, wondering how the hell this leaked out to her.

"Who told you that?" he demanded.

"You see these things," she began, her eyes at first glassy, then showing a hint of moisture. "You see them in dreams. That sounds crazy to you, doesn't it? It sounds…irrational. Yes, I know. It is very irrational. Joey couldn't remember his dreams. I discovered that while working with him. He's never experienced what it is like to dream. Well, I'm sure he's experienced it, but he didn't *remember* the experience, which is just as bad as never having had a particular experience at all. He couldn't keep his own life experiences in his head, and I can't keep them out. He's still in my head. I see him there, while I'm awake, but also when I'm dreaming.

"During dreams the frontal areas of the brain that govern our claims of reality are shut down. Reason and rationality are trespassers in the dreaming mind. So you can do or see anything, no matter how 'irrational.'" – She made quotation marks with her fingers. – "You can see and talk to loved ones…or departed friends. I talked to Joey. He told me that he wasn't here anymore; that he was somewhere else. I woke up crying."

Rosalind suppressed her tears. They were not for her two guests, but for her and Joey alone.

"I cried," she continued, "because he came back to tell me that he was gone. That was when it hit me – he remembered who I was… He *remembered* me."

Her forbidden tears finally freed themselves, rolling down and stopping somewhere on her cheek, where she could wipe them away. She looked at Addison and Stan and decided that she didn't care after all that they had witnessed this part of her. It didn't matter because they couldn't share in her feelings.

They didn't believe.

"Of course, if you don't believe in dreams you can always turn on the TV," she finished.

"What are you talking about?" Addison and Stan both asked together.

"Your own agency seems to keep you out of the loop. They announced Joey's murder this morning at 5 a.m." Rosalind answered. "His face has been all over the news ever since."

***

Joey's face had been Xeroxed several dozen times over, adhered to picket signs, and raised above the heads of over a hundred protestors, standing outside the research labs of ETGR. His black and white, grainy, polarized visage was punctuated with other messages; many of them decidedly religious, promising swift punishment for encroachment of divine will.

Police officers formed a line outside the front perimeter of the building, deterring violence and vandalism. Several cars pulled up along the fringes of the fray, and a team from the FBI's BioEvaluations division emerged, along with field agents offering protection. Immediately they were surrounded by a mob of demonstrators. The agents held out their badges in one hand and guns in the other as they forced their way through the teeming bodies and inside the ETGR Labs.

Stan and Addison were dilatory in exiting their car, each for their own reason. For Stan this was déjà vu all over again. This was the third time that he'd set foot in ETGR. Each time, like the proverbial river, the building offered new events and circumstances. It felt as if he were locked within some time loop, where, no matter how often he tried to alter his course, he was transplanted back to the same destination.

"So this is what they mean by destiny," he said aloud to himself, forgetting that Addison was right there next to him. The words made no logical sense to Addison, with the exception of the word *destiny*. His body reverberated at the sound of the word, effectively countering everything his mind had ever told him about the fallacy of destiny. *He had been here before*. If Saracki was right, this is where he was made. Somewhere inside this *home*, stored in industrial-size refrigerators, were bacterial strains with information about Joey. Perhaps stored right alongside Joey's strains were biodrives containing information about his father and him. Addison was here. He had returned home.

The existential trance dispersed as protestors confronted Stan and Addison inside their car, shouting through the windows. The angry density of their words collided together, rendering them inscrutable. However, the intensity of their fiery words was meaning enough for Addison. *They were here for him, for people like him.*

"Ready?" Stan asked Addison, looking over at him.

"Yeah," Addison answered, though hardly convincing. Stan heard the trepidation in his voice, and, for the first time that Addison could remember, Stan offered him the kind of reassuring smile that could only come from someone he would call a friend.

"Don't worry. I got your back."

With those words both men grabbed at the door latches, opened the doors, and stepped bravely into the chaotic waves of dissention, pushing forward to destination and destiny.

***

The good news was that bacteria, preserved in glycerol and stored in agar dishes, were far less cajoling than gazing at deformed fetuses stored behind glass. In fact, there was not much to look at.

For Stan, it was the benign equivalent of staring at a small cup of Jell-O, or, considering that glycerol is also used in explosives, he could equate it to staring at a bomb. Knowing that expository information was embedded somewhere inside these cups of goo was a surreal thought. Then again, so was the thought that information could be stored within *anything* at all. As Stan and Addison watched the BioEvaluations Team remove the agar dishes and prepare to extract the strains, Stan wondered about the divide between a cylinder shaped flash drive and the rod-shaped cylinder strain of bacteria.

He pulled the flash drive that he kept attached to his key chain from his pocket and measured it against his hand – the size of his thumb. On the edge, printed in white letters against its black coating, were the words 20GB. To him this was an ample quantity. 20GB, *whatever the hell that really meant,* could be "stored" in a device the size of his thumb. Yet, somewhere in this glycerol Jell-O Bomb were microorganisms holding 100,000 times the capacity of his flash drive. Unlike his flash drive, these microorganisms were...*alive.*

The BioEvaluations Team walked away with the dishes. Stan and Addison didn't bother to follow them.

"Is life just a program?" Stan asked. Addison looked at him, understanding the question and remembering that, at one time, he believed he understood the answer. Now he wasn't so sure.

Is life a program? Addison repeated the question to himself, his eyes ruminating.

"An environmental program?" he began. "Yes, at least, that is what we believe."

"Who is *we?*" Stan asked.

"Scientists," he answered, "and maybe Christians too. If I'm not mistaken, the name *Adam* means '*From the Earth,*' which I suppose is true. Our transition from inanimate matter to amino acids means that we are, quite literally, products of our environment. Our oldest earthly ancestor is the earth itself."

With a simple blink Addison's existential, cogitating gaze flickered out, and he was back in this world. He looked over at Stan, who didn't miss the transition. In fact, he was somewhat spooked by it.

"I looked up the meaning of my name," Addison continued.

"What does it mean?"

"*Son of Adam*"

Stan looked away, smiling. Addison easily noticed his smirk.

"I read that the name *Adam* has another meaning," Stan explained.

"What?" Addison asked flatly.

"That's right. How did you know?" Stan's smile broadened, enjoying the conundrum.

"What?" Addison asked again, furrowing.

"*Adam* means '*what.*' Numerically, at least. It's based on the number 45."

"Let me guess. You learned that from Allan's book?"

"Yup."

Addison closed the ridiculous conversation with silence. His eyes traveled over to the glass freezer where the biodrives were stored. His mind wandered in the direction his eyes took him. Every dish holding every isolated strain was dated and labeled. He looked for his father's name *and his own*. He abandoned the search after only a few minutes, realizing that he was appearing conspicuous.

"What now?" Stan asked, looking around the room.

"I guess we wait."

"For how long?"

"We'll be here awhile," Addison replied throwing his arms up.

"Shit."

"What's wrong?"

"Nothing." Stan pushed away the question, but Addison could clearly see that his partner was antsy.

"What???" Addison pressed again.

"I have to pee."

"Then go!"

Stan rolled his eyes and head at the presupposition that this was a simple thing. Addison had no idea what Stan had been through the last time he detoured to the Little Men's Room, nor did he want him to know. Knowing that *not going* would demand an explanation, Stan, with great hesitation, surrendered to nature's call, dragging his feet on his way out of the room. This gave Addison a chance to continue searching for his and his father's names among ETGR's biodrives.

***

Stan cursed to himself as he stood outside the men's bathroom. He reached out his hand, pausing first to notice his injury. He pushed the door open, half expecting the boogieman to jump out after him. Of course, no such thing happened. This only added to his anticipation that it would.

The restroom was crammed with silence. Stan could hear every single one of his own footsteps as he walked over to a urinal.

The quick pattern sound of his zipper seemed to roar. The sound of water breaking apart as he relieved himself was audible enough to be embarrassing. He looked around, wondering if anyone was watching. Then the flush.

His head jerked, and in the span of an eye blink The Gemini was there, then gone again.

What was his mind doing? What was his memory doing? Haunting him? Do our memories follow us everywhere, even beyond the grave?

These were not thoughts but impulses that flashed through Stan's nerves as he quickly refastened his lower half and exited the restroom as quickly as possible.

***

When Stan returned, he found Addison probing the bacteria storage. Addison quickly aborted his mission, attempting to look bored and casual.

"I had a theory about life while taking a piss," Stan volunteered, raising a single dry finger in the air.

"Did you wash your hands?" Addison asked with a look of revulsion.

"No. So my theory is that our souls come to earth to escape bad memories from previous lives. In that book I borrowed from Dr. Shapiro it said that Pythagoras, who invented that whole number to letter thing, believed in reincarnation. Yet he said that, when we take on bodies, matter clouds the memory of the soul, making us amnesiac. I don't have a problem with reincarnation…but my question would be: 'Why would anybody want to come back to this world?' Then the idea flashed in front of me – we're running away from our memories.

"Still, I think maybe it's also to reconcile those memories. You know, so memory is like a thread that connects us from one life to the next. Of course, with each new life, new memories are developed and the thread gets longer."

Addison didn't seem put off by this nonsense, perhaps because his mind was still preoccupied with other matters, but he decided to entertain Stan, nonetheless.

"How do we stop the cycle?" he asked.

"When there are no more bad memories. This means that, somehow, we must stop all the bullshit that goes on in this world," Stan answered with an obvious tone.

Addison nodded his head to this.

"Anyway, Joey had no memories," Stan finished. "Lucky bastard doesn't have to come back here. He gets to go home."

***

"Wake up, genius. Your idea didn't work."

Stan opened his eyes, having fallen asleep on the lobby couch. He opened his mouth to respond and immediately felt saliva trailing down the side of his face. Too tired to be embarrassed, he wiped it away with his hand. The BioEvaluations Specialist curled her lips in slight revulsion at the sight. He looked up and saw Addison stand next to the Specialist.

"You were right about the biodrives, but the password sequence you gave us isn't working."

"Why isn't it working?" Stan asked, cleaning his moistened hand on his pants leg.

"Because you were wrong!" the Specialist snapped, her temper seething. Stan was much too dogged to feel the prick from her words. He stood up. She held up *The Black Plague* illustration, slapped it back in Stan's hand, turned, and left. Addison and Stan hurried to keep up with her.

"While you were napping," she began, talking as fast as she was walking, "we were busy isolating the marked cell data carriers, sequencing the DNA, decrypting and defragmenting their base code. Somewhere between all that was a lot of words like *fuck, shit, damn, son-of-a-bitch, and what-the-fuck!*" As they approached the Bioinformatics Lab, she stopped at the door. "Actually," she continued, "*what-the-fuck* came when we looked at your so-called password sequence."

She walked inside, leaving Stan and Addison to follow after her. Stan expected the other technicians to share in her acerbity but was relieved to find that they were all too drained and fatigued from verbally assaulting one another to adopt any new victims. Only Heinrich, who was also part of the crew, hadn't lost his alacrity.

"Mr. 11415 has arrived," Heinrich said, smiling.

"Is that my code name now?" Stan replied, half-smiling back.

"Yup, before it was –"

"You don't have to say it. I can imagine."

"I'm sure you can. To say that your imagination is vivid would be an obvious understatement. Not that I don't see the leaps that you made here. In fact, I'm the only person in this room who still thinks that you're onto something. Just as you surmised, we have no fewer than five data fragments, which correspond with our five-digit password sequence. Unfortunately, we're hacking our way into these fragments, so we don't have the luxury of getting them to re-link themselves." Heinrich waved Stan over to a computer monitor that displayed a segment of the nucleotide strings. "See here," Heinrich pointed.

TGCAGTCCTTGTTTTCTAGTCCGGGTCGAGTCATAAGGGAAATTGGGCAAGGCACGT
GAT GCCTGATAAGAACTAGATGTTGACAGAACTAGGGTCAAACAAGACTCACCTCACC
ATTAAGCTGTAGGTACGTCCTCACATGGTATTCCCCACTATCTTTATGGGGGCGGCA
GAG TACGGACGGAGGACGGCATGAATAGAGGCTACGCGAGCGAGCGAGAGGCTACG
TGTAATGCTTTCCGGGTCTCTGATGGACTTCTGTGCTATTAGGTACTCTTCGAGGGCT
CATCTCGGCCTTCCTCCGGAGGAAGTAGGATGAGGGCGGGTGGCGGCTTAGTAGCC
CAGTTTTTTGAGATATCTTGGTAGATGATGCGTGATTGACTAGACACGTATAAGTGTCCC
TCGGTGCGGCTAAGCCACTAACCTCCCCTCAGCTATCTCCTCTATGAAATTGCTTTCCA
GTCCCTATATTTACAGCTGACGGTTTGTTTACATGAGCTTTCACCTCAGGTGTGTATAAT
GTTGGATTGTATCTCTTATGTTGTTAGGATCCCATTCATTGCTTGAGCCGGCATGCAATT
CGGGTGTATGCCTTTTATCTTGGAATATTTAGCAGGCCTTGTCCCAACTTGTCGAACTG
ACTGGACCGGTAGCAGCCGGGACTTATTAGTAGCACAGGGACTCTGTGTTGCATTGTT
GGAAACTGTGGTGAGCTGGGTAGTGGCTAACTGGTTAGAACTGTACAATAACATGTCC
ACCACTGCTGTTTATGAGCTCCTTACGAGGGGGGAGCAGCAAGACTTGTCTAACGATTT
GCCTAGACGAGCCCTGACGTCTCTCGGTGAGTCTCGCCCAGCCAGCAATTACAGATA
GTTATTCCACGAAGAAAGATCCCGCAGCTTGGAGATCCTGCGTATACGGCCCGGTTAC
ATACAGGCTAGAAACTTCTGAACCGGATCTCCGGAGCGCCAGCCGGCAAACTAGCGG
ACCGCAAGGACTTCCCAAATTTTGCTTCCTAGCAAGGAAAGCTCGCAACGAAGGTAAC
CATGCTTCGCTCCAAAGAAAACCGTGATAGCAAAGCCGGCAGCGCATTCCTCCTGTTA
ACCTGGCGTGTTAGAAATAGCTCAGACCGCGACAATAATCGATACTTCTGGTGGTACT
GCTTGGCTAAGCGTGGTACTGGGCGCAAGTATATCTTAAGGTGTCGCAATAGCAAGCT
TCCCTCCCAAAATTGCTGAGGCACGGGGAAGTCAAACGGTCGGAGAGGATCCGGTG
TTTTACTCTAGTTTAGGAAATATAGCTGTCCTTACCAATTACCTCTAAGTCAAGTCGCGG
GGTGACACGTGGAATGTAGAGACTAACCACCACTAGCGCCCCTGGAACACATTCTTAC
AAGAAATGGGTGACTATCTTTACTTTATATGGAGCTATTTGCCAAGTTCGGACCTTTCAT
TATCATCTGTTGTGACATATAATGACTCGAGCTTTCCAAACCCACCACGGTTAGCACCC
GGTAAATCTCTCGAAGGATCGGGTTCTTACGGGTTACCTTGACTGTCTTCAGCGCTTAA
TCAATTCTAATGTTGCAGGGCCCTAACCTCATATCATATAACTGGGCGGTACGGACCGA
CTTTGGACGGACCTATGAAGCATATCTACTTCCTACCCGTAGAAGCTTGTTTTCCCACA
ATGGTTCTGCCAACAGACTCAGCAAGCCATGCACCCGATGGATTAAAAAGCCTCTCGC
TGCTATTGCTAAGCTCCTAACGAGGGAATATCGGACAACCACCGAGGTGAGGTGTCGT
CGGGACAATGGTTAAGATTATGAGCGAGCAATCATCTACACAGAACTTACTGAGCGATA
ATGCTCAATGCCTCTACCCATGACTCTTGCCGGGGTCCGATTGAACAATTCTAGCGGG
TCTATTACATTACTTAGGAGCTAGGGACCCGACGATGTTAATAACAGCCGGCGTTACAA
CGGAGCGAAAGAATTTACGTGAGTACAGACTTCGACGTTGGTTAACTGTTCTGCTGAC
GTTACCAGATGCCGGGAGATCGGGATGTGGCACACAGAATGCTTCCAGTAATATTCGT
CTCTAAACATTCGCTGCCATTTCATCCTCTAACAGTTCCACTTCTCCACATTGAATCGTA
ATCAAAGAAGGCTATCAGAGTACTTCAATTACCTTCGTCATCTTCATAGATGGCACCTG
CTCGAACAGAAATACTCCCGAAAACACGACTCGAATTTCGCTATCGCCAGATTCGCGG
TCTATCACAGCTACCTGCACAGCCAAGGAGTAGAATCAACACGACGGATGCGCACGTA
GTAAAAAGCGGCGGTTATATGGGATGCGTAAGTTTTGCCTTCACGTCCTATTTGTGTTG
GAAAAATCACTTTGTCAGTATGTACGCATCGGGCGGGAGCCTCATAGTGGTTTATAAGT
CCTGAATCTTAGTCTGTCGAGTGTAGTTTCGGCGATGCGTGAAACGGAGCCGTTCGG
GCACTCCACTCCAAACCGTGGGCGGGACTATCCAAGACGCCCTCGCCGAGGCATCAT
ATCACGGATCGGTAAATTCAGTTCATGCGAGGTGTATATAGAATCATTGGAGGAGTCCT
AGACAGTACTAGCTGGCTTACGACACTGAGTAAACCAGACTCGAAGTGATATATGGCC
GAAAGAGCGACCGGCCCATTGCAGGACAAGGTGTCAATTCTCTCGGTATCCTTGCCT
GTCGGGTGAGTTAGCCCAAGTCGTGTAGCTGACTCGTGAGCATTACATTTGGCACTTG
CGAGATCCAAATCAAGCTCTAACATCGTTGAGGGTCTGTCGAATGGGCATTTGCGGGA

```
GGACACATTTCAAACGGTTCATTAATCAGCCAGCCATCTTAACTTATAGCTCTTAGGGAT
AAAATCTATGGATGGATGAAAGCATTAGCGCTCTGCATCAAACGCATAAACGCGCCTTC
GTAGTAACGGAATTGTACGATCAAGTCCTGGTCTGCTCTCCGTAAGTCGATATCTCCGT
TAGGGTCTTCATGAAGTCTCTTGGAATAACGCTCAGAGATGATTAAAGATCAGTTGGCA
CGCATCATAGAGGATCCTGGGTAACACGGATATCTGTTGTATAGCATGTTATATTTCCGC
TTTCGCAAGCAGTCGGATGAATACTTCATAATCTAGGACCTGCAGTCCACCTGGGTCA
GAGCACCCGGGTAATCACTTGCGCGTAATGCCGAGACAAATGAACAGGTCGGTGGTC
AAAGGTACGCGCCGTGGAGTAACTCTAACCGAATATATACGAAATCCGAGGCCAATAAC
ACAGGTCTTGCGAAGGGACGGACGTCGCCCTCTTGTATCAATACAGACACCGTACGC
CAACATGATATCGCGCGCTCCGGCCTACACAAGGAGTCGCGATGTGTAGACTCGTCAT
GTGTATCGCCGACCGGCGGATGTATTCGAGCTTACAAGTTTAAATCTAATGTACAGTGT
CATAGATGAGCATTAAACAGAATCTGAAAGAATAGATTTTGAAGGAGAGTATATATGCCC
TACGATTGAGTTAGCAATGAATTTTCTTAAGCCGCGCAGTCACTTGGGTTGGTGCAAAT
AAAAAGCACATTAAATGTTGTCTGTGTAATTGGGAGACTTGTTATGAGGGCGCCGGTG
GAGATACACGCTAGGCAGAAGGAGTTTTGAGCAGATGGGCCACCCATTTGGTTAGGC
GGCTTCAGGTTGATTCGAGGCGGGCGGCGACCGCTCCACCTAGTGATACAGAGGACA
TATCCTGGAAGCAGACTCTTGCGGTGGGCGTCGTTCGGTGCATTGAGTATAACTGTGT
TCGCGCTGCCACCTGAGGGGACACGGGGATCTTCAAACCTGTATTCTAATGTCGACAA
ATGTTCGACCTCTTCGTGGAGCCATTCATTATTGACTGCGATCAGCTACTCTCCCTTTTA
TAACCGTTATCAGGCAATAGCAGGCACTGGCGATTCGTCCGGGAGAGGGGGTGGATC
ACAGGGGCGTTCGCCATGGAACCTGAGCGTCAGTCTAAGGACTCAGTGCTGACAATA
GCACAGGCGATCGCTAAGAAAACTTTCTTGAACTAGCTGATCTTCGTAATAATGGGACT
ACCTCTAAATGTGGCCCTGCAAAGGCATAGAGGAATTTAGTTTAAACTTCAATATCTCCT
GGCGCTTTCCTAGAGCCTAAAATTCATTGCGCCCTTGTTCAACTTATGGACACCCAAGT
CCGCGAGTGATCTATTTGTACAGACAACACAATCAAATCGCCTCCTCTAGGTCACGCC
GGACCGACCCATTAACGGTTGGCCGCCCCATACTTTAAGTCTGTGCAGATAAGTATTTC
GTCCATTCCTGGATCAATGGCCGCTAGTAATAGCAGTCCTCGGGTGGAGTGGGCGAA
GCTGATATAGCAACCGACTGGACATCGTGAGTGGACTTGCGTCCACAACCCAGCGCT
GTTAAGTTGAGAAAACCCCGATTGTAACTCTCGTTGGATTTTCGCGAGCTAATATATCGA
TTCCAATTGTTGTAGTGTCTAGACGAAGAACGAGACATGCCGGAGGGTCTCTGCGGT
CGTTAGCGTGCTAATATGCGTTGTACCAGACTTTTATGTTTGCGATGTCCAAAATAACTA
ATGGGCTTGTTTTCCCATTCCCGGAAGACTGAGGTCTTAGTTGGAGGTGCGGCGCTA
GCTATTCAACAGATAATCGCACGTGACTTGAATCCGTCTGTCGTAACCGCTTTCTAGTG
ACCACATATGGACAAGCTCGACTCCAGTGCTCAACGCCTTGGATCCTGCCCCGTGTAT
AAGCGTTGGCGCATCGAAATTTGGGACATAACTTTCCGTATGTGCTCAACGGATGGTC
AAGTTTCCGGGCCACAAAGGTGAGAGTCTACTGCAAGGTCGATAGTCATGCCGCTAC
CAGGTTATCGAAACAGCTAAACGGATTACGAAACGTTTGATGCCCTCAGCAGGCTGCG
ACTCGGCACTTATAGTCCGTACTGGGTGGCGGCAAGTACACCCGGCGGAGGTAAATG
AGTGATCGTTATGATTGTAAATAGACACTGCGGCGGAGTCGCGGGATCCCCAACCCTC
CCCGCTAACCGTTAAAATACGGACTCCCCCTTAATGGAAGATAGCGGCTTTTCCACCTC
TATATATGCTCAACTATCGACTTTACGGCGGAGTCCTCGGCGGGCCGAATATCGCCCAAT
GCTGCCAAAAGAAAGATTTGACTTCGGCGGATGTGTTTGGCTGCATTCATCTGAGCAG
TTCAAGGCCTGCATGCTTGTACAGCACCTGGATCATGCCTCAGTACATTTCTTAGAACT
TAGGTTCAACGGAGCGGCCCTTCATGCCTATCCTAGTTTACCCGCCTGAAGGTGCCG
GAGGGAGCTATGGTAGATCTCAGCCAGACAGTCCTGTCTAAGTGCGTCACGGTGGTTA
TACGGCACAGGAGTACTGCTGCGTGAGTCTGCCCTCCGAAGTGTCCTGGGGAATGG
CACGTGAGGGCATGA
```

"Holy shit!" Stan exclaimed.

"Our words exactly," the Specialist added, her mordant mood

192

seeming to have finally softened. Addison hastened over to get a closer look at the code, imagining that these letters were an elucidation of him. Of course, even to his scientifically refined eyes, this run-on string of letters was little more than chaos. Yet knowing that beneath this illusion of chaos was an underlying order strengthened his resolve to sort out the tentative chaos of his own life.

Life, if bereft of meaning, is replete with order.

"There's a lot more where that came from," Heinrich continued. "Now, we just have to figure out how to stitch it all together. Specifically, we have to write an algorithmic function that will take this crap and pass it through all of the possible permutations of your password."

"*11415* didn't work?" Stan asked.

"You're catching on. Good for you!" the Specialist called out.

"You're a smart woman," Stan said back to her, "and smart is better than smart-ass, so why don't you take it down just a bit?"

"No, 11415 didn't work, sorry," Heinrich answered Stan's question in as neutral a voice as possible.

"It's a fluke, fallacious, farcical, a fantasy, a fable…a fucking fairy-tale!" With her asperity now rekindled, the Specialist decided to sulk away her frustrations by sentencing herself to some distant part of the room. There, she sat down and rested her head aggressively on a fisted hand. For a moment everyone watched her in silence.

"Okay! So who's up for lunch?" Heinrich said, breaking the silence with a smile.

"You've been working so long, you forgot that this place is surrounded with demonstrators," Addison replied.

"Okay, so we draw straws to see who does pick-up," he answered.

"I vote for the guy who brought *The Black Plague* upon us all."

All eyes turned on Stan. His objections were cut off by the sound of stomachs grumbling.

"You gotta be kidding me."

***

As soon as Stan stepped back out into the crowd, a melee of demonstrators was upon him, grabbing at his jacket. Police officers were wedged between him and the many hands clawing at his body. As he fought his way through, Joey's enlarged and photocopied face continued to obscure his sight of his car. Getting inside the car proved even more difficult. A horde of bodies tried to force itself inside after him. Hands and fists slapped and pounded at the surface of his car. As he backed out, finally the bodies began to peel away. Only after he was a mile away from the ruckus did he roll down his window and released a cathartic expletive.

"Shit!"

Accelerating as fast as he could through the hills, Stan had no idea that he was driving along the same road, passing through the same location, where Allan Shapiro had discovered Joey.

He arrived at Adam's Diner, where a sexy, middle-aged waitress greeted him, prompting him to sit down. Stan was all too happy to oblige. The waitress came back with a menu.

"I'm feeding an entire crew. Is there any chance I can walk out of here with a few boxes of pizza and maybe some wings?"

"This is a diner, sweetie, not a pizzeria… How about some burgers or sandwiches?"

"Perfect."

"Okay, which kinds?"

Stan paused, realizing that he had no idea what anyone wanted to eat. Abashed, he smiled at the waitress, reaching inside his jacket for his cell phone, holding up a finger as if to say: *Give me a minute.* The waitress smiled back and strutted away.

"Oh…uh, can you turn on that TV?" Stan pointed at the TV mounted on the wall. The waitress nodded obligingly. Stan stole an opportunity to check out her figure as she reached up to push the power button. The monitor defaulted to news reports of city-wide demonstrations. The waitress watched the report for only a handful of seconds before blitzing through a series of channels, pausing long enough to allow sound bytes from pundits and orators.

Channel 2:

"…and these people, who pose as so-called 'enlightened' members of our society, will have us believe that religion is the vehicle for mankind's ignorance. If that's true, then I say in response that science is your vehicle for arrogance."

Channel 4:

"Scientific literacy too often proves to be a costume worn by the scientifically illiterate, specifically by those desperate and impoverished minds that lack a sound scientific argument to oppose a sound scientific argument."

Channel 7:

"…I am not defined by Their patronizing science, Their cold technology, Their lifeless statistics; Their vague theories, Their abstract philosophies, or Their baseless currency. I am a human being, and, whether They like it or not, so are They…"

She changed the channel once more, this time stopping on an image of Allan Shapiro; no doubt as part of a report about Joey. She left this channel on, recognizing Allan's face and allowing herself a smile to the fond memory of her favorite regular.

Stan watched the coverage from his peripheral view as he flipped open his phone and began punching his keypad. His thumb suddenly came to a dead stop as he stared at the numbers – *and letters* – distributed across the miniature keys.

A mixture of sagacity and skepticism entered his eyes. He leaned backwards and began probing his own memory of what he had read in Allan's book. He hastily pulled a pen from his pocket, pushed away the fork and knife at his table to grab the napkin underneath. He began scribbling the first nine integers and mapping out the alphabet beneath them. Again he paused, staring at his fabrication:

$$1 \quad 2 \quad 3 \quad 4 \quad 5 \quad 6 \quad 7 \quad 8 \quad 9$$

A B C D E F G H I
J K L M N O P Q R
S T U V W X Y Z

Finally, he matched his scandalous password, 11415, with their corresponding letters, to produce the scandal's offspring:

JAMSE

Disheveled and picked over, with both arms full, Stan returned with food for the troops. Almost as earnestly as the protestors outside, the troupe of researchers, and even Addison, voraciously pounced upon him, pulling the bags away from his arms and grabbing at whatever contents they could get their hands on.

"I have good news and bad news," Stan announced. No one cared. They were too busy stuffing their faces. Only Heinrich, with his good manners and good nature, seemed to be attentive.

"What is it this time?" he asked, biting into a sandwich he hadn't even bothered to identify.

"The good news is that I figured out the password."

Still, everyone ignored the talking crackpot. Even the Specialist, who had made sport of assaulting Stan with her sharpness, found her mouth too preoccupied with sustenance to be bothered with her primal appetite for sarcasm.

"Okay," Heinrich laughed, "what's the bad news?"

"It's the same password as before."

Heinrich lowered his sandwich. *You're kidding, right?* was written all over his face.

"This time it will work. I'll bet my share of lunch on it," Stan assured him.

"Deal!" Heinrich hopped up, walked over to his computer and began punching away, calling up the five data fragments. "There are 243 possible permutations of the numbers 11415. What's the magic number?" He looked over at Stan smiling. However, before Stan could answer, he continued with a word of caution. "I hope you understand the risk you're taking here. If you get this wrong, you don't eat. That's worse than going without sex."

"Reverse the last two numbers." Stan said, ignoring the warning. Heinrich paused at the simplicity of the revision. He turned and looked at his monitor and then once again stared dubiously back at Stan.

"11451," he asked. "Is that your final answer?"

"Yes."

Heinrich went to work, programming the new sequence, then leaning back in his chair, waiting as the computer processed the instructions. The animation of letters shuffling into numbers was enough to solicit an audience. Everyone gathered around to stare at the monitor. Finally, the operation ceased, and all eyes gaped at the never-ending chain of code that filled the screen:

```
11101220121102001033130212211213122112320200123312120200102212
33121113210031003111101220121102001303131012331302132102001233
12120200100310301033103210110200120312111232131012111302130302
00120113021233131112321210020001201020012021233132102001232120 1
12311211121002001022123312111321020013131220123302001303121112
11123113030200131012330200122012011312121102001202121112111232
02001202123313021232020013131221131012201233131113100200131012
20121102001201120212211230122113101321020013101233020013021211
12311211123112021211302020012011232132113101220122113232121302
00121113201203121113001310020012201221130302001212122113021303
13100200123212011231121102320200111012201211020012211210121112
01020012031201123112110200121213021233123102001201020013021211
12011230023112301221121212121102001022123312111321020013131220 12
33020013131233130212231211121002001313122113101220020012311211
02001201130302001201123202001221123213101211302123202001212 12
33130202001222131113031310020012331312121113020200131013131233
0200132112111201130213030232020010101311302122112321213020013
10122012011310020013101221123112110200122012110200120112321210
0200102102001202121112031201123112110200121213021221121112321 2
10130302320200100113100200130312331231121110200130012331221 1232
13100200122112320200123313111302020012121302122112111232121013
031220122113000200102102001303122012011302121112100200131312 21
131012200200102212331211132102001201020013031221123212131311 12
30120113020200121013021211120112310200131012201201131002001021
02001220120112100230020013101233020013131220122112031220020010
221233121113210200130212111300123012211211121002001313122113 10
```

198

122002001220122113030200131113031311120112300200123012112113101012
201201130212131221120302001312123312211203121103220200200001301
021020012321211131212111302020012101302121112011231023202000102
113030200130312331231121113101220122112321213020013131302312331
232121302001313122113101220020012311211033302001001130212111123
220001211310020013001211123313001230121102001303131113000130012
331303121112100200131012330200121013021211120112310333200001310
200020011131220121112320200102212331211132102000130313001211120
112231303020013101220121113021211020012011302121102001201020011
213130212112011310020012311201123213210200121012111230120113 2
113030230020012111303130012111203122112011230123013210200013131
220121112320200122012110200122113030200130212111303130012331233
212101221123212130200131012330200120102000130113111211113031310 1
221123312320232020011101220122113030200120312331231121111303020
012121302123312310200120102001210121113121211123012331300123 11
211123213101201123000200121012211303120112021221123012211310132
102001221123213121233123013212211232121302001303123012331313 0
200130013021233120312111303130312211232121302001233121202001 22
112321212123313021231120113101221123312320200120213210200122 1
221130302001202130212011221123202320200111312200121112320200102
212331211132102000131012331230120120020012311211020013101220120 1
310020012200121112000120102012211210123220001211310020012101302 1211
120112310200010210200120312331311123012010123220001211310020012 2
012111230130002001202131113100200131012330200131312331232121 1
211130202001221121202001221131002001313121113021211020012101 1
112110200131012330200131012201211020012031233123212101221131 1
221123312321303020012331212020012201221130302001202130212011 22
112320232020011001303132112031220123312301233121312211303131 1
303020013131233131112301210020013031201132102000131012201201131
002001022123312111321020001210123312111303020012101302121112011
231023002001220121102000122213111303131002001210123312111303123
220001211310020013021211123112111231120212111302020013101220 2
111231023002000131312200122112031220023002000123312120200120312 33
131113021303121102300200122113030200120312331231123112331232 2
001310123302001201123012300200123312120200131113030232020010 21
123202001201020013031211123213031211020013131211020012011301 2
110200120112301230020012301221123312110200102212331211132 200
122112320200131012201201131002001313121102001220120113121211 2
001210130212111201123102000120112311232121113031221120102001311
1300123312320200131312011223122112321213020013111300023202 10
210200122012011312121102000123112011232132102002000130121013021
2111201123112301211130313032000131020012321221121312201310 303
020012211232020013101220120113100200130212111303130012111120313
10023202001002131113100200131312201211130212110200102212331211
132102000122113030200121012211212121212111302121112321310020012

2113030200131012201201131002001212123313020200003020301020013 21
1211120113021303020012201211020012201201130312322000121131002 0
013021211123112111231120212111302121112100200120102001303122 11
2321213123012110200121013021211120112310232020010321233131002 0
012331232121102320031003110210200120312331232130312211210121 11
302020013101220122113030200120213021221121111212020012111320 120
312201201123212131211020013101233020012021211020012010200130 01
221131212331310120112300200121113121211123213100200122112320 20
012311321020012301221121212110232020010221233121113210213130 30
200131313231302121013030200121212301311123212130200123112110 20
012201211120112100200121212211302130313100200122112321310123 30
200130113111211130313101221123312321303020012011202123313111 31
00200123012211212121102300200122013111231120112321221131013 210
2001123212100200013101220121102001220131112311201123202001 20
212331210132102001310122012011310020010210200122012011210020 01
2301233132321213020001303122112321203121102001201120212011232121
012331232121112100230020012101311121110200131012330200131012 201
211020012211232120112021221123012211310132102000131012330200 130
0130212331210131112031211102001201123213210200013031201131012211
303121213211221123212130200120112321303131312111302130302320 20
010211232020012010200130313101233130213210200012301221122312 110
200100310301033103210110200131012201211020001220131112311201 123
2020012021233121013210200120212111203123312311211113030200120 10
200130313211231120212331230020012121233130202001221131013031 21
112301212023202000100102001303132112311202123312300200122113 030
200123112111201123213100200131012330200120312011230123002001 20
113101310121112321310122112331232020013101233020012010200123 01
201130212131211130202001221121012111201020001310122012011232 020
013101220121102001201120313101311120112300200120113021203122 01
211131013211300121102320200200013011101220121102001002123312 10
132120001310230020013101220121113021211121212331302121102300 20
012211303020012010200130012111302121212111203131002001303132 11
231120212331230020012121233130202002000130103113210200100212 33
121013212000131023202001110122012110200123012011310131012111 30
2020012021211122112321213020001313120113210200012311233130212110
200130012111302130312331232120112300200131012201201123202001 31
012201211020012121233130212311211130202320200111012201211020 01
303121112321303120113101221123312320200102102001220120113121 21
102001313122012111232020010210200131012011223121102001233131 31
232121113021303122012211300020012331212020012311321020012021 23
312101321020012211303020013121221130313111201123012301321020 01
211123212031201130013031311123012011310121112100200120213210 20
013101220121102001031121112101221120312011230020010211230123 01
311130313101302120113101221123312321303020012331212020010221 20
112031301131112111303023110212011202122112111232020010131201 1

31113101221121113020232020011111232123012211223121102001310123
31210120113212000121130302001231121112101221120312011230020012
10130212011313122112321213130302001313122012111302121102001201
12321321020012211210121112010200123312120200120102002000130130
21211120112300200130012111302130312331232200013102001221130302
00120112021303121112321310023002001013120113111310122112111302
20001211303020012211230123013111303131013021201131012211233123
21303020013031220123313130200123212331310020012221311130313100
20013101220121102001202123312101321023002001202131113100200131
01220121102001300121113021303123312320200131312201233020012021
21112301233123212131303020013101233020013101220120113100200120
21233121013210232020010311233130313100200123112111210122112031
20112300200122112301230131113031310130212011310122112331232130
30200123312120200131012201211020011021211123212011221130313031
20112321203121102001201121012201211130212111210020013101233020
01303131013021221120313100200120113021310122113031310122112030
20012131311122112101211123012211232121113030200120112321210020
01302121113031311123013101211121002001221123202001310122012211
30302001210131112011230122113101321020012331212020012011302131
00200120112321210020001303120312211211123212031211023202001101
22012111321020013031220123313130200120112320200123313121211130
21230120113000200123312120200123112011232200012111303020013101 3
02120112321303122113101221123312320200121213021233123102001310
12201211020013021211131212111302121112321310020013121221121113
13020013101233020013101220121102001302121112101311120313101221
12331232122113031310020013121221121113130200120112021233131113
10020013101220121102001220131112311201123202001202121112211232
12130232020000310031100112301230020012331212020013101220121102
00120312201201130212011203131012111302130302001233121202001003
10301033103210110200120113021211020012010200123012011303131002
00131212111303131012211213121102001233121202001313122012011310
02001221130302001201120212331311131002001310123302001202121112
03123331231121102001201123202001201123212011203122013021233 1232
12211303131012211203020013101321130012110200123312120200122013
11123112011232020012021233121013210200131312201221120312200200
12311201132102001201123013031233020012311211201123202001310 12
20120113100200131012201211020013101211130212310200020212201311
12311201123212211310132102020200120112321210020000202122013111 2
31120112321211020202000123112011321020001201123013031233020 01203
12201201123212131211020001210130212011231120113101221120312 0112
30123013210232020011101220121102001203122012011232121312111303
02001201130212110200120112301302121112011210132102001220120113
00130012111232122112321213020001201130302001310122012110200 1202
12211233131012111203122012321233123012331213122112031201123002
00121112321230122112131220013101211112321231121111232131002001233

121202000131012201211020003020301130313100200100312111232131013
1113021321020012211303020012211232131212011230122112101201 1310
1221123212130200123110211232132102001233121202001233131113 0202
0012301233123212130200122012111230121002001303130012211302 1221
1310131112011230020012011232121002001231123313021201123002 0012
0113201221123312311303023202001113122113101220020013101220 1211
1303121102001202120113031221120302001212123313111232121012 0113
1012211233123213030200120212111221123212130200120112301230 0200
1202131113100200120312331231130012301211131012111230132102 0012
1113021233121012111210020010210200123212331313020012011303 1223
0200123113211303121112301212032200310031111312201201131002 0012
2113030200120102001202123312101321020013131221131012201233 1311
1310020012010200130312331311123003330031003111131220120113 1002
0012211303020012010200130312331311123002001313122113101220 1233
1311131002001201020012021233121013210333003100311021121202 0013
1012201211130212110200120113021211020012331310122012111302 1303
0200123313111310020013101220121113021211020013131220123302 0012
0113031223020013101220121113031211020013011311121113031310 1221
1233123213030230020010210200122012331300121102001003103010 3310
3210110200131312211230123002001201122112100200131012201211 1231
0200122112320200121012211303120312331312121113021221123212 1302
0012121233130202001310122012111231130312111230131212111303 0200
1303120113101221130312121321122112321213020012011232121002 0013
11130312111212131112300200120112321303131312111302130302 32

Chapter Ten

"What do you mean it worked?" Stan objected. "It went from letters to numbers."

"Just hold on," Heinrich said, smirking and punching a few more keys. "This is like binary, only its quaternary. We just have to –" Heinrich stopped short of finishing his thought, the sound of his fingers tapping away at the keyboard practically finishing the sentence for him. His final key punch came down, decisively, like a slammed gavel. As the quaternary code began the slow conversion to ASCII, a progress bar appeared on the screen...

0% Complete...

5% Complete...

15% Complete...

27% Complete...

33% Complete...

The conversion program stalled. Like John Q. Law, Murphy's Law had shown up, made a routine stop, and threatened to make an inopportune arrest right at the threshold of victory. Everyone in the room held their breath as the progress bar remained static, still thinking or fatally stuck in thought. It moved slightly. Then made a promising leap forward…

88% Complete…

100% Complete…

Everyone exhaled.

For all its unnerving suspense, the completion message was typical of the computer personality. It was to the point and uneventful, displaying a declarative success icon for only a few brief seconds, then vanishing. A desktop folder appeared, auto-opening its window and revealing three files sharing the same name, distinguished only by a number:

"James Ontogenetic Investigation 1"
"James Ontogenetic Investigation 2"
"James Ontogenetic Investigation 3"

"JOI 2" Stan whispered, his eyes zeroing in on the middle folder.

"Open the files!" Addison ordered, but Heinrich was already way ahead of him, right-clicking each file in succession. **"James Ontogenetic Investigation 1"** opened, revealing a substantially long documentation with a cover page summary:

James Ontogenetic Investigation 1:
CONGENITAL SUMMARY: CONGENITAL PHYSICAL ANOMALIES INCL. POLYDACTYLISM, ANENCEPHALY. SOMATIC CELL ORIGINAL: **JAMES PRICE**

After a short delay, the second file opened, also displaying a cover page summary:

James Ontogenetic Investigation 2:
CONGENITAL SUMMARY: CONGENITAL FACIAL ANOMALIES, HIPPOCAMPUS DISORDERS
SOMATIC CELL ORIGINAL: **JAMES PRICE**

Finally the third file opened, covering up the other two:

James Ontogenetic Investigation 3:
CONGENITAL SUMMARY: NORMAL
SOMATIC CELL ORIGINAL: **JAMES PRICE**

A hush swept across the room, each face quieted by the haunting undertone of the word "anomalies" followed by a deceptively more prejudiced term: "normal." No "*perfection,*" just "*normal.*" This is what it was, what it came down to – normalcy, the pursuit of normalcy, a cult of normalcy, control of normalcy. The word seemed inoffensive to everyone but Addison. For him, there was distaste to the word that made his mouth blench. As all minds turned and jostled, rearranging themselves to make sense of it all, Heinrich spoke out, breaking the silence:

"Not bad"

All heads turned in his direction. This wasn't what anyone had expected to hear. Heinrich, in turn, was taken aback by their surprised looks.

"Their batting average wasn't bad at all," he explained. "Dolly was lucky number 277, which meant that, at varying stages of development, the other 276 didn't do so well. There are only three records, and here's lucky number three right here," he finished, tapping that word "*normal*" on his screen.

Addison looked contemptuously at Heinrich from his peripheral but decided to say nothing. *The loudest voice in the room is always the most ignorant one until experience comes along to silence it,* he thought to himself, making this his final ruling.

"So…James Price," Stan said, his voice surprisingly deflated. As is usually the case, the chase seemed better than the kill. Perhaps the buildup had simply been too great for it all to culminate in something as obvious as a pedophile ex-pharmaceutical executive. Had the records read "SATAN," or even "Jesus H. Christ," well, that would have been satisfying, but *James Price? Par for the course,* Stan thought to himself.

Addison thought otherwise.

"Okay," Stan exhaled, "let's print and bind it, so we can get out of here."

***

Several reporters and cameramen were standing outside the ETGR Building amidst the swarm of demonstrators. By now, the word that the Feds had spent an entire day here circulated through their news circuits. When the doors opened and the entire BioEvaluations Team exited, camera lights turned on and reporters pressed their way inside, hoping for statements. The team, however, forced its way through, silently passing by all lights and mics. Stan clenched tightly to his documentation of James Price's clones, holding it securely to his chest with one arm while shoving aside obstructing bodies with the other. This was his fourth time muscling his way through the crowd and he had become something of an expert. Addison kept pace behind him, taking advantage of his partner paving the way to their vehicle.

When they made it to and inside the car, the shut doors blocked out the noise of the outside chaos, enough for Stan to notice the ominous silence of his partner.

"Well… It's over," he said to Addison, with closure in his voice.

"This part is, at least."

"Yeah… We still need to get to the Bureau and submit this to Saracki. We'll need to –"

"You can do that without me, right?" Addison cut him off, recalling their unpropitious conversation. He decided Saracki wasn't exactly the first person he wanted to see after an entire day of gene sleuthing, especially when his own genes were also in question. Of course, he never volunteered these thoughts to Stan, who peered at him as if probing for an explanation.

"Drop me off at my place, please," was all Addison could muster, his voice plagued with fatigue. Though feeling censured, Stan complied, concluding that, whatever Addison's reasons for bailing out early were, they were his own.

"Okay," Stan said, turning the ignition. He backed the car up quickly and somewhat recklessly, practically plowing away the cluster of bodies that surrounded the car. Dozens shouted and cursed after him as he drove away.

***

The car came to a rolling stop in front of Addison's home. Addison stepped out and, with no parting words, closed the door. Stan pulled away. Addison didn't bother to watch him as he drove up the road and turned the corner. His hand fumbled in his pockets for his keys as he walked towards his own car, but he didn't step inside right away. He turned and leaned against the driver's door. For the first time since he had moved into this neighborhood, he began to diagnose his environment. The large, spacious homes rested at comfortable distances away from each other and boasted of architectural dignity. They had been thought out, planned, blueprinted, and designed. Their creators carried memorabilia of these oversized marvels of engineering in their portfolios, which they used to procure other assignments. No doubt, their next creations would be as individualistic and discrete as these. Every home Addison observed, including his own, was a fingerprint of the designer and the dweller. In this way, they were connected. Addison would never know or meet the man or woman who parented the space where he lived. This, perhaps, was not unlike man's relationship to the gods, who perhaps carry their designs of humanity in their portfolios, setting out to design new life in some new planned and prepared environment while fondly remembering their firstborn…if humans were even the firstborn.

Yet in the torn world where Addison had nearly lost his life, the gods were eager to abandon and forget their creation altogether. The gods, in this case, were men. The architects and planners of crowded spaces, dilapidated by time and neglect, were absentee fathers with a simple agenda – build and bail. They left no fingerprints of their collusion. In fact, they made a point of erasing them, lest they be incriminated and pinned to the engineering of congenital paucity.

The environment is a geonome – a determinant in the expression of genes.

Buildings, as bodies, share in the genomic expression of their inhabitants. The dwellers leave marks and signatures of their lives in every open canvas of their environment. The decay of surface is a reflection of decaying lives – cancerous in-growth. *Here*, where Addison stood, the *geo*nomic expression was refined. *There*, refurbished at best.

There is theory in these designs, perhaps engendering my convoluted musings about them. He smiled at this admittance, and he forgave himself for rambling around these tortured theories. It is human to intervene in our environments, just as it is quite human to

209

question our intervention afterwards. If answers are discovered, which usually they are not, they must be shared with the world, or, in his case, his brother.

***

"I apologize that I didn't return your call right away," Addison said, walking alongside Nancy Bailey. "Trust me, if I told you what happened, you'd think that I pulled the story from out of a dime pulp novel."

"It's okay," Nancy replied. "I kind of made the assumption that something important must have come up. Usually, you're more punctual than even the staff here."

Nancy was a young woman, floating somewhere in her mid-twenties, though her heavy voice and big bones gave her the aura of someone much older. She had the chameleon appearance of a woman who could effortlessly oscillate between mother figure and MILF. Right now, she was the former. This was her work face, plain and lacking in ornament, her hair pulled back and tied. She peered at Addison through the corner of her eyes, remembering how attractive she found him. While they walked, she decided to poke for details about his pulp novel life.

"I didn't know life at the FDA was so exciting."

"It's not although I guess, technically, I'm with a different agency now."

"Job promotion… Why didn't you tell us?"

"I don't know that it's a *job promotion*. If it is, it's a lateral one. The short and skinny of it all is that human clones don't really fall under the category of Food or Drugs, but the FDA has to pretend that they do, ever since the technology for cloning became realized. The solution was to form a sister agency, where we collaborate with the FBI. So here I am."

"Wow, so you're an FBI agent now?"

"No, I'm FDA. My partner is FBI. The two agencies have worked together before, notably, *Operation Cottonmouth*. Don't ask me who comes up with these names, but that's what they called it."

"So who did what?"

"Pseudo-drugs, black market"

"So this was one of your cases?"

"No, it was part of the required textbook reading before accepting this 'job promotion.' You know, so that I knew what kind of crazy stuff I was getting myself into."

"Ah…" Nancy smiled, deciding she would now slip in the question she *really* wanted to ask. "So, does this pulp novel workplace also include any dangerous dames?"

"One," Addison laughed, seeing right through the question. "But I think she's more interested in my partner than me. It's okay though. Trust me; I'll take a textbook over the pulp novel any day."

Addison could practically hear Nancy thinking to herself: *no fun!* He could tell from the clumsy silence that followed that she was disappointed that the details weren't juicer. He fumbled with the silence, trying to find some other topic to fill the space while being escorted by an office flirt.

"Has my brother been okay, otherwise?" he asked. The question worked, and she shifted gears, putting her work face back on.

"Yes, actually, thank you for reminding me. I did leave a second message on your answering machine to let you know we were moving him to a new room. He needed more space to accommodate some of the new equipment he's working with now. I have no knowledge whatsoever of computers, aside from basic data entry, but apparently the technology he's using facilitates – if that's even the word – neuro-impulses and keyboard commands…" Her words trailed off, leaving the sentence unfinished as she struggled to decipher her own explanation.

Addison was half-listening anyway, his mind had now drifted somewhere else, deliberating how exactly to tell his brother the truth about their history, their origin. One way was just to be direct and to the point. *There are two of us,* he thought to say. *To quote the asshole I just spent the entire day with – I'm lucky number two.*

Another option was just to say nothing at all.

Nancy was still talking and sorting out makeshift terms like *neuro-impulses* as they approached a room. She courteously knocked first, then opened the door.

"Surprise! Guess who's here?" she announced.

They walked in to find Addison's brother facing a wall of technology. He turned around, his mouth agape in a contorted smile. Excitement rushed through his face. Using his chin, he pushed a lever strategically positioned below his face to set his wheelchair in motion.

Addison watched him silently.

***

The worst part of Saracki's day was the very minute he was relieved from his work and free to go home. Usually, he'd waddle around his office, poking and prodding for anything left unfinished, postponing the inevitable – *sooner or later, he'd have to go home.* That word – *home* – was a difficult one to figure out. He could get his head around it easily enough; his heart was where he ran into problems. He couldn't remember the last time his dungeon felt like a home. Maybe the problem was that he could, and that it was a painfully long time.

During the drive to the dungeon, he remembered briefly what home was – what it used to be. It was a fleeting thought that he immediately chased away. He had entertained the memories before and was disappointed when he figured out that memories only allow for temporary residency. Fond memories are hospitable until the time comes for them to eject your ass back into a cold reality, slamming the door shut. Now, don't look back because there is no forced re-entry. Memory itself decides when to let you back in. That could be the next day, next month or next year. If the memory is really distant, you may never see the inside of her home again. Memory has forgotten you.

Saracki had not quite reached this point just yet, but the way he excommunicated his own memories, he seemed hell bent on speeding up the process of forgetfulness. The drive home, the time stuck in traffic, the vanishing time while in motion – none of these moments were for memories anymore. They were reserved for other thoughts, usually hankering meditations that hardly passed for memories at all – like fantasies with a co-worker. *Who hasn't had these thoughts, and whoever remembers them?*

Yet, at least, such fantasies carried him home. This time, as he pulled up in his driveway, he found a welcome change. His home was not a private ghost town. He had a visitor waiting for him – *Stan.*

Like a loyal dog companion, work had followed him home. *Oh goodie!* He was relieved to finally have some company waiting for him; though there was no way in hell he would ever confess this to Stan.

"How long have you been waiting?" he asked, walking up to the door, searching himself for his keys.

"Not long, I pretty much know your schedule."

"Looks like you have some headline news for me there." Saracki tapped the stacks of reports in Stan's arm, then motioned for him to come inside.

"Yeah, looks like our old friend Ja–"

"Hold on a second, Stan. I want to show you something," Saracki cut him off, then walked over to his staircase and shouted: "Hellllooo…anybody home?" He paused and waited for a sound, but there wasn't even so much as an echo. He turned, looked at Stan, and flung open his arms exclaiming, "Welcome to my graveyard."

Stan smiled uncomfortably, not sure what to say at first.

"Where is she this time?" was all he could think to ask.

"Who the hell knows? That's her business, not mine, apparently," Saracki said, seething. "Children claim their parents fail them. I say they fail us!" He pulled out a cigarette but only held it in his mouth, fighting back the urge to light it.

"Children can't fail their pa–"

"Bullshit!" Saracki snapped, waving away Stan's rebuttal. "Do you know what an axiom is? It's an accepted truth. Not necessarily

214

a 'fact'…just an accepted truth. Supposedly because they're self-evident. '*Children can't fail their parents*' is an axiom, and I say it's total bullshit. That's like saying children can't be cruel. Children can be any fucking thing adults are because, at the end of the day, they're people, just like us. What the fuck do we think they become when they grow up? They can fail big, just like us. We buy into that bullshit that '*they're innocent*' and '*they're the future.*' Why? Because we're desperate. We need something to believe in. If God and Santa are out of the picture, the only thing left is our children. Bah!" Saracki flipped his hand in disgust.

"Children learn from us," Stan retorted, finding himself defending children although he himself wasn't exactly very fond of them.

"Until they get tired of learning from us…or get tired of learning, period. I guess we figure that doesn't happen until they're all grown up. Bullshit. It happens at any age; depends on the kid."

Stan could clearly see he wasn't going to win this one, so he kept quiet. Saracki barely felt the awkward silence, his mind still preoccupied with his tirade. "Daddy's Little Girl" he muttered to himself, now remembering his talk with Addison. "Where the hell is Addison, anyway?"

"I dropped him off at home. I don't think he wanted to come here. Have any idea what's wrong with him?"

"Wrong question. The right question is: How do we make what's wrong with him *right*?"

"I'm not sure I follow you." Stan was beginning to feel that his boss was losing it.

"Never mind." Saracki finally gestured Stan to sit down while plopping down on his couch himself.

"Okay, so what do you have?" he asked.

"James Price"

"James Price what?"

"JOI is a clone of James Price, Ex-CEO of GAIA. GAIA owns ETGR. The only piece left in this puzzle is to confirm ETGR's connections with The Gemini."

Saracki's response was listless at first. Then his eyes lit up: "Our Thailand guy, right?"

"Same one!" Stan replied. "Did you ever bring him in?"

"Little more complicated when you're doing something like that overseas," Saracki answered, then paused, the thought of the Thailand girl inadvertently spinning his thoughts right back around to his own daughter.

"Children inherit our sins, don't they?" he asked. Stan nodded, accepting that, for whatever reason, his boss' immediate attention refused any detour from this subject.

"Maybe that's why they hate us," Saracki concluded, his voice full of resignation. He also surrendered to the will of his habit, finally putting a small torch to the tip of his cigarette. Shit flavor or not, his nerves needed a tranquilizer. As soon as he inhaled, his nagging nicotine-addicted nerves were satiated. Saracki leaned back savoring, if not the thrill of victory, the repose of surrender.

Stan took it all in, reserving judgment for later…or never. He had no family of his own and knew nothing of the business of it. As far as he was concerned, children and family were a necessary evil, and he was all too happy to pass that responsibility to others. *Children and family make the world go round…true that,* he thought to himself. *Then again, the world isn't exactly a well-rounded place.* Stan pulled himself from his thoughts but saw Saracki submerge even deeper in his ruminations.

"James Price?" Stan's voice snapped Saracki from his trance. He blinked, realizing that he had unwittingly wandered back into Memory's house. He re-focused his eyes and re-calibrated his attention to his work. He replayed the name in his head: *James Price. That's right, James Price.* He looked up at Stan, resolved.

"Let's get that son-of-a-bitch."

***

Animals can sense death, especially their own. James Price was sensing his.

He had aged about five years since the Thailand scandal. At least, that's how he appraised himself in the mirror. He had long since stopped running and hiding. He decided that he wanted to be home – a private home, away from Maria, away from complexity. Maria knew nothing about this space – his sex temple, where he walked around naked, scratching and rubbing himself where he pleased. He considered letting the Feds find and arrest him in the nude. Hell, maybe there would even be a camera crew to film him while he strutted from private seclusion to public exhibitionism, entirely naked.

That would be his final lesson to the world – to indulge the body, not to deny it…

Or maybe not. He decided he didn't have anything more to give to this world and opted for clothing.

Besides, at his age, size, and weight, benign movements had become troublesome. He didn't exactly walk with a swagger anymore.

217

Maybe that was the reason for his obsession with sex; it was an absolution from age. He always forgot who he was or even where he was. There was only him, his body, the body of another (or others), and the rush of a sensory addiction. The body itself is an addiction, the world of matter – doubly so.

Why deny this gift? he thought to himself. The gift of pleasure and pain, or even the gift of shame, knowing that a transgression has been committed – a delicious breach of policy and the high of temptations fulfilled. *Shouldn't that be a good thing?* he asked himself. *Why deny this body? It's all we have, and we only have it once.*

With these thoughts on his mind he stared at his *Adamic* self, not running from the voice of God but subsuming it to become a god himself. Adam exposed, consummated through shameless, egregious intercourse, reborn a buck-naked deity – a god. He held his clothing in his hand, accursed fig branches that they were, and cast them to the floor. *Fuck it, they can get me like this.*

He felt every second of the clock ticking as his animal-sense informed him of destiny approaching and made up his mind to ignore it. He swaggered, as best he could, from his bedroom, through the living room, and out on a back patio where he kept his grill. Twenty-five minutes later, the winds carried the aroma of steaks and burgers. Strangely, he was grilling for more than one. *I'll offer them some flesh when they get here,* he thought.

He slapped away the small stings of mosquitoes prickling at his fully exposed flesh. Grilling in the nude was something he had never done before. Now that he was doing it, he was wishing he hadn't waited so damn long. It was primal and spiritual all at once. The feel of air – *this air* – far removed from the city, enveloping his body and tickling his skin, was gratifying.

He walked away with the first burger forked fresh off the grill and looked around, realizing he had forgotten to bring the buns.

He scratched his buns, too lazy to go back inside. It's a minor detail. *Animals don't run in the wild with bread attached to their bodies, so fuck it.* He sat down in his recliner chair, attempting to pull the burger from the fork. Immediately he jerked back his scalded hand and shook his fingers vigorously. *Burns good, like lust.* He sent his fingers back into battle, indulging the heat while biting into a quarter-pound of grilled animal flesh and loving it. He scratched at the crevice between his legs and his balls, then took another bite.

Then came his favorite part: *beer*. He didn't forget that. He cracked one open.

Five beers later, the Feds arrived.

***

Fully clothed, James Price maintained a stolid expression throughout the entire conversation between his lawyer, Saracki, Stan, and the Bureau's General Counsel. It was almost as if he was unaware of the potential charges being levied against him. Despite the absence of affect, there was an unknown brooding behind those eyes, an animal's acuity, really. He was checking out the Bureau's Counsel, a woman roughly the same age as himself. He wondered what she looked like beneath her officious business uniform. How he could undress her and find a padded bra holding up a nice set of dumpy tits, then remove it and let the Double-D's spill in whichever direction gravity took them. It amused him to have such predatory thoughts without anyone knowing. Well, almost – *she knew*. The prey always knows what the predator is thinking. Women can feel when they are being undressed by unsavory eyes. He could see in her eyes that she knew. She knew and she refused eye contact. That's how it always works. It's in the script. While he reviewed the playbook of predator and prey in his head, the conversation that would determine his freedom ensued, and he was missing every moment of it.

"In absence of substantial evidence you are without the jurisdiction to hold him." Price's lawyer spoke with the usual dour demeanor of an attorney. Underneath it, however, was a man not so sure about the innocence of his client. In fact, even he was certain of Price's guilt. It was a rare incident where Price actually turned out to be faultless. The lawyer did his best to keep a no-nonsense, stern expression, but the whole time he could feel his unflappable veneer of confidence peeling away. The Bureau's Counsel sensed it too and responded by confidently placing the Rosalind and JOI Files on the table, then sliding them across for review.

"These are explicit and substantial documentations collected during an investigation at ETGR, all of them citing James Price as the 'somatic cell host,'" she responded. Stacked, one atop the other, both files made for a small paper mountain that no one would ever read.

Price's lawyer reached for the lowest hanging fruit, grabbing the Rosalind files first and quietly paging through them, combing the text for any mention of *James Price*. While everyone watched him tediously paging through the files, Stan covertly pulled out his cell phone, held it at waist level below the table and punched in a message to Amber:

"Want some action?"

"My place or yours?"

"The office?"

"On my way."

"My client's name is not mentioned in any of these." Price's lawyer set the files aside, as if to suggest that they were irrelevant.

"Try the others," Stan said, slipping his phone away.

Price's lawyer ignored the prompting and pulled from his own bag of tricks a small stack of papers. He placed them on the table, then slid them across as his counter-point. The BGC picked up the stacks, giving them only a cursory glance.

"What is this?" Stan asked.

"All of the people in the Los Angeles area with the name 'James Price.'"

"Which means what?"

"JOI could be a clone of James Price…but which James Price?"

"Come on!" Saracki protested, finally speaking up.

"Excuse me," Price's lawyer fired back. "What makes any of you so sure that of the 200+ James Prices in this area, this man here is your 'person of interest?'"

The room fell silent.

"Is it because of the reputation the media has imposed upon my client, or has the Bureau accumulated some other block of *unrelated* evidence that it is using to make him a target?"

"Look," Saracki cut in, leaning forward, "I'm not interested in this game that you're playing."

"There is no game here," Price's lawyer countered, "but it needs to be clarified which Ja—"

"Fine! We'll do a genetic test of every damn James Price in Los Angeles – starting with him!" Saracki pointed at the only James Price in the room. This finally snapped him from his sex-trance.

"I'll do it."

All heads turned towards Price, surprised that he had conceded so quickly. His lawyer moved to object to the decision, but Price held up a hand silencing him. He then looked over at the Bureau's Counsel and smirked as if to give her an invitation. She rejected his gaze to look at Saracki instead for confirmation of the testing.

"Okay," Saracki said, "let's arrange this right now."

***

JOI's corpse lay motionless on the autopsy table, inviting eye contact with *the void*. His vacant, quieted features were haunted by the absence of a soul.

A doctor and his assistant entered the room, slipping on latex gloves. Their faces and their approach towards JOI's body were decidedly unpronounced and neutral. The doctor went about obtaining a blood sample from JOI's body.

"Krieke, remember when sequencing DNA took a week?" the Doctor said while handing the sample to his assistant.

"Remember when it took *years*?" the Assistant added.

"No, and neither do you," the Doctor quipped. "Okay, I'm sure I don't need to say this, but please be sure to not confuse JOI's sample with James Price's sample. While you run the sequence and analysis, I'll let our friends know that we should have results within 24 hours."

"Jesus, the way people talk about him, you would think he wasn't human," the Assistant said, accepting the sample.

"Are you talking about JOI or James Price?"

"JOI, but now that you mention it, I would say both. I still see a few news reports about James Price and that young girl."

"There will be even more news about him for the public to graze on now."

"Well, maybe now they can stop talking about JOI like he was some kind of animal. I mean… Who is the real animal here?" the Assistant replied. "Maybe our taxonomy shouldn't be contingent on the biology of a life form after all. Maybe it should be contingent on the *behavior* of that life form. For instance, if I build a clock and the clock failed to work, would it be accurate to call it a clock? If it can't do what clocks should do, it would be no more a true clock than a drawing of one.

"James Price looks human, and he has all of the biological parts of a human, but his animal-like behavior could mean that he is decidedly *not human*. We have standards of conduct for what constitutes human behavior, but most 'humans' don't meet those standards. So here's my new theory: the term 'human' shouldn't be determined by our biology, but by our behavior. That means our taxonomy should be contingent on psychology."

"You really thought about this, huh?" the Doctor stated, looking up at his Assistant, then noticing behind him a poster of a medical schematic of the human muscular system.

"Not really," the Assistant replied, "it only hit me just now."

"You know…you might actually be onto something. I stopped at a coffee shop on the way here. While I was in line, two kids came in. They were loud and rowdy and started intimidating the customers. Everybody was too scared to do anything about it, even the manager. Then, after they got a sufficient rise out of everybody, the kids left. They were like animals – dogs, let's say – barking for the effect of intimidation."

223

"Exactly!" the Assistant exclaimed. "Those kids weren't human. They're actually animals. Maybe it's a mistake to think that they have the psychological capacity to be human. Maybe their psychological capacity is limited to that of an animal. Therefore, they're limited to that type of behavior. So, you can't reason with those kids anymore then you can reason with, say, wild dogs. You can tame them, but you can't reason with them. A human being can control his behavior based on critical and discriminatory reasoning. Animals don't control their behavior unless they are trained to do so. Essentially only through government social engineering can we truly manufacture a society of human beings. Without social engineering we have a society of animals."

"In other words," the Doctor concurred, "the function of government is to *domesticate* the people. People have to be trained: to sit, to stay, to shake hands…" He winked at his Assistant, laughing.

"Ah, see there – *humor*!" the Assistant pointed at his new accomplice in his contrived pseudo-philosophy. "That's a good sign. That qualifies you as a human being."

"I didn't know I was being tested," the Doctor said, raising an eyebrow. "However, before you get too cocky, I should remind you that you're still forgetting one important orthogonal point to your theory. If taxonomy is to be based on psychology, and human beings are to be categorized as animals based on behavioral criteria, can animals then be categorized as humans based on similar criteria?"

"Absolutely, I've known dogs that are smarter than some people."

"You *knew* them? Close friends, were you?" the Doctor chuckled.

"Yes," the Assistant finally winked back at his mentor, "on a first-name basis."

Stan sat outside his former office, nursing his injured hand, grunting slightly as he flexed it. He heard footsteps approaching. He looked up and saw Amber come towards him, also clenching at the troublesome injury at her side. She stopped directly in front of him. Two wounded friends, re-united.

"How's your hand?" she asked.

"How's your side?"

"Hurts like hell," they said together, then chuckled. They shared a moment of silence.

"Okay, so where do we do this?" Amber asked, conjuring up her sexiest smile.

"Follow me."

He led her up the hallway, to the elevator. The doors slid open. It was empty. They got in. The door closed and they stood together, practically shoulder to shoulder, quietly sharing mutual vibes of closeness. Stan blinked, frowned, and then his nose twitched. He looked over at Amber.

"Wait a second," he said and then leaned over to smell her.

"What's wrong?"

"Were you at Addison's place?"

"What? Why?"

"'Cause if you weren't, some other woman who wears the same perfume was!"

She responded with a grin, keeping her secrets to herself. Stan was hardly prepared to accept her silence as an answer, but, in this instance, he had to. The elevator door opened, and she was already walking away, grinning smugly.

"This isn't over." He pointed to her back and followed behind her.

As they approached an interrogation room, guarded with its own security check point and manned by two agents, they ran into Carl, also on his way to the interrogation. He was not surprised to see Stan but frowned at the sight of Amber.

"What are you doing here? Aren't you supposed to be on leave?"

"Stan invited me," she replied, thumbing over to him.

"Aren't *you* supposed to be at the FDA office?" Carl said, now looking at Stan.

"Just came here to see an old friend and make sure you treat him right." Stan quipped.

Carl glowered at this, opening the door and deliberately forgetting the etiquette of letting the two guests go first. Stan followed after, then turned around to prepare Amber.

"Brace yourself," he said, winking before walking inside.

Immediately upon entrance, Amber's eyes widened. In the span of a mere second, the face of the man who had nearly claimed her life was here again in a flash of resurrection. Though now he seemed hardly a threat, resembling instead a broken animal, caged within a featureless government room. Cuffed, bruised, and battered, The Gemini's face was healing terribly.

"A clone?" she asked, quickly shaking the initial shock.

"No, a twin," Stan replied. "Same difference though, right ol' buddy?" Stan slapped The Gemini on the back, mocking him.

"How's your hand?" The Gemini asked Stan.

"It's about the same as your face."

"We can all be clever with each other later," Carl chimed in, patting Stan on the shoulder to chill him out. Then he turned to the suspect:

"For the record, are you Gemini One or Gemini Two?"

"What difference does it make?"

"We have to keep accurate records of the people we kill," Stan jabbed again.

"Stan!" Carl snapped, giving Stan a censurable look.

Unintimidated, The Gemini obliged the stare down with Stan, but his attention was soon diverted over to Amber, who still hadn't walked much further than the door.

"You look like you've seen a ghost," The Gemini sneered at her.

"Hey!" Carl snatched The Gemini's collar. "Now you're pissing me off. I don't think you want to do that."

"No? Why? Are you a tough guy, like Mr. Stan over there, who hides in bathroom stalls?" The Gemini delighted at the sight of Stan grimacing at these words. "Oh, so you never told them? Can I be the one to fill them in?"

"Some other time," Carl interjected, "let's talk about who hired you and your brother."

"Sure... Shall we have some tea while we chat?"

"You really don't want to play with me like this."

"I don't? But I'm having so much fun."

"Yeah, but I'm not. My boss is a very demanding son-of-a-bitch. That's not good news for you, my friend. You'd be amazed at how motivated having my boss' goddamn foot up my ass can make me."

"Bring your boss in here and I'll ask him nicely to remove his foot from your ass."

"You're an ex-CIA asset, aren't you?" Carl replied. "That's good news for us because they couldn't give a shit about what we do to you. That's going to be very useful while we do whatever's necessary to get you to talk. Do you know how easy it is to force information from a man who doesn't exist? I mean, after we cut your dick off and stuff it in your mouth, who are you going to tell?"

"Actually, he can keep his dick if he wants," Amber said, stepping forward. "So you're the 'Memory Killer,' right?" She looked him right in the eye. "What kind of drug were you using?"

"I'm not a chemist. I'm a cleaner. If you really want to know, get a textbook," The Gemini replied dismissively.

"I wouldn't have pinned you as the type to lie around reading textbooks. Maybe while catching up on your favorite biochem literature you came across something called SP-17-2."

The Gemini was silent from confusion. He had never heard of it, neither had Stan nor Carl.

"C'mon! A former CIA asset has never heard of SP-17-2?" Amber continued. "You've been out of 'The Company' too long. Okay, let me show you then."

She pulled a syringe from her jacket pocket and held it at eye level for The Gemini.

"Quick history lesson: The KGB invented a truth drug, code-named SP-17. They called it the 'remedy which loosens the tongue.' The beauty of it was that it was tasteless, odorless, colorless, and, unlike the drugs pushed by pharmaceutical companies, it had zero side effects."

Amber dramatically removed the safety cap.

"It was a great tool for the KGB, because subjects didn't remember a damn thing after being injected with the drug. They would tell every detail of their lives, including how many times a week they jerked off and wouldn't remember saying a word. The problem with SP-17 was that it was too humane. Human beings aren't known for their humaneness."

Now she squatted and began swiveling the syringe back and forth between her fingers within dangerous proximity of The Gemini's face. He tilted his head as far back as he could manage, his eyes saturated with terror.

"So someone – I'm not going to say who – invented SP-17-2. It does everything that SP-17 does, except this one has a side effect. Once it's in you, it burns like a mother-fucker. They called it 'The Scorpion Drug' because it feels like somebody set you on fire from the inside…"

She made a dramatic pause.

"And the pain lasts indefinitely."

Hearing this, the Gemini flinched, struggling to pull himself away from Amber. Stan and Carl instinctively rushed and grabbed his arms, holding him still. Amber, scarcely missing a beat, leaned in closer, holding the syringe to his neck. She could see and smell the odor of sweaty terror effervescing from his body.

"Here's the best part..." – She aimed the syringe for a large vein protruding from his sweaty neck. Stan wrestled his hands around The Gemini's face, forcing his head back. – "While SP-17 erased your immediate memory, SP-17-2 doesn't erase shit. Whoever gives it to you, wants you to remember just how much the truth can hurt."

"Wait! Wait! Wait! Okay! Okay!" The Gemini pleaded.

"Good boy, now start talking," Amber said, lowering the syringe.

"It was GAIA, godammit! GAIA!!!"

"We need names."

"David Lee."

"David Lee is dead."

"Then talk to his fucking brother. GAIA wanted the kid cleaned up. That's all I know. That's all I needed to know."

Stan and Carl relented their hold while Amber stood up. The Gemini didn't fail to notice that she had not yet put the safety cap back on the syringe:

"Why is she still standing there with that fucking needle?"

***

Saracki was waiting outside the interrogation office with a burning cigarette in his mouth. Once again, he succumbed to the habit. The door opened and his three agents walked out, immediately inspecting his face to diagnose just how much he had overheard.

"What did he say?" Saracki asked, waving the three on to walk with him.

"Merritt Lee told David how to contact The Gemini, which means The Gemini has done work for Merritt before," Carl answered. "It confirms the ETGR link although we can't circulate The Gemini as a source in this."

"We don't need to," Saracki countered. "In three days, I want you to submit Merritt Lee's name to the press as a 'suspect' in JOI's murder, then find out where he is and make the arrest."

"Why three days?" Carl asked.

"Because, in 24 hours, we're going to have confirmation on the DNA test of James Price and JOI. That gives the Attorney General and the President 48 hours to plan and prepare announcements and protocol after we cite GAIA and ETGR in this scandal."

Saracki looked over at Amber. "Who the hell brought you back here? Are the letters *R&R* not simple enough for you?"

"Actually," Carl interjected, "she's the one who loosened the lips of our friend back there."

"How'd you do that?" Saracki asked.

"The old fashion way – coercion," she answered.

"Just checking… As long as it wasn't torture…" Saracki stopped at the elevator. The door opened. He and Carl stepped in. Amber took a step behind them, but a resistant yank of her jacket from Stan made the interception. She looked at him and stayed put. Saracki and Carl waited a moment, then looked at each other knowingly.

"Whatever" Saracki rolled his eyes at the corny romance that filled the air. He pushed a button to close the doors.

Alone in the vacant hallway, Stan turned his head to his friend, his penetrating gaze alone demanded an explanation: *What the hell is SP-17-2?*

She grinned devilishly, then held up the syringe…and squirted it, causing Stan to flinch.

"Colorless, odorless, tasteless…" she announced with a voice befitting a TV commercial. "*It's water.*"

"Where'd you –!" Stan yelled but caught himself, looking around to make sure nobody could hear him. "Where did you get that?" he finished, his voice lowered.

"What do you mean?" she smiled coyly.

"C'mon…you just *happened* to have a syringe on you? Where did you get it?"

"Addison's house."

"I knew it!" Stan said pointing at her, flaring with jealousy.

"Knew what?"

"That was your perfume at his house. I knew it!"

"Stalker!"

"I didn't have to stalk you; all I had to do was *smell* you. Why were you at his house? You two are friends now?"

"We were just talking."

"About what?"

"Girl stuff," she said walking away, teasing out, and taking away her little secret. Then she stopped, turned and looked at Stan.

"Stan, you don't need to be jealous. If you want some *more* action, just text me."

***

A crimson sun broke first light across the Los Angeles landscape. The usual hustle and bustle of the morning traffic crowded the city. A small mini-van broke away from the density of vehicles, pulled off to the side, and parked illegally on the sidewalk. A young white man emerged from the car, walked over to the trunk, and pulled out a long staff wrapped in cloth, which he set ablaze with his lighter. With one hand, the young, passionate man extended the small fire to the sky, holding it up as if it were a second sun. With his other hand, he pulled a second sign from the trunk of his car:

"IT WILL BE REVEALED WITH FIRE, AND THE FIRE WILL TEST THE QUALITY OF MAN'S WORK."
1 COR 3:13

Holding both signs, he walked over to join a flood of other protestors, all of them donning their own handwritten or printed messages – not all of them in agreement.

SCIENCE CAN PLAY GOD IF IT WANTS,
BUT I'M STILL AN ATHEIST

THE EARTH IS OVERPOPULATED,
EVEN WITHOUT CLONES

CLONING IS EUGENICS 2.0

233

**WE DO NOT WANT TO BE PERFECTED
WE ARE PERFECT ALREADY**

**THE GENOME GIVETH AND IT TAKETH AWAY
ESPECIALLY WHEN YOU KEEP FUCKING WITH IT**

WE BÉ-BÉ KIDS: WE DON'T DIE. WE BOKANOVSKIFY

**I PREFER MY FOOD AND MY FRIENDS
TO BE ALL-NATURAL**

Amidst them all, were quiet pickets of JOI's face floating above one simple word:

MURDER

***

"The test results show that there is no genetic match between my client and James Ontogenetic Investigation 2, commonly referred to as JOI 2," Price's lawyer announced in a straight yet victorious tone.

Saracki and the Bureau's General Counsel met his statement with a conceding silence. There was no smile on James Price's face, but the gloat of celebration lay just beneath his composed expression. If not visible, it was palpable.

"I want to remind you that you cannot bring Mr. Price back into detainment without additional and court approved evidence," the lawyer added.

"We are within the right to request future tests if we find, at a later date, that the tests we made were inadequate or inconclusive," the Bureau's counsel retorted.

"You will need to provide us with adequate documentation showing why the tests were indeed 'inadequate' or 'inconclusive.' If necessary, we will ask to have such documentation presented to a court to make sure you aren't harassing my client."

Price and his lawyer stood up, signaling that the meeting was over. Saracki looked over at the Bureau's General Counsel, who could only give back a look of defeat.

"I want to have a talk with Mr. Price before he leaves," Saracki said, stopping Price just before he exited. "In private please," he added, looking at the Bureau's Counsel.

"Okay," she exhaled, stacking her papers and leaving the room.

Staring obstinately, Price's lawyer watched Saracki, suspicious of his intentions.

"It's okay," Price said retaking his place at the meeting table.

"James, you don't have to talk to him," his lawyer objected.

"I know," Price replied. "We can talk."

Saracki held tightly to his thoughts until the lawyer left the room. The door closed softly, and finally, two very powerful men, similar in weight, age, demeanor, and authority, were left alone. Yet there was no tension of a showdown or stand-off. It was only a talk.

"You and I are people of power, aren't we?" Saracki began. "Of course, it's a different kind of power. My power is because someone appointed it to me. Yours is the old fashion power. It comes from money.

"The thing with power – and I'm sure this is also true for money – is that once you get it, after a while, you don't know what the hell to do with it. So you start doing something stupid. I'm sure you can imagine the stupid shit some of my guys do with their appointed power, and I already know at least one of the things you did with yours."

"JOI is not my clone. I think we've already determined that," Price stated flatly.

"I wasn't talking about JOI. I'm talking about the 15-year-old Thai girl you raped."

Price's stoic expression reflexively shifted to something more defensive. His first impulse was to speak up, to react, to object; but he remembered from his legal coaching to always stay silent. *Let them talk.* Saracki recognized that Price was clamming up, so he continued:

"I'm sure your lawyer is still wondering why we were watching you in the first place. Would you like to know the answer? *We weren't.* It was one of your own guys who came to us. I'd tell ya, but I'm not allowed to. Not yet anyway, but if you think real hard, I'm sure you can figure it out."

Saracki pulled another cigarette from his breast pocket, placed it in his mouth, and held the lighter close to its tip, but he stopped short of lighting it. He removed it, resisting the power of habit. This time at least. It was always back and forth like this, but today he decided to win.

"My daughter is 16," he continued. "She's at the age when she still thinks not giving a fuck about anything makes her special. It's her way of protecting herself. That's how we all protect ourselves. We decide that we don't give a fuck. That's the only protection we have against people with power.

"My daughter used to break my heart every time she pretended not to care about anything, especially when her apathy was directed at me. Then, I reached a point where I became like her – I stopped caring. I stopped talking to her, but when I heard about what you did to that girl, I started caring again. I had to.

"You see, I finally understand how this power thing works. It's my daughter's job *not* to give a fuck, because it's the only power she has in my house. She resents the fact that she has rules to follow. And do you know why I give her rules, James?

"Because I give a fuck.

"So… If it's her job to not give a fuck, then it's my job to give a fuck; that's how power works. That's how this country works. That's how it works with God, and that's how it's going to work with you and me. One side gives a fuck. The other side doesn't."

"What the hell is your point?" Price asked, annoyed.

"One of us has to choose a side." Saracki leaned forward on the table, clasping his hands together. "If you decide not to give a fuck, well, then I guess you know what my job is. You've got two bad cards in your hand right now. One is called 'Thailand' and the other 'JOI.' JOI may not be your clone, but the test shows that there *is* a genetic relationship between you and him. JOI and Thailand are all I need to be a permanent thorn in your ass. I don't give a fuck what your lawyer just said. I am the F-B-fucking-I. I am a man of power. I'll do whatever the fuck I want, until I get exactly what I want…"

Saracki unlocked his hands and leaned back in his chair.

"Or… *you* can be the one who gives a fuck. That means I won't, and if I'm the one who doesn't give a fuck, well then all of your past sins will go away."

The proposition was made; the cards were on the table. Price's eyes showed evidence of wheels spinning. He easily worked out the name of the Thailand snitch. From there, it didn't take him long to figure out who the accomplice was either. It was a suspicion he carried for a while now. The only question was if he would use Saracki's offer as retaliation…

"We are men of power, Mr. Price," Saracki pressed. "Do you give a fuck or not?"

Price quietly made up his mind. He stood up, walked to the door, and turned to give Saracki his verdict.

"Talk to my wife," he said, opening the door. "She's the one who doesn't give a fuck."

With those words he closed the door, leaving Saracki to himself. Now it was Saracki's turn to let the wheels spin. He replayed the words in his head, staring somewhat absently inside himself. Then the wheels came to a sudden halt, and Saracki's eyes glowed with revelation, followed by a knowing smile.

Chapter Eleven

Resting quietly along the shores of California's Monterey Peninsula is the Asilomar conference grounds. Here, in 1975, a sizable gathering of scientific minds convened for the first time to discuss the advent of genetic engineering and question its prospects. Today, on this placid morning, with the sun just barely peeking above the horizon line, a new coterie of scientists came together to finish the conversation from decades ago. They have even given themselves a name – The Biotech Consortium.

The buzzing voices from inside the resort were enough to disturb the tranquility of the surrounding environment. Linda, the introductory speaker for the morning, walked to the podium. As she prepared her notes, she ignored the humming clamor of overlapping voices in the audience. When, at last, she was ready, she pushed a button on the podium's control panel, calling up a large title screen on the digital projector behind her:

"So Animal The Human"

The audience murmur slowly came to a hush. Linda paused dramatically, scoping out the attendee faces. All eyes and ears were on her – the person who had managed to unify both colleagues and competitors into a single body that would represent the voice of progress.

She turned and looked at the title on the screen. Its white serif lettering floated in a sea of ominous black. The design was simple, yet theatrical. She was not averse to a touch of theatrics right now. It was sorely needed if she was to have any hope of exciting the measured composure of her audience. Conversely, there needed to be a balance. Such minds were wary of sensationalism and would quickly spot and castigate an attention-seeking performer. Her solution was a tried and true one – stand on the shoulders of giants.

She held up a book by René Dubos, titled *So Human An Animal.* "It's not plagiarism when you confess right away where you stole your ideas from," she opened her presentation. The audience laughed knowingly. *So far so good,* she thought, then turned again to look at the title, then back to the audience: "Albeit, I had a bit of fun with the title." More laughter.

"This book, written by microbiologist René Dubos, had long been a favorite of mine. After news about JOI was released, and, of course, the public reactions to that news, I thought it prudent to re-evaluate what we are doing as members of the science community and also as members of the broader community at large. I returned to my roots," – She pointed to the book again. – "I consider this book to be an important part of my professional heritage.

"At the very beginning it reads very much like a manifesto for our Modern Age, which Dubos calls 'The Age of Anxiety.' Actually, he didn't call it that at all. Instead, this term was the 'universal' buzz word used by all to describe the growing public antipathy towards science.

"I want now to show you a painting that Dubos mentions in his book."

Another push of a button changed the title screen to a painting of a young man, holding his right arm up in defiant protest, inspiring, or perhaps merely rousing, a group of onlookers to follow him in the path of rebellion.

"This painting," Linda continued, "was done by – I'm going to demonstrate my paltry French now – *Honoré Daumier.* So I don't embarrass myself any further, I'll give you the English title of this painting – *The Uprising*.

"At first glance, the painting appears to be a romanticized depiction of rebellion. In a democratic society, there are few who do not respond, somewhat idealistically, to the very notion of the prevailing will of the people. It appeals to our idyllic conception of what justice ought to be in the face of corruption.

"However, Dubos tells us to inspect the painting closer, to see that the attention of the people is not fixated on a particular principle. Their fixation is, quite simply, on a person – a very charismatic person, whose force of will and personality has attracted them to his cause even if they themselves do not know exactly what that cause may be. Indeed, even if *he* does not know what his own cause is.

"This is the nature of the human animal: mimicry.

"The human animal is an imitator. He is a clone of his fellow citizen, replicating the attitude, language and behavior of his peers. He will, of course, believe himself to be discrete; believe that his ideas are distinct. Yet as Daumier so wisely observed, *popularity is persuasion* for the human animal.

"This is not to say that every convicted catalyst is without cause, but the cause very quickly turns into a meme and the meme into a misguided movement. Again, I quote Dubos: *'Marching in a parade is easier than blazing a trail through a forest...'* This is largely what we are seeing right now – not a rebellion or a revolution against reckless science, but rather a reckless parade.

"Of course, one could argue that the Biotech Consortium is also little more than a parade of imitators, which is why we must demonstrate otherwise. This is a fledgling union, and though I do not think we have reached the point of having any official leadership, I know that I have, by default, assumed the role of the man in this painting. Yet this organization is not about me, or any one messenger. It is about the message of science. That message is to show that the human animal as imitator can also be an *innovator*.

"I am here, first, to announce my official resignation as the *unofficial* spokesperson of the Biotech Consortium and, second, to officially open our conference to a plethora of speakers, who, I believe, represent what this organization is all about."

The audience applauded as Linda turned over the podium to another speaker. As she exited the stage, she noticed a member of the audience raising a hand, presumably for a Q&A session. She turned back to the podium.

"I apologize, sir. Do you have a question?"

"I do," the man replied. Linda focused her eyes for a better look at him: middle-aged and padded with weight that matched his years. His face seemed permanently pensive, as if smiling were a rare occasion. She didn't know him.

"Because we are a new group," Linda began, "before you ask your question, maybe you can introduce yourself to the rest of the audience."

"Of course, my name is Professor Virchow. I teach pharmacology at the University of California. My question is, *'Where is everybody?'*"

"I'm sorry. How do you mean?"

"Well, everything you said sounds good enough, but there are only scientists in this room. If we are going to discuss ideas that are pertinent to the future of our society, shouldn't the rest of society participate, or, at least, be privy to the discussion?"

Linda stood in place, staring absently at the question. The audience waited silently for her answer. She had none.

***

No one ever expects rich, old white guys to be gun carriers, when actually they take their *right to bear arms* as seriously as their right to a free marketplace. Not that Merritt Lee was a rich, old white guy; not yet, at least. In another twenty years, when his hair transitioned from salt-and-pepper to just salt, he'd be *that guy* – the old white guy who goes hunting at ranges because it makes him feel alive with testosterone; because he can talk about the hunt and the kill. Merritt would be that old guy who keeps a few guns in his home because old age is no excuse for vulnerability.

Right now, Merritt was just a middle-aged white guy *with a gun*. As far as he was concerned, a warrant for his arrest was still no excuse for vulnerability. He sat at the edge of the deluxe bed in his hotel suite.

Spread out across the sheets, were all the stripped down parts of a Glock 30: frame, magazine body, barrel, and cartridge. His hands assembled the parts effortlessly.

He pointed the empty gun at the door, as if an army of agents was waiting for him on the other side. He pulled the trigger and the hammer clapped as it snapped forward. The strong black nylon-based polymer body of the gun was ominous in his hand. The look on his face was detached and amoral.

He rested the gun near his leg and rehearsed several scenarios of escape and disappearance in his head. Every scenario included Maria Price.

He picked up his cell phone and called her. When she answered, his usual voice of a fool in love was replaced with that of a fool obsessed. He was determined to make everything go the way he had planned. No longer was he the sap hurried off the phone by an ambivalent lover. He now adopted a take-charge personality that assumed any conversation was his to control. *Control.*

This impulse fired from every neuron and precipitated throughout his entire body. *Control.*

"You need to focus, okay... I want you to focus..." he instructed Maria. "Everything is going to be fine, but you'll need to do everything I ask you to do, exactly as I ask you to do it..."

He paused as Maria protested on the other end. She wasn't buying it. She was not conceding absolute control to him. Everything would not be okay.

"Maria...listen to me... Yes, I saw the news... Maria...lis–"

Control, his mind kept telling him. *Control.*

"Maria, SHUT UP!" he ordered.

The phone went silent, on both ends.

"Maria, we have to be calm, okay?" he tried again, adjusting his tone. "Stick with me on this. I'm going to leave the hotel now. Just meet me at the airport, okay?"

She didn't answer. He paused, waiting, listening to the muted vacancy. He repressed the urge to say another word. He used her silence against her. Finally, she relented:

"Okay, Merritt."

That was all she gave him, but she didn't hang up. She remained on the other end. Merritt wanted very badly to believe that this had been the tipping point, and it was. Something in her voice had tipped in some other direction. He heard it. He felt it.

"Okay," he said softly, realizing that his own voice had also tipped.

Something had changed, but he wasn't sure what. Perhaps it was the realization that, wherever they were running off to, they were doing it together. This felt more binding than even marriage;

certainly more irrevocable than a scandalous affair. He welcomed the permanence.

"Okay," he said again, deliberately reversing his tone. He hung up the phone and remained still. For all the prior urgency in his voice, he suddenly found himself feeling quietly inert. He sat down on his bed and stared at his luggage, packed and ready to go, but he didn't move. His eyes drifted over to his gun, followed by his hand.

The thought finally crossed his mind – *suicide*. He had blocked it out for as long as he could, knowing that it would revisit him eventually. It was an option that one did not have to accept, but certainly had to consider; like a rites-of-passage for the pursued and desperate.

He removed the block from his mind and replaced it with the hard, pressing barrel of his Glock 30, then pulled the trigger. Brains flashed everywhere and the lights went out…

Or maybe the lights don't go out. Maybe then, and only then, is when the lights *turn on*. He pulled the trigger again, this time not vanishing into the dark but escaping the darkness of matter, surprised that a soul as benighted as his could be so luminous. He stood before other luminous beings. They detected the thread of love that tied him to a woman still on Earth.

This was a primal love; not unconditional, but unconditioned, unrefined. This love required more pain and more pressure, more fire and hammering. Only then would it be finished; not by Cupid's arrow, but his sword – a sword to strike down the wretched stupidity of the other lover. "*This is not a fool in love*," the luminous jury decided, "*just a fool.*" They sent him back.

Merritt blinked. The thoughts had passed. The rites-of-passage were over. His brains were still intact. He returned the road blocks in their place, barring any further thoughts of suicide from ever passing through his mind again.

He hurried to his feet, grabbed his gun and his luggage, and left.

He pushed through the hotel lobby, past all amenities, concessions, and services, making his way to a parking ramp of several concrete layers. Every sound of his feet stomping the floor and his luggage jostling about bounced and rebounded off every hard surface, engulfing him in an endless echo of his own frantic haste. His feet abruptly slammed into a frozen halt, and his head swiveled, at the clamorous and overpowering sound of engine and wheels suddenly excited. Before he could grab his weapon, a large, tinted SUV stopped with screeching tires right in front of him.

The Feds? he wondered, while the passenger window rolled down.

No, not the Feds…

James Price.

"Please get inside, Merritt."

Merritt obliged, taking the passenger seat. Price raised the tinted window to its place, turning their encounter into a private meeting.

"Where are you going?" Price asked.

"I have to leave, James," Merritt replied impatiently. "I can't stay here."

"Relax, I'm just asking." James looked down and noticed that Merritt's hands were anything but relaxed. In fact, they seemed *prepared*. Price, of course, was also *that guy* who hunts and kills and keeps weapons in his home. He knew an antsy gun hand when he saw one. "It was unfortunate what happened with your brother. I liked David," he said, hoping his sympathy would work as a sedative for Merritt's tension.

"I'm sorry," Merritt replied.

"What are you sorry for? He was your brother, not mine."

Merritt's eyes snapped and locked on James Price, who stared back through his primal flesh covered eye.

This was a stare down – *a show down*. James didn't flinch.

He saw what was behind Merritt's eyes – the thought of bashing his skull into bone splinters with his gun handle. James was all body; he relished every experience it offered. The thought of the initial "*thump*" that would strike his meaty head intrigued him, enough so, that he had no intentions of interfering with Merritt's assault.

No doubt, his fat head would insulate him from unconsciousness. It would take three or four of those "*thumps*" to free him from the sensorial pleasure of murder. If Merritt was too much of a pussy to pull it off, *then* he would retaliate. He'd add to his résumé of aphrodisiac experiences, the stimulation of taking a living body and destroying it. He was now eager to instigate Merritt's rage, to push him over the edge, to make him a murderer.

"Maybe you're apologizing for telling the Feds about my personal business in Thailand?" – Price waited for Merritt's animal stare to return, but it didn't. He blinked and snapped from his murderous trance. He was back in reality. – "Maybe you're just sorry about fucking my wife?"

Merritt blinked again, this time his pupils dilating from having been discovered.

"You're not sorry, Merritt. You're just scared." Finally, it was Price's turn to blink and reveal through his distorted eye a soul ripped apart by fear. "Don't worry…I'm afraid too. There's nothing left to protect us. I'm not the CEO of GAIA anymore, and you're not the big man at ETGR. Hell, after all of this shakes out, you won't even be a lawyer anymore, will you?"

"I don't have anything to say," Merritt replied, exhausted from tension. "I just want to leave."

"Right… Are you going alone, or is my wife going with you?"

"She is."

Price nodded solemnly.

"Merritt, I will give you one last word of advice. Not because we're friends, but because that is still my family you're taking with you.

"You may be willing to die for what you think is love, but we both know that GAIA is willing to kill for money. They've invested a lot of money into ETGR, and because of you and my wife they've lost it all.

"Don't forget that, because they won't."

Merritt didn't wait for the words to sink in. Recognizing that the stand-off was over, he opened his door and stepped out. The sight of James Price vanished from behind the veil of the tinted passenger window.

Merritt tried looking through the darkened glass, knowing that Price was looking back, but all he saw was his own disheveled reflection, which he pompously used to fix his hair.

Price, offended by the vain and sneering gesture, zipped away; the screeching sound trailed behind him as he turned the corner, leaving Merritt Lee to his fate.

***

A fawn-colored Pug wandered around a spacious, demarcated backyard, happily sniffing around an array of exotic flowers that peppered the grassy perimeter. Suddenly, his attention was arrested by sounds and smells he had never encountered before.

With a sudden jerk, his demeanor switched from casual to cautious as his small, square, compacted body stiffened with vigilance. His small nose, practically lost on his flattened, wrinkly face, twitched several times, evaluating the approaching scent. Finally, he abruptly bolted towards the front of the yard, barking at the two strangers approaching.

Addison and Stan walked slowly through the long, linear driveway. Stan stopped to acknowledge the watchful presence of the Pug. The Pug responded in kind, freezing in place and angling his head to the right while observing Stan. For a brief moment, there was mutual curiosity, but the moment Stan began to walk away, trying to catch up with Addison, the Pug's instincts kicked in again. He ran along side Stan, keeping pace with him, yapping away.

"Hercules! Hush!"

A woman's demanding voice traveled from the inside of the large estate-home, reaching Hercules' ears and causing them to flicker. He recognized his name. He also recognized the censuring tone and obediently clammed up at the command.

Before Addison could reach the end of the driveway, the door opened and Maria Price walked out, insouciantly appraising her *expected* visitors. She walked back inside leaving the door unlocked. Addison, however, still knocked gently at the door.

"Mrs. Price?" he asked through the screen door.

"It's open," she called back.

Addison walked inside and found Maria holding a lighter to her cigarette. She glanced briefly at Addison from the corner of her eye, then returned her attention to her lighter. Satisfied with her light, she removed the cigarette from her mouth and, with good smoker manners, exhaled the smoke in the opposite direction of Addison. Finally she allowed eye contact, so Addison could see that she was both fatigued and relieved by their arrival.

For a moment the two said nothing, taking a few seconds to make estimations of each other. Right away, they detected the spools of tangled complexity that ensnared their lives. Their silent exchange shared, not empathy, but familiarity.

The door opened and their brief evaluation was interrupted. Maria looked over Addison's shoulder to see Stan walking inside, not bothering with knocking.

"Maria Price?" he asked.

"It's open," she repeated, trying to make a point, but Stan ignored it.

Maria seemed less interested in assessing Stan. She decided that the instant impression was information enough. For Stan, the snap-judgment was mutual. One look and he knew everything he needed or wanted to know about this woman. Maria walked away to her counter, picking up her pack of cigarettes and motioning in the direction of her guests.

"Either of you smoke?"

Her question elicited an unexpected chuckle from Stan.

"That was a question, not a joke," she said, genuinely perplexed by his sense of humor.

"I'm sorry. It's your cigarette," Stan replied, still trying to curtail himself.

"Cigarettes make you laugh?"

"They do now. I heard some funny shit about them from one of... Oh, never mind," he said, waving it all away with his hand.

"So, James must have sent you here about JOI," Maria said flatly, changing the subject tersely.

"Why James? Maybe it was Merritt who sent us over," Stan replied coyly.

"Please," Maria rolled her eyes, "Merritt would snitch on his own mother before he'd ever snitch on me."

"Where is Merritt?" Stan asked.

"Correct me if I'm wrong, but I do have the right to remain silent, don't I? Shouldn't I be talking to my lawyer?"

"Sure, call your boyfriend Merritt. He's a lawyer, isn't he?" Stan replied, offering her his cell phone. Maria just looked at him, unimpressed. Her eyes may have been world-weary, but her body language still suggested that she wouldn't abdicate her power easily.

"You're investigators. You should be able to answer that without my help," she responded curtly.

"You can play this game if you want, Maria," Stan replied, "but you won't win. I'll tell you why. No, actually, I'll show you why…" – Stan now forced his badge into her face. – "See this badge? Those three letters, F-B-I, are called an acronym. They stand for, 'BOY DID YOU FUCK UP.'"

"Cute." Maria exhaled smoke from the corner of her mouth, not turning her head away.

"Fine, let's cuff this bitch," Stan muttered aloud to himself, reaching for his handcuffs. This is what Maria waited for – a chance to go down on her own terms, in her own playing field.

"Calm down. Merritt is on his way to the airport. While I'm at it, I'll tell you where I am… *I'm right here.* Maybe you didn't notice that there aren't any packed bags sitting near the door. Doesn't look like I was rushing to get out of the house, does it? I was supposed to have left long before you two arrived. Why do you think I'm still standing here?"

Addison turned towards Stan, wondering what to do.

"I'll have Carl pick him up," Stan said, walking away with his phone to his ear. As soon as he exited, the room returned to its previous climate. Addison and Maria were examining each other again.

"Why *are* you still here, Maria?"

"Because it's over; it was over a long time ago. Merritt wanted to fly away into the sunset. For a lawyer, he's not very practical."

The sound of feet fast approaching made Addison turn around. Maria, recognizing the pattering feet, turned away from the conversation to put out her cigarette. She didn't smoke around her children. A second door, leading to another room opened. A young boy, no older than eight or nine years old, ran inside energetically.

"No running in the house Jimmy!" Maria ordered with a firm, disciplinary tone. "Where is your brother?"

Instead of answering his mother, the boy spun around in his tracks and ran back the way he came. He knew the drill.

"Wai–" Addison tried calling out after him, but Jimmy was already gone. Addison didn't get a chance to take a good look at the boy, so he couldn't be certain of what he saw. He looked over at Maria, his eyes begging for confirmation, but there was no response in her eyes. She looked at him, easily deciphering his stunned expression.

The door opened again. This time, Jimmy came in holding the hand of his older brother, who was slow-footed and unstable in his walk. Addison finally got a chance at a second look. Next to each other, their similarities were unmistakable. They shared hair and eye color. The straightness of their small lips and the puffiness of their boyish cheeks were homologous, but they were not identical. The older brother's features were asymmetrical. Though he was a likeness of Jimmy, he was an exact simulacrum of JOI.

He was JOI!

Jimmy looked at his mother for approval.

"Thank you," she said, trying to smile for him. "Please try to remember what I've always told you: Your brother needs you to help him. He depends on you."

Jimmy, having already earned validation from his mother, barely paid attention. He pulled harder on his brother's arm, rushing him out the door. The moment they stepped outside, Hercules began yapping vivaciously. Addison walked silently to the door and watched the two brothers outside through the screen. They passed through a fence door where they were greeted and relentlessly licked by Hercules.

Addison turned again to face Maria.

"JOI!"

"No, not JOI...just James. Jimmy was cloned from his older brother, James."

She reached over and grabbed another cigarette, studying Addison's face while lighting it up. He didn't say anything.

"Do you have any idea what a mind-fuck it is to look at your first born child and know that your genes are responsible for his body and mind not being normal?" she continued, taking another smoke. "The anger you feel – at yourself, at the world, at God. Then you have those smart-asses who tell you 'There is no God.' Okay, well, that takes one asshole off my hate list. What about the world? What about myself?

"Then you start doing your research, and you learn that your faith is better placed with science than God. Yet they actually do have a lot in common – unanswered prayers."

"You think that your son is someone to be *fixed*?" Addison asked.

"Save the lecture, okay? I'm an extremely wealthy woman. Do

255

you think that I haven't been on every side of this issue, donating money, attending fundraisers? I've heard all the platitudes before: *'They're fine the way they are.'* Bullshit! Not in this world, they're not. Not even when you've got a rich father who works for the very industry that should be able to *fix* you!" Maria paused, biting down on her lip, almost grinding her teeth. Addison saw in her face a melting pot of history and anger. He opted to say nothing.

"Not that James gave a shit in the first place," she continued bitterly. "Typical male! I wonder how many other children he's sired and abandoned."

"You had Merritt Lee do this?" Addison asked with disbelief in his voice.

"You're with the Hybrid-Division, right?" she asked, ignoring his question "So which half are you? FDA or FBI?"

"FDA."

"Suddenly her look changed. No longer did she gaze upon Addison as if he might have been some familiar face that she had seen in passing. He was now a familiar foe. She pointed two fingers that choked the end of her cigarette in his direction.

"Go back to your bosses, or whoever the hell writes your checks, and tell them that if they'd remove some of their goddamn yellow tape that keeps cures off the market, then maybe people wouldn't have to turn to illegal technology to fix their children."

"Maria, yes, I work at the FDA. Yes, just like you, I've heard it all before too. From your side of the fence, the FDA delays cures; from the other side we sanction poison. Yet there's another side that you didn't even stop to consider –"

"Are you a parent?" Maria cut him off.

"No, but I'm a sibling!" Addison snapped back. "I'm telling you –

unequivocally, *I'm telling you* – that not all people with disabilities want to be 'fixed!' Cures are what *we* want for them. What they want for themselves are their *rights!*"

Maria took another drag from her cigarette and quickly exhaled a cloud of smoke, hoping to veil her own turbulent feelings. She remained silent, her face still coarse and hardened, but her eyes trembled, showing that emotions were forcing their way out after years of denial.

Stan returned to the room, stashing his phone back in his pocket. At first, Maria was thankful for the diversion. She turned her head away, hoping to steady her emotions, but then Stan's words shattered the wall she was struggling to keep erect.

"They spotted Merritt. Carl and Amber are pursuing him now."

Maria looked down at her feet. Perhaps if the conversation with Addison had never happened, she would have been able to keep her usual distance from her circumstances with Merritt. However, her foundation was shaken, and she couldn't fight back the regret swelling up within. It was the first time she had felt anything for Merritt.

She wasn't sure what the feeling was, but it was no longer nothing. She felt something. She only wished she had felt it sooner.

***

"No, don't hit the strobe lights just yet," Amber advised. "He's too far up. Wait 'til you can get closer."

Carl accelerated. Almost as quickly as he did, the car in front of him decelerated, forcing him to punch the brakes. Amber jolted forward, bending inward on her wound. She sucked in her bottom lip, repressing a painful moan, hoping to keep her discomfort away from Carl's attention, but he saw it. He looked at her.

"Jesus, why the fuck did I let you —"

"Right lane! Right lane! We're clear!" she ordered.

Carl reacted to the command like a true soldier. He yanked the wheel to the right, rocketed into the next lane, and sped forward. Merritt's car had taken advantage of the same opening but had not yet receded from sight. Their cars sped forward through a maze of traffic but came to another stop under a collage of monolithic overpasses cutting across the sky. Only four cars separated them from Merritt. Carl considered putting the car in park, running directly up to Merritt's window and making the arrest.

"Don't do it," Amber said, reading his mind. "It'll be just our luck that traffic clears up the moment you get out of the car. He'll get away."

Sure enough traffic began rolling forward.

"Right, now what?" Carl replied, exasperated. "At this rate, we're just escorting him to the airport."

"Then we'll take him at the airport. We'll have other ag–" Amber stopped mid-sentence, as traffic began to break apart, and the cars directly in front of them splintered off into adjacent lanes. As if it was a gift from the gods, Merritt's car lay directly within sight. Carl immediately hit the strobe DeckBlaster and pulled up behind their target. For a moment Merritt didn't move. His car remained fixed and static in his lane while a sea of cars continued to flow past. The strobe lights continued coruscating, eventually bringing all traffic to a rolling stop. Merritt saw his opportunity and hit the gas pedal. His wheels burned against the pavement as he sped off.

"Shit!" Carl shouted.

"I told you to follow him to the fucking airport!" Amber chastised, grabbing her CB radio to request back up for the pursuit.

The chase induced panic further up the freeway as Merritt zipped dangerously past other cars, making haphazard cut-ins that sent several vehicles veering to the side of the road. One vehicle lost control and gyrated into a skidding stop, perpendicular to Carl's head-on approaching car. Tactically, Carl managed to angle away from the T-Bone, forcing another driver off the road.

Whether he had planned this chaos or not, Merritt seized his chance to disappear from the radar. He made a last-second swerve, just barely catching a bending exit.

The turn was too soon, too sudden.

He clenched the wheel tightly, trying to force his car to complete the winding turn, careening into iron rails, sending sparks everywhere. His speed, combined with the screeching turn, popped his rear tire. Time seemed to turn static for him as he desperately tried steering out of a tail-spin. As he ejected from the winding exit, he found himself struggling to avoid the impact with oncoming pedestrian traffic and side street vehicles.

Somehow, through some undeserved miracle, he came to a skidding stop, unscathed. His victory, however, was short-lived. Directly above him was a police helicopter. *They had found him!* He felt the slump at the back of his car from the flattened tire but ignored it. Flat tire or not, he had to keep going.

He took off.

There was no more strategy in his driving. Now he was a desperate prey taking any turn, up any random street, trying to avoid the looming eye of the overhead chopper. He knew it was hopeless, but panic pushes all desperate souls to the very brink of reason. There was no map, no plan. Like a captain navigating his ship within the eye of a terrible storm, Merritt clung to the steering wheel as his anchor. Each detour up a side street came as abruptly and violently as a wave crashing against his ship. He was whipped back and forth with no control, until finally the current flung him to the random shores of a decaying, desolate neighborhood.

Though his eyes were open, he had seen nothing of this erratic escape. Everything was a haze. He paused, waiting for his hands to cease trembling, for his blood flow to return to normal. He blinked and blinked again until finally his vision restored. He looked around. He had no recollection of where he was or how he had even arrived here.

He opened his door, stepped out and walked aimlessly forward, before turning in a semi-circle, to appraise his surroundings. With one good look-over, he diagnosed himself as being stranded on a deserted island...

Or was he?

His ears detected the ominous sound of air being chopped incessantly. He knew the sound, looked up, and saw the helicopter hover far above him like a vulture circling its prey. Still, the eyes of this bird were fixed elsewhere, somewhere further up the road. This time, his ears picked up an entirely different terrestrial sound, the sound of feet marching and a vociferous cluster of people. His eyes soon confirmed what his ears had heard.

He was not alone after all, quite the opposite. His hope quickly turned into despair. Turning the corner was a parade of protestors marching as a fragile union. Merritt felt his heart plunge into his stomach. His eyes, filled with dismay, zeroed first on the scores of fast approaching bodies, next on the picket signs in their hands. He didn't run. In fact, he didn't do anything at all. His attention had been arrested by the hazy image of one picket sign. From this distance it resembled an inkblot, inviting his mind to decode the meaning of the image. It morphed first into his own visage. He saw himself.

Are they here for me? he thought. *No, they're here for Price.*

His thought shifted as his mind transformed the image into the face of James Price. Next, his heart took over where his brain left off, morphing the image into Maria Price. His eyes softened.

Maria is waiting for me. She's at the airport waiting for me. I can't stop. I have to go…

As the mob drew dangerously closer, the image revealed its true identity. Merritt's love-stricken, delusional gaze dissipated. The clouds cleared from his eyes. He could see. The inkblot crystallized, taking on defined lines and contours until it painted the unmistakable face of JOI.

This brought him back to *now*, back to reality. His face stiffened. He turned and fled back to his car, a foolish move that triggered the animal instincts of the protestors. They chased after him.

Merritt started the car, pushed into reverse, and attempted to speed away backwards. His escape foiled after he carelessly backed into an abandoned car. There was no time for a second attempt. There was no Plan B. The demonstrators had already ambushed him, surrounding his car from every angle. His eyes full of terror, he looked up and saw a swarm of faces that were not like his own – faces full of color and conviction, race and rage.

He reached for his gun. He wasn't thinking. He was acting. He didn't even aim. He didn't have to. There were targets all around him.

He pulled the trigger. The glass shattered and a young man was hit.

Not a moment too soon, Carl and Amber's car came screeching into the scene, their strobe lights still flashing. The protestors, though recognizing the lights, were hardly intimidated. Their rage had found its next target, an outlet even more satisfying than Merritt, an enemy that symbolized all sins ever committed against their community.

Courageous as ever, Amber sprung from the car with her gun drawn. The crowd surrounded her. Carl tried to eject from his seat to her rescue, but several clamoring bodies obstructed his way. He forced his door open, succeeding only in allowing stray hands to claw at his body and drag him from his vehicle.

They picked him up by every limb and hovered him above the ground. He arched his head up, bellowing. Then a powerful foot struck his jaw, jerking his head violently to the side and snapping his neck.

His body abruptly shifted from life to death. All that kept him alive – tension, purpose, soul – were gone in an instant. His head hung low and lifeless.

Meanwhile, Merritt continued to fire shots at his attackers. The bullets penetrated more bodies but barely put a dent in their blinded wrath. They were after retribution and would not stop until it was had.

They forced his doors open and filled the space inside with punches and kicks at his defenseless body. He was surprised to find that the pain had been blocked out by the voice of his body.

His body was talking to him.

It was telling him it was over; that he had reached the end of his time on this earth; that he would be leaving. With those silent and final words, his senses began to shut down. He pulled his knees and arms into his chest as he prepared for the inevitable. He would die the way he was born – in a fetal position, in the womb of this car, as mounds of bodies denied the passage of light.

He felt the spray of broken glass. He felt the trickles of his own blood. He felt a sentient and unfathomable darkness claiming him, leaving a mass of abandoned flesh to the will of the mob.

Amber was fighting; fighting back the raging mob; fighting for her life – as if she had no memory of her wound; as if she was immortal.

Punching and kicking, she clasped the testicles of one attacker, forcing an inhuman cry from his jaws, snapping the life of another in a single punch to his throat.

Her plight to survive was her last tether to her human body, but the awe inspired by her power, her will, and her refusal to die promised her immortality.

She was beating back the fire of mass hysteria. She was smothered by this fire. She had to be. Fire exists to animate the spirit of the human animal, but also to cremate the body, releasing the spirit within.

The animals were upon her. Reason had been renounced. Savage instincts reclaimed. Appetite prevailed as the men ripped apart Amber's clothing, exposing her chameleon flesh that mutated from the color of life to the discolored shades of injury and mutilation. With every aggressive grope at her breasts, every forbidden pressure imposed upon her body, she was being desexualized and made into an object of violent ridicule.

BANG! BANG! BANG! BANG! BANG!

A series of gunshots dispersed the mob. Flashing red and blue lights surrounded the horde, scattering dozens of retreating bodies, some to their doom from falling and being crushed in the panic-ridden escape. A picket sign, plastered with JOI's face, fell to the ground, disfigured by trampling feet.

Amber's fallen body watched the shadowed, fleeing legs of the animals, but her body wasn't hers anymore. She was Kami – a god.

The fire of the masses was now burning itself out. The flames had done their job, setting free her spirit.

It rose.

High above the gunfire and the scattering clouds, high above the vertical pillars and the chaotic waters of civilization, it rose. Above and beyond the heavy air that hangs over this tumultuous city, it rose.

All that was below – the people and places – were little more than tiny, quantum particles of uncertainty, fabricating into a world defined by its own certitudes. Their dichotomous conflicts of existence were hassles only for the body and matter, but not for her. No longer the soul's journey, no longer the soul's concern, it traveled somewhere.

It rose to its rendezvous.

Chapter Twelve

284

A decal of numbers remained affixed to the door that used to be Amber's office. Stan stood alone, staring at the numbers with wordless thoughts running through his head. Of course, if he wanted to clothe his emotions with words, he could. His most intrinsic feeling was to ask himself why he felt so compelled to revisit Amber's office when she was no longer there. It was no longer *her office* anymore. It was now simply Office 284...

Or was it? After all, just below the number was her name. Why should her name still be here, lingering, if she was no longer around?

Material objects somehow take the characteristics of an immaterial echo of the departed. The number, the name, the space – *memorabilia* – if that is indeed what they are. Life's artifacts, maybe; life is wont to leave evidence of itself, reminding death who is really in charge here.

Are they death's artifacts...or nothing at all?

It depends on what the person relishes: life, death, or none of the above.

A sliver of light divided the edge of the door and *its way*, indicating that the door was not shut entirely. Perhaps it was Memory's invitation to Stan, welcoming him inside its new home. He reached out his hand, touching her nameplate, and gave the door a gentle push.

As the door slowly glided open, it revealed an empty temple.

Three days later, the gods departed.

He walked inside, with hands in his pockets, and stared absently at the *nothing* that filled the room. One would have thought he was taking in an eyeful, the way he lingered and looked around. His body was his eyes now...and his ears. He listened to the emptiness.

Silence is its own sound, and there was plenty of it *here* in this empty temple. Memory prefers silence. It loathes noise. It scurries away from interruption, even if it be only a mild creak from feet and floor.

Stan turned to find Addison standing behind him.

"I didn't see you back at the office, so I came here," Addison said softly.

"I had to go over some details about Maria Price with Saracki," Stan replied.

"So, what's going to happen?"

"She'll be prosecuted with everybody else who broke the law, but for her son... I don't know. What do you do with an illegal being that is a legal citizen? I don't know."

Stan paused, thinking about his own words and the often violent words of the world.

"It's a shame, the life that children inherent from their parents," he said to Addison, but mostly to himself.

"The perfect child, in an imperfect world... Who the hell would want that burden to carry?" Addison returned in-kind, keeping most of his response for himself.

The two friends shared a mutual silence together, each acting as quiet witness for the other while sorting out their own thoughts, emotions, and lives.

"Well, I'm going to head back to the FDA. Will I see you there later?" a friend asked.

"Yeah, you will," a friend replied.

A friend left, pulling the door shut behind him.

The light that peeked through the door now filled the office. The sun must have waged a dramatic battle against a cumulous sky and finally won. Now it was curious, and of all places on Earth for it to wander about it had chosen to visit this place, shoving aside obstructing clouds to get a closer peek inside the abandoned temple. Stan knew it was here because he saw his shadow stretch across the floor. He meditated on this image of the sun and of himself, remembering a quote, which he felt compelled to vocalize, to materialize thoughts as sound.

The human body is the best picture of the human soul.

He looked once more at his own shadow and a realization awoke inside him – *The Temple is not empty. I am here.*

Every space we enter is Memory's house. We are welcome guests, for as long as we are there.

The sun had satisfied its curiosity and left the room. The shadow faded.

"I'm sure we'll see each other again, Amber," Stan spoke aloud, "some other time...

"Some other place."

Stan left, closing the temple door behind him. He took one last look before leaving this Holy place and returning to the concerns of the secular world. His eyes fell back on the numbers but eschewed them in favor of more poignant memorabilia – a name.

"AMBER"

The hand of a friend removed the nameplate...

And silently walked away.

Addison left the FBI office. For a moment, he wasn't thinking of his life or the sprawling city that surrounded it. He was simply thinking of life, though a pliant word like that, floating around in a mind as austere as his, would demand clarification.

Life was what was lost, but only for now while he quietly mourned for his friend. The moment he'd step back into the FDA office, life would become a function again – a process, a biology. Life is what we make it – literally. We engineer life. We steal nature's magic to fabricate new machines to call our own.

There is also the life right in front of us, and all around us. Look up and there it is – *Life*. It is a reason to marvel, wonder, and express awe; at first with our eyes, next with our words, beginning with a name. We name life.

"Addison!"

He turned around at the sound of his name to find Pearson Fueller walking rapidly to catch up with him.

"I didn't know that you were still being held here," Addison said.

"I'm a free man now," Pearson replied, opening his arms in liberation. "Apparently, I don't need to be protected anymore."

Addison smiled approvingly. He felt a change in the dynamic between them. He now appreciated Pearson's role in all that had transpired. He could also see in Pearson's face and body language his denouement of the fantastic drama that Addison had lived, endured, and survived.

"I guess I can tell you now that I know about your background," Pearson divulged.

"I'm not a clone of my father," Addison replied confidently, with a face that was nothing but designer genes.

"You've had the comparative test done already?"

"No. I just know."

"You *just know*? Not the words of a scientist." Pearson smiled.

"No, they're not, are they?"

"Well, I've always been a firm believer that we are more than just our genes, in the same way that the whole is greater than the sum of its parts."

Addison had a response to this, albeit, a somewhat tetchy one, so he decided to keep it to himself. Beneath the silence, Pearson could sense the struck nerve and tilted his head slightly in humble concession.

"OK, you're right. Philosophy class is over."

"I'm sorry. It's just… Platitudes always go down a little too easy."

"They do, don't they?" Pearson chuckled. "Although…these days I think I'm quite fond of platitudes. I've choked enough on answers too big to swallow."

On this, Addison could agree. His most recent events and revelations had all been too big to swallow, and, maybe, if he knew what was good for him, he would thank life for its merciful clichés. They are, after all, clichés for a reason. They have the element of time, having been around long enough for our welcome to have weathered and withered away, yet the legitimacy of their truth remains.

Pearson and Addison stood apart from each other in silence, unsure how to end the conversation. The dilemma, really, was how to close a chapter. Which parting words were the right words after such circumstances? *See you soon? Hope everything goes well for you? Good luck on all your future endeavors?* These were stock departures reserved for acquaintances, not friends, but Pearson and Addison were hardly friends either – journeymen, perhaps. *What does one say at the end of a journey? What does one see at the end of a journey?* This thought compelled Pearson to look around at what surrounded him – a space teeming with life.

"The poet Gwendolyn Brooks reminded us that '*Wherever life can grow, it will. It will sprout out, and do the best it can. You don't get all your questions answered in this world,*'" Pearson recited, looking around at life.

"Something tells me, Pearson, when I reach your years, you and I will be very much alike."

"We already are. We're both assholes who have all the answers."

Addison smiled in agreement. "So what's next for you?" he asked.

"Apparently, a TV interview. Now that this is over, I'm to be the official asshole with all the answers…

"What's next for you, Addison?"

"I have a visit to make."

"What I meant was… Are you going to search for your genotypic twin?"

"I don't have to," Addison smiled knowingly, "I already know him."

"Adam?"

Addison's brother, hearing his name, rotated in his wheelchair and turned to face Addison. He smiled broadly, a strained sound finding its way through his windpipe. His disabled voice was *enabled* by a small monitor facing his visiting sibling. Adam's arms and hand, though limited in mobility, were situated near a miniature keyboard at the end of the arm rests, where his touch-trained fingers typed away:

You again? ;)

Addison read the message and smiled.

"Yup, me again."

Addison re-appraised the accumulation of technology in Adam's apartment. From the outside, it was a simple apartment hidden in an oversized group home. Inside, it looked more like a satellite headquarters for NASA.

"Who set all of this up for you, Adam?" Addison asked.

Nancy,

I think she likes you.

"Yeah, I know. You better delete that before she walks in."

Adam smiled but obliged, and the message vanished.

"So, explain to me again... What the hell are you trying to do here?"

Okay, but maybe you should
give yourself a tour of the new room.

This could take a while...

Right. While Adam typed away, Addison began pacing the room in small steps, his eyes making bigger leaps around the apartment... until finally stopping on a framed caricature illustration of his parents. He remembered this. He remembered when it was done – long ago, while walking along Venice Beach with his family. It was done in twenty minutes, as promised by the artist. It cost only twenty dollars, one dollar per minute.

Addison leaned in to look at the mostly unreadable signature of the artist and remembered him as being fairly aged, even back then. *I wonder if he is still alive,* Addison thought to himself. *Probably not.* Though his name was right there, scrawled in illegible cursive letters, Addison could not recall anything about the artist, other than his person. He remembered his frugal appearance and his faithful smile, guaranteeing a parodied likeness of any person or pet in only twenty minutes. This man, doubtless, died in obscurity. He may have even wondered if it were all worth it. *Was his a wasted talent?* No, it was a worthy one. The answer was right here on the wall. He was immortalized here. Addison's eyes now travelled up the painting, taking in every exaggerated detail that triggered his memory of his father's many flaws. He began to smile. *You made me laugh, whoever you are.* Addison sent this thought out to the artist before turning away to rejoin his brother.

"Okay, time's up. So... What kind of mad science are you up to here?" he asked, then waited as Adam finished his dissertation. Finally the screen filled with text.

I am working on two things.
The first one is still in development, as I do not yet have all
of the equipment I need (yikes!). Once I do, I plan to hook
all kinds of plugs and wires into my own head, so I can
digitize my "self" and upload a copy of my "self" into my very
expensive computer. When that is finished, I will have a very
elite conversation with my "self," and thereby prove to the
world that one can talk to oneself without being labeled as
completely fucking crazy.

That brings me to the second thing I am working on…

I am building a case for Neuro-Diversity. No offense, but
science has had its say and so has religion. I'm interested
in what lies between the two. The human brain provides
a spectrum of modes of thinking; it is unlikely that we've
explored the entire frontier of this spectrum. We have to get
out of this Dark Age of Intellectual Dogmatism. We are long
overdue for the next Enlightenment. It is time for others to
have their say, including people like me, who are completely
fucking crazy.

Addison looked at the screen, then at Adam.

"Jesus," was all he could say.

Then the screen went blank again, and a new message appeared
in its place:

So, what's up with you?

Addison laughed, scratching the back of his head. He flapped
his arms to his side, flabbergasted. He thought he had come here
with the breaking news, but all of a sudden his "breaking news"
felt like the equivalent of celebrity gossip. *What the hell, I'm here;*
might as well get this over with.

275

"Well… I'm sure you heard about that kid JOI on the news? What would you say if I told you that you and I are clones? Well… not you… You're fine. But I'm your clone… What would you say to that?"

Adam looked at him, thinking: *He's completely fucking crazy,* then typed away:

> *You may be a clone,*
> *but I still have one up on you.*
> *Look at me…*
>
> *I'm a Cyborg!*

Gabriella piffled around the kitchen, putting the finishing touches on a low-carbohydrate meal she prepared for Claudia. Walking quietly into the living room, where Claudia sat in her wheelchair, watching television, she placed the meal in front of Claudia on a fold-out table.

"Thank you, Gabby," Claudia said graciously.

Claudia picked up her remote and changed the channel to yet more news footage about the JOI trials.

"Uh, you do know that the voice command is working, right?" Gabby asked.

"Yes, but I'm in a nostalgic mood today," Claudia said, waving the remote. Gabby smiled and took a seat next to Claudia, who changed the channel once more to footage of Rosalind Hagen giving her testimony about JOI.

"JOI wasn't born without memory, but he was born with cognitive disabilities, the formations of which couldn't be explained without examination. ETGR kept him for analysis of his disorders. Learning what caused the disorders is instrumental in preventing them with future developments. However, that level and duration of detainment is cumulatively stressful, so a proprietary drug called Antiase was used. This drug is an enzyme-inhibitor, breaking down proteins used by neurons specific to higher-learning functions, as well as short and long term memory. I was responsible for the administration of this drug..."

A third click of the button summoned the familiar face of Pearson Fueller on a panel show, discussing his version of the JOI case and his memories of his old friend, Allan. Claudia set down the remote. *Finally a program worth watching.*

"Why was Dr. Shapiro so curious about JOI's memory impairment?" an interviewer asked Pearson.

"He wasn't. He was more curious about what JOI could remember, which was only his first name.

"I'm sure if Allan had been privy to the circumstances that resulted in JOI's memory loss, he would have condemned it. Yet he also would have secretly marveled over JOI's retainment of his name, while memory of all else was discarded.

"Even those people who suffer complete amnesia, forgetting even their own name, distress the most over not remembering exactly who they are. There's something about the self that seems to demand an identity, and that identity in turn demands a name. But a name is just a sound really. It's a vibration resonating with some hidden aspect of ourselves.

"This reminds me of a poem by Joseph von Eichendorf. I came across it in a manuscript that Allan had finished just before his passing. I have it written down..."

Pearson removed a small piece of paper from his breast pocket and unfolded it. He paused briefly as he rescanned the poem, refreshing his memory. Then he placed the note back in his pocket and recited:

> *"There slumbers a song in all things*
> *Dreaming on and on*
> *And the world set out to sing*
> *If only you strike The Magic Word."*

Claudia extended the remote in her hand, pushed the power button, and the TV flashed to a blank screen. The room was silent.

"That's it?" Gabby asked.

"Yes," Claudia replied, a slight grin on her face, "I'm going to do some reading now."

"Sounds good," Gabby said, standing up, "let me know if you need me."

"I will."

Claudia watched Gabriella leave the room, feeling overwhelmed with gratitude and thanking her lucky stars that she had let Allan talk her out of firing her caretaker before. Gabriella was all she had now. She remembered Allan's words: *When life snatches away something from one hand, be sure to hold tight to whatever you have left in the other.* He had a lot of sayings like that. Some of them were completely disposable, others were pure treasures. He, of course, made sure to leave his little collection of trash and treasures in his book.

His book…

Well, it wasn't a book yet. It was still a manuscript, but it would be a book soon – *someday*. Until then, she kept it near her, ensconced in her lap. Yes, it would be a book someday. It was finished. It even had a title. Claudia looked down in her lap, at "the book" and the name she had given it. It was the perfect name for a must-read:

"THE MAGIC WORD"

By DR. ALLAN SHAPIRO

End

About the Author

A.A. Jordan is one part writer and one part graphic designer. He writes novels with an anime tone, which only means that his creative process begins with visualizing anime-style characters (the kind without the whiny voices). He was born in Buffalo, NY and lives abroad.